The Soup Kitchen Girl

Libby Ashworth was born and raised in Lancashire and comes from many generations of mill workers. It was while researching her family history that she realised there were so many stories about ordinary working people that she wanted to tell.

Also by Libby Ashworth

The Lancashire Girls

The Convict's Wife
A Mother's Fight
The Runaway Daughter

Cotton Crisis

The Soup Kitchen Girl

Libby
ASHWORTH

The Soup Kitchen Girl

canelo

First published in the United Kingdom in 2026 by

Canelo, an imprint of
Canelo Digital Publishing Limited,
20 Vauxhall Bridge Road,
London SW1V 2SA
United Kingdom

A Penguin Random House Company
The authorised representative in the EEA is Dorling Kindersley Verlag GmbH.
Arnulfstr. 124, 80636 Munich, Germany

A CIP catalogue record for this book is available from the British Library.

ISBN 978 1 83598 4 772

This book is a work of fiction. Names, characters, businesses, organizations, places and events are either the product of the author's imagination or are used fictitiously. Any resemblance to actual persons, living or dead, events or locales is entirely coincidental.

Cover images © Dreamstime.com, Shutterstock.com. Front: Arcangel: Abigail Miles

Printed and bound in Great Britain by Clays Ltd, Elcograf S.p.A.

Look for more great books at
www.canelo.co | www.dk.com

1

MIX
Paper
FSC™ C018179
FSC
www.fsc.org

Chapter One

Blackburn 1861

Sally Grimes would never forget the day in May when the looms had powered down and she'd followed her father out of the mill, her ears still ringing from the incessant noise.

'Hast tha seen this, Jimmy?' Old Eddie had asked her father, waving a copy of the *Blackburn Times* under his nose. 'The Confederate states of America have attacked the northern union. They're saying it's a civil war.'

'Daft buggers!' her father had remarked, giving the paper only a cursory glance. 'Nowt to do with us,' he'd concluded. How wrong he had been, thought Sally. They'd had no idea back in the spring how much the war was going to change their lives.

Now it was the second week in December, and when she pulled her shawl over her head and stepped out onto the street Sally felt the ice beneath her clogs. She hesitated, wondering whether to wait for her father and brother or go straight home. A few of the other weavers came out behind her and mumbled their goodbyes. Everyone was subdued and worried. They'd known it might happen. A lot of the other mills had been on half-time a lot longer than Haworth's, but being told there was no more work just before Christmas made the blow of the final closure even harder to bear.

There was no sign of her father. He'd probably stayed behind to speak to Mr Haworth, she concluded, so she began to walk towards their house on Primrose Lane where her mother would be waiting. It would fall to her to break the unwelcome news, although she reasoned that her mother wouldn't be surprised. Her father had been preparing them for it all week.

'There's been no delivery of cotton bales for a month now,' he'd warned, 'and the warehouse is almost empty. Once it's all woven up, it'll be the end. The mill will have to shut. Mr Haworth doesn't want it. But what choice has he? And who knows when there'll be cotton again?'

A light flurry of snow had begun to fall and although Sally had been hot as she'd worked at her looms, she was shivering by the time she reached the door and was glad to get inside.

She walked through the front parlour, which was only used on special occasions, and into the kitchen beyond. Her mother turned inquiringly from where she was peeling potatoes at the sink in the scullery. Sally shook her head and saw her mother's face fall into despair.

'Closed until further notice,' she said as she took off her shawl to shake the snow from it. 'At least we got our wages,' she added as she put the six shillings on the table. It was only half of what she usually earned. They'd been on short-time working since October and Sally knew that since her mother had lost her job at Perseverance Mill, her parents had been dipping into the savings set aside for a rainy day.

Six months ago, they had been able to save because they had all been employed to work cotton. Even her little sisters, Florrie and Ellen, had worked as part-timers for half the day, attending the Girls' Charity School for the other half. Only the seven-year-old twins, Isaac and Esau, hadn't been bringing in a wage. The family's combined weekly earnings had amounted to four pounds, which was ample to pay the rent on their three-bedroomed terraced house and buy food and clothing. There had even been money left over for treats, such as visits to the music hall and occasional trips to Blackpool to take in the air or have a dip in the sea.

Now, Sally knew that her father was concerned about how they would pay their way. He came in with a glum expression as she was helping her mother to lay the table ready for their meal.

'I've been speaking to Mr Haworth,' he told them as he hung his hat on the peg behind the door. 'I asked him when he thought he could get hold of more cotton, but he wasn't optimistic. He says there is some in the warehouses at Liverpool, but the brokers are wanting so much for it that he'd be manufacturing at a loss if he paid their prices. He's looking at other options – bringing it in from India or Egypt instead, but they don't produce the same quantities and he's not sure if it's worth his while.'

Sally watched her father as he spoke. His voice was subdued and his face gaunt. She knew that the responsibility for keeping them all housed and fed weighed heavily on him.

'It was the same at Perseverance,' said her mother. 'And every other mill in the town. How will people survive when we have no idea how long this will go on for?'

'They said the American war would be over in six months,' agreed her father. 'But from what I've heard it's just a stalemate, and wars can drag on for years.'

'We can't manage for years without jobs. What will we do?' asked her mother.

'I don't know. I really don't,' he replied.

They all gathered around the table in a downcast mood. Even the twins, who were too young to understand the implications of what had happened, were uncharacteristically quiet and ate their potato pie without their usual chatter about what had happened to them at school that day. Florrie and Ellen were silent too and even George, who at fifteen considered himself an adult, had nothing to say.

Every now and again, Sally's mother sighed as she looked around the table at them. Sally knew she was worried about where the next meals would come from once this week's wages had been spent.

'Surely there'll be some help,' she said at last. 'Can we not appeal to the Guardians for some relief?'

'I'll not go, cap in hand, to beg for charity,' declared her father. Sally could see that the thought of it was making him feel angry and ashamed already. 'I'm not like the ruffians and ne'er-do-wells who expect to get summat for nowt,' he went on. 'I've always worked hard, and my parents before me. We've never gone begging to the gentry and I'll not take their handouts now. A man should work to earn his wages, not be handed money like giving scraps to a stray dog!'

He pushed the last of his meal into his mouth and set down his cutlery with a clatter, before pushing back his chair and going to the hearth where he liked to sit in the evening and enjoy a pipe of tobacco. Sally watched as he took his pipe from the mantel, looked about for his baccy tin, then remembered that it was empty and had been for a few weeks – his last bit of comfort snatched from him by their growing poverty. He sat down with a frown and waited until her mother handed him a cup of tea.

Sally felt on the brink of tears. She'd never seen her parents so despondent and concerned. Of course, there had been problems and challenges before, but they'd always had a solution – such as extra hours at work to buy something special, like the piano in the front parlour that her mother loved to play. She'd never seen her parents without a way to cope before. This war on the other side of the ocean had stolen their livelihood and there wasn't a thing they could do about it.

Chapter Two

Caroline Haworth and her mother were hosting an 'at home' in their townhouse on Richmond Terrace when the conviviality of the afternoon was spoiled by her father's unexpected arrival. It was unusual for him to come home so early from his mill.

His face was stern, and he took her mother aside and spoke to her in low tones as Caroline continued to say her farewells to their guests, apologising for her mother's negligence. She hoped the ladies who had visited them would forgive the rudeness. As she did, she strained to overhear what her parents were discussing. It was obvious something was amiss and her imagination ran away with her as she visualised all sorts of scenarios – a fire at the mill, a serious accident, even the death of the queen.

It was only later that evening that she discovered the real reason for her father's distress. He had taken the decision to close the mill completely and lay off all his workforce – just before Christmas too.

'I had no other choice,' he repeated as they sat at dinner in their candlelit dining room, the flames making shadows on the papered walls as they ate the lamb chops prepared by their cook, Mrs Jenkins. 'I hated doing it,' he added. 'I think it was the hardest thing I've ever had to do.'

'How did the workers take it?' asked her mother as she popped a morsel of meat into her mouth and took a sip of wine from the crystal glass beside her plate.

'Surprisingly well,' he admitted. 'I think they'd seen it coming. Brookhouse and Paradise shut down last week and Perseverance laid off most of their hands two months ago. Jimmy Grimes hung back to speak to me, asking when there would be cotton again, but what could I tell him? That his guess was as good as mine?'

'Is it really all gone?' asked her mother. 'I overheard my father discussing bales that were piled up in the warehouses at Liverpool. Is it not possible for you to buy some of those and keep the mill open?'

Caroline watched as her father frowned over his meal. 'The merchants have set their prices sky high,' he explained. 'My broker keeps telling me it's the law of supply and demand, but no one can afford to pay what they're asking. The mills would run at a loss. I don't mean to criticise your father,' he said after a moment. 'But he isn't a cotton manufacturer.'

'He's a businessman,' replied her mother, showing a flare of the temper that both Caroline and her father feared. Her mother's rages were something they both tried strenuously to avoid. To the outside world she was a dutiful wife who supported her husband and appeared to be meek and compliant. But within the confines of their home, she often challenged her husband, believing that he was her inferior.

They must have loved one another once, thought Caroline, although some days she doubted that they even liked one another. Today was one of those days. Her parents glared at one another across the white linen tablecloth, the twinkling decanters of wine and the bowl of fresh fruit, delivered from the exotic glass houses of her grandfather's home at Feniscowles.

Caroline watched as her father considered whether to counter his wife's statement. He had been angry with everyone since he'd come home and she knew it was because he was upset at having to close the mill doors. The spinners and weavers were just workers as far as her mother was concerned, but Caroline knew that her father regarded them as individuals, friends – family almost. He felt he had a responsibility towards them and leaving them with no jobs and no income was hurting him deeply.

'I suspect your father is speculating on cotton which makes him part of the problem,' he said irritably.

Caroline's heart sank as she watched her mother rise from her chair, pick up her glass and walk around to where her father was sitting. She threw it fully into his face, leaving him looking shocked as the red wine dribbled down his chin and onto the tablecloth where it formed several pink stains that the maid would struggle to remove.

'I should never have married you!' screamed her mother.

'You were left with little choice!' her father replied. 'Or perhaps you would have preferred me to walk away and leave you a ruined woman?'

'I should have got rid of it. My mother said it was possible.'

'Amelia!' Her father grasped hold of her mother by the wrist to prevent her leaving. 'How dare you say such a thing in front of our daughter?'

Caroline watched and saw her mother hesitate. Their eyes met and she saw the regret at her angry words. 'I didn't mean it,' she told Caroline. 'It's just that your father makes me so angry sometimes. He's so stubborn.'

She pulled her arm free. 'Tell Mrs Jenkins to fetch my coffee upstairs,' she called over her shoulder as she left, gathering her full skirts to aid her progress through the doorway and up the shallow staircase to her private sitting room.

Her father referred to these scenes as flouncing. Caroline's mother flounced regularly and neither of them paid it much attention any more. But throwing wine was new, thought Caroline as she watched her father wipe his face on his napkin. He dabbed ineffectually at the tablecloth then gave it up and threw the napkin down on the remains of the meal on his plate.

'I'm going to my study,' he said, and left. Caroline sat alone at the table, staring at her half-eaten supper. Her appetite had deserted her and she felt sick at the sight of it. Not wanting to eat alone, she pushed back her own chair and went to the parlour where the fire was burning brightly and the coffee cups were arranged on the table. She sat down at the fireside and began to cry. Some days she wished that she never had been born, because she knew that she was the cause of the recriminations between her parents. It was her existence that made them loathe one another and although she loved them both there were days, like today, when she wondered if they loved her at all.

When she heard Mrs Jenkins tap on the door, she made an effort to compose herself and wipe her eyes.

'Would you like me to pour you a cup of coffee?' asked the cook. Caroline nodded and watched as Mrs Jenkins poured the dark liquid, added cream and a heaped spoonful of sugar, just the way she liked it. 'I'll take a cup up to Mrs Haworth,' she said.

'Pour two. I'll take one to Father. He's in his study,' Caroline said.

Mrs Jenkins nodded, but her look was sympathetic. Caroline knew she understood. She'd been their cook since Caroline was a small child, and the troubles that occurred within the walls of the house were nothing unusual to her although she never spoke of them; never referred to them. Caroline knew she was far too loyal to ever gossip and she was grateful.

When Caroline went into her father's study and put the coffee on his desk, she saw that he was examining sheet after sheet of paper covered in numbers – the accounts from the mill.

'There was no other way,' he told her.

Caroline nodded. She didn't know anything about the business of the mill. It was something her father did. The mill and its workers moved in a different sphere to her mother and herself, and to some extent her mother moved in a different – even higher – class from her father. Her mother's belief that he was inferior to her had some truth. Her father didn't come from the same class as her mother who was a daughter of Sir Walter de Lacy of Salesbury Hall – a family that claimed it could trace its ancestry back to the Norman conquest. It wasn't news to Caroline that her mother had been forced to marry her father when she fell pregnant. It was an accusation thrown in her face often enough by her mother when she was in one of her notorious tempers, an attempt to lay the blame, as if Caroline existed simply to spoil the chances she might have had.

'But you must have loved him,' Caroline had replied on one occasion, wondering what had happened to change her mother's opinion of her father.

'I was young and starry-eyed,' her mother had told her. 'I fell for his good looks. I was a fool. I ought to have gone through with the engagement to Sir Gilbert.'

Caroline knew the man she meant. She'd met him at a dinner party at her grandparents' house. He was much older than her mother, with a big bulbous nose and an even larger belly. He was rich though. He owned a house at Wiswell that was by all accounts twice the size of her grandfather's residence. She'd wondered what it would have been like to have him as a father and the thought had made her shudder. Even the sight of him repelled her and she couldn't blame her mother for choosing differently. It was just a pity that what love there had been between her parents hadn't lasted. And things would be even worse now, she realised. With the mill closed, her father would have no income. That much she did understand, and she knew that he would be too proud to ask her grandfather for help and have all his failings thrown back into his face.

Chapter Three

'No one has money for luxuries any more,' sighed Ruth Hodgson's father as he stared out of the door of their confectionery shop onto Queen Victoria Street. There was no one about. Most of the mill chimneys stood smokeless, and there was an unusual clearness in the air. Her father had mostly kept his own counsel until now, not wanting to alarm her, but Ruth knew that his anxiety had been growing for weeks if not months. Some of the sweets that had been made back in September remained unsold. The pear drops, humbugs and aniseed twists, which had been boiled up in the huge vats in the room behind the shop, still filled the glass jars that ranged the shelves, and it had been almost a fortnight since he'd made anything new, whereas normally the smell of the sweet making pervaded their house every day, drifting up into the rooms above the shop where they slept and lulling Ruth to sleep each night with the scents of fruit and mint and honey.

'I was going to make sugar mice,' he said. 'They usually sell well at Christmas, but we've had so few customers I'm not sure it's worth the effort.'

'We don't want to disappoint people,' pointed out Ruth. 'Maybe they've been saving their money to indulge in some Christmas treats. And even if the mill workers are unemployed, there are the businessmen and the mill owners. I'm sure they will still be able to afford them.'

'Perhaps you're right,' said her father, turning away from the door. 'Maybe I'll make a few and hope that trade picks up. Otherwise, I'm not sure what we'll do. I'm worried,' he admitted for the first time. 'I don't know how things are going to end, but with such a lessened income and the increase in rates in the new year, we're going to struggle. Still, not to worry.' He smiled to reassure her. 'We mustn't grumble,' he said. 'There's plenty of folk worse off than we are.'

It was true, thought Ruth. Last Christmas the town had been prosperous. Customers had come to their shop eagerly to buy sweets for the celebration, and on Christmas Eve there had been a queue out of the door, and her father's only fear then had been that the sugar mice would run out before everyone was served. Later, she'd gone out to the market to buy their own provisions. The stalls had been busy with sales of geese and turkeys. The fruit stalls had been piled high with shiny red apples and exotic fruits shipped into the docks at Preston from overseas countries – some of which she couldn't even name. There'd been a brass band playing carols. Bunches of holly and mistletoe to festoon tables and hearths had been for sale, along with evergreen trees to be taken home and decorated – a new fashion brought from Germany by Prince Albert. How Ruth had longed for one, but they were too big for her to carry with all her other purchases and she knew that her father would say it was an extravagance. Since her two older sisters had both left to be married and her mother had died, their Christmases had been subdued, without too many excesses, but it was a time of year that Ruth loved.

This year, there were not so many stalls on the market. The pie man and the hot chestnut man had stopped coming weeks ago. It had been months since she'd seen the shrimp woman from Southport. Staple foods like potatoes and bread were still on offer, but the women who bought them purchased smaller quantities. They handed over coppers and looked glad to have anything to eat at all as they hurried away with their threadbare shawls pulled tightly around their pinched and pale faces.

'I have a committee meeting later at the town hall,' her father told her. 'We're going to discuss what can be done for the unemployed. Mayor Hutchinson thinks the town needs to do more. He says things can only get worse,' he told her gloomily. 'He predicts that some of the mills may have to close for good. He wants anyone who can afford it to donate to a fund so that some money can be distributed to those worst off before Christmas comes. I hope he doesn't ask me to donate,' her father went on. 'It's not that I'd be unwilling if I could afford it, but he takes no account of how the shopkeepers and publicans are suffering through loss of trade.'

'Perhaps we could give a little,' suggested Ruth, remembering the mother with three young children she'd seen the day before, wandering around the stalls with a tattered basket over her arm, asking the price of some turnips that looked only fit for cattle fodder.

'We'll see,' her father replied and it made Ruth wonder how bad their situation was. When the shop was doing well, her father was always eager to help anyone. He usually made a generous addition to the collection plate at the parish church each Sunday and gave his time freely as a councillor for their ward to assist in the running of the town. But he never discussed money with her, and neither had he with her mother. He said it wasn't fair to worry her about finance and business arrangements, and

Ruth had accepted that. She helped him to run the shop and he handed over more than enough money for her to buy food and necessities for the household, as well as a generous allowance to spend on herself.

She'd seen him adding up the takings and writing the amount in his account book and she knew that he ordered and paid for the ingredients they used, sometimes grumbling about increases in price. But the sugar and the spices came regularly by horse and cart from the warehouse on the edge of the canal and she'd never thought to question it or wonder if one day things might change.

At six o'clock they decided to close for the day and Ruth drew down the blinds in the shop window and covered the displays with white sheets to keep off the dust. Her father locked the outside door, and Ruth went into the scullery to fill the kettle to make tea. Their daily maid, Agatha, had ironed the laundry and put on a mutton stew to cook. It smelt appetising when Ruth took a cloth and opened the oven door to check on it. The gravy had thickened and was bubbling.

'Will you eat now?' she asked her father when he came through. 'There's a nice crusty loaf to mop up with and Agatha's made an apple pie for pudding.'

'Aye. Plate it up,' he agreed. 'The meeting's not until eight, so there's plenty of time.'

'Will you be late home?' Ruth asked as they ate their meal, hoping he would say no. She disliked being alone in the house, much preferring to have companionship, even if her father said nothing, but read his newspaper as she devoured the latest novel.

'Probably not. Unless they argue,' he continued. She knew that the constant bickering amongst the councillors and their lack of resolve to make any clear decisions often irritated him. 'But I don't think they will about this,' he went on. 'The distress is plain for all to see and something needs to be done. It wouldn't be right to watch people starve.'

Ruth felt slightly guilty as she finished the food on her plate. She found it hard to imagine what it would be like to be hungry. She knew that she was fortunate. Even though the shop was quiet, her father had not reduced the amount of money he gave her to buy provisions, and although he was clearly worried about the cotton crisis, she doubted that it would affect them too much. Customers would come for the sugar mice and the other Christmas confections, she was sure.

She washed up the pots after her father had gone to his meeting. Ruth liked to help where she could and it was no hardship to wash the cups and plates even if she did leave the pie dishes soaking for Agatha to deal with the next morning. When everything was tidy, she added more coal to the fire, lit an extra candle and sat down to read until her father returned.

It was late when he eventually came. She had heard the distant chime of the church clock strike eleven before his footsteps reached the door and his key turned in the lock.

'Are you still up?' he asked when he saw her sitting beside the dying embers of the fire. 'I thought you'd have gone up long since.'

'I waited to hear what had been said,' she replied. 'What did they decide to do?'

'They're planning to open a soup kitchen,' he told her as he sat down and held out his hands towards the remains of the fire. They looked blue and cold, and Ruth regretted not reminding him to wear his thick woollen gloves. 'I told them that they could have the use of our vats.'

'But won't we need them?' Ruth asked, puzzled by his offer.

'I've decided to shut up the shop once Christmas is done,' her father said. 'I've been thinking about it for a while now, but this soup kitchen idea has brought it to a head.'

'But what will we do?' she asked, shocked by his decision.

'They need someone to supervise the kitchen,' he told her. 'I've said I'll do it and I've been promised a small wage in return. It'll bring in more than we've been making in the shop these last couple of months.'

Ruth didn't reply. She didn't know what to say. The idea of her father shutting up his shop was unthinkable, and she felt like crying at the thought of him being reduced to working in a soup kitchen.

'What will I do if the shop is closed?' she asked him.

'I've said that you'll work in the kitchen as well.'

'Doing what?' she asked, horrified by the idea. 'Making the soup?'

'You sound like you think it's beneath you.'

'No!' she protested. 'I didn't mean that. It's just that I wouldn't know how to begin.'

'Don't worry. You won't be the only one helping,' he reassured her, 'and it'll only be for a while. I'm hoping the soup will only be needed to get folks through the worst of the winter months. There'll probably be cotton by the springtime – if not from America then from another country. The mayor told us that the manufacturers are looking to buy in from India and Egypt. Once people can go back to work and earn wages, we'll be able to open the shop again.'

Ruth thought of all the sweets that would sit uneaten in their jars in the meantime. Would they even be fit to eat by the time spring came? Or would they all have to be thrown away? That would be a terrible waste, and she wondered if her father was making the right decision. But she kept her thoughts to herself. It wasn't her place to question what he was going to do. She just hoped that there would be a Christmas rush and most of the stock would be gone before he closed the doors.

She banked up the fire and put the guard around it. If they were lucky, it might still be alight by morning and they would be able to make a pot of tea before Agatha came. Ruth hoped that they would still be able to afford to employ their maid when they worked at the soup kitchen. Ruth relied on Agatha to do most of the laundry and the cooking as well as clearing out and laying the fire. It would be arduous work if the maid didn't come because all these tasks would fall to her. If it was hard to envisage her father running a soup kitchen, she knew that it would be a miracle if he turned his hand to helping her wring out the soaking-wet bedsheets on a Monday morning.

Upstairs, she undressed quickly in the icy cold bedroom, pulled on the flannel nightgown with the high neck and long sleeves and got into bed, wishing that she'd put some hot coals in the bedwarmer to take the chill off the sheets. When she'd glanced out of the window, she'd seen that there was a hard frost, covering the roofs and cobbles in a veil of sheer white. At least if it was clear, it wouldn't snow. She hated having to go down the yard to the privy when there was snow on the ground, and her father didn't always have time to clear a path and put some ashes down.

Ruth shivered as she rubbed her feet together, trying to create a warm spot in the cold bed. People sometimes told her that she was a lucky girl to have the luxury of a bed to herself, but on nights like this she envied the mill workers who crowded three or four to the same mattress, knowing that the proximity of so many other bodies would help them to keep warm.

Unable to drop off to sleep, she mulled over her father's words. She didn't like the idea of working in a soup kitchen at all. She would have much preferred to keep the shop open. The shop was what she was used to. She understood what was required of her and she couldn't imagine how soup would be made in the huge vats her father used for toffee and the other sweets. She'd seen Agatha chopping vegetables in their kitchen and making soup or stew in a pan, but the number of vegetables and potatoes that would be needed to fill those vats was a huge amount. Where would it all come from? The prospect seemed impossible and she wished that her father hadn't volunteered her for the task without at least asking her.

Chapter Four

Sally Grimes woke at her usual time the next morning. She was about to brace herself to get out of the warm bed she shared with her two sisters and brave the cold of the bare-boarded floor, when it occurred to her that there was no need to get up straight away. She had no work to go to.

The thought would have cheered her if it had been a holiday, but this was just an ordinary Saturday when she would normally have been in the mill, attending to the threads on her looms.

She stretched out a foot, but quickly moved it back to the place that had been warmed by her body. She listened to hear if anyone else was up yet. She could hear her parents talking although their voices were too low for her to make out what was being said. But they sounded anxious and Sally knew they were worried. They'd never been without work before, and no one knew what such a bleak future would hold.

When she heard her mother and father go downstairs, she gritted her teeth and pushed back the pile of blankets. The cold from the floor struck up through her legs, making them painful as she broke the layer of ice on the water in the wash bowl. She hastily scrubbed at her face and underarms then layered herself with as much clothing as she could before shaking her sisters awake and going down the steep stairs.

Her father was kneeling at the hearth, trying to get the fire to light. The kindling and the coals were damp and although it was smoking, he was struggling to get a flame. Her mother was slicing bread and putting it on plates – two slices for her father, but only one each for the rest of them on which she was spreading the merest smidgeon of black treacle.

'I'll ask about to see what other work there is this morning,' her father said when the fire had taken hold and the kettle put on to boil.

'I'll come with you,' said George. 'There must be some vacancies somewhere.'

Sally saw that her mother was unconvinced they would find anything. The only work in Blackburn was in the mills, or in industries related to the mills. The engineering works and foundries were dependant on the prosperity of the cotton manufacturers and had no purpose when the mill owners had no need to buy new looms or engines. So, no work would be had there. The whole town had prospered on cotton, and now that there was none, there was nothing to support the inhabitants except charity – and even that might not be enough, because the generosity of the manufacturers couldn't be relied upon when they themselves had fallen on such hard times.

Sally ate her slice of bread and drank a cup of weak tea without milk or sugar. The room had barely warmed since the fire had been lit and she was still cold. When her father put on his jacket and hat and went out, she helped to clear away the pots then decided that she couldn't sit at home all day doing nothing.

'I'll go to look for work as well,' she told her mother. 'There must be something I can do.'

She walked through the town, calling at all the mills that were still open, but she was turned away at every one.

'We've had to lay off most of our own workers,' an overlooker told her. 'There's nothing to be had at all – and it'll not improve until master can get hold of more bales of cotton.'

Sally nodded. It wasn't news to her and she knew she would have to look for other work if she was to earn anything. She went back to the town centre and began to call at all the shops to ask if they needed an assistant. She hated it. She had to force herself to open each door to go in and ask for work.

'I'm sorry. We have no vacancies,' she was told over and over again.

When she reached the sweet shop on Queen Victoria Street she lingered for a moment outside the window, looking at the dishes of colourful sweets on display. It was a long time since she'd last called here. This time last year, she'd come to buy sugar mice as treats for her brothers and sisters. She'd even got some for George and although he was always telling her that he was a grown up now, his eyes had lit up at the sight of the little pink and white sugar creations with string for their tails, and she'd seen he was delighted that he hadn't been left out of the gift giving.

Sally pushed open the door and the girl who was the daughter of the confectioner came hurrying out from the back room with an optimistic expression.

'What would you like?' she asked.

Sally's fingers closed around the penny in her cloth purse. It was all the money she had and she knew that it would be needed for something more necessary than sweets.

'I'm looking for work,' she confessed, feeling awkward when it was clear the other girl had been hoping she was a customer. 'Do you need any help? I can cook, so I'm sure I could learn sweet making.'

'I'm sorry,' the confectioner's daughter said. 'My father's closing the shop after Christmas because we're doing that badly. No one has any spare money for sweets. Have you been laid off at the mill?'

'Aye. Haworth's. They closed yesterday.'

'I'm sorry,' she said, looking genuinely sympathetic. 'I wish I could help.'

'Thank you,' Sally said, retreating to the door. It was clear that it wasn't only the cotton workers who had fallen on hard times. The whole town was suffering from the cotton famine.

Chapter Five

Ruth had hoped that the mill girl was going to ask for sugar mice. Her father was busy making them, stirring up the sugar solution and then adding flavourings and pink colouring before pouring it carefully into the moulds and adding a length of string to each 'mouse' for a tail. She'd hoped it was a sign that trade was beginning to pick up in time for Christmas. But the girl had come to ask for work, and she wasn't the first. There were more people coming to the shop seeking work than there were coming to buy and Ruth hated having to turn them away.

'Customer?' asked her father. It was a remarkable occurrence now.

'Just another girl looking for work,' she told him.

Her father went back to his task with a frown and Ruth could see he was hoping that his efforts wouldn't be for nothing.

She looked at the empty vats, scrubbed clean and piled onto the wooden table. It was strange to imagine them filled with soup.

'Where is this soup kitchen going to be?' she asked her father. 'Will people be coming here?'

'No. The council have been offered a place on Cleaver Street by Mr Yates. His foundry isn't at work and the premises are ideal. There's space to put vats over the fires that are usually used for working the metals and there's room for tables and benches if people want to eat there, or if they bring a pan, it'll be dished out for them to take home.'

Ruth nodded. It was hard to imagine what it would be like. She'd never seen inside the foundry. It was a place for men and although she'd sometimes seen the workers coming out at the end of the day, pink-cheeked from the heat, all she knew was that they built boilers and steam engines for the mills.

It wouldn't be like this for sure, she thought as she watched her father adding eyes and noses to the mice that had cooled and been shaken out on to the table.

She heard the ping of the little bell above the door and hurried back into the shop, hoping that this time it would be a customer and not someone else asking for work. The young woman who stood waiting in the shop couldn't have been more different from the mill girl. She was dressed in the latest fashion with a huge skirt of a rich blue, striped with navy, which was held out wide by a crinoline frame that took up almost all the space on the far side of the counter. Her coat was trimmed with pale fur and her bonnet, fastened with a huge bow, sported delicate lace and dried red flowers. On her hands she wore tight, kidskin gloves that exactly matched the colour of her cornflower blue eyes as she raised a hand to push away a stray strand of her blonde hair.

For a moment Ruth could only stare at her, as if she'd sprung to life from one of the fashion plates that she sometimes yearned over in the women's magazines. She was perfection and Ruth felt shabby and insignificant in her shadow as she straightened the plain white apron that she wore over her daisy-printed cotton gown.

'May I help you?' she asked.

'I wanted sugar mice,' said the vision of perfection. 'I know you haven't any on display, but I was hoping there might be some?' She smiled and Ruth returned the smile warmly, pleased that she could fulfil this request.

'My father is just making them, but I'm sure some are ready. If you would wait for a moment I will go to enquire.'

'Oh, that's kind of you! I do hope they're ready and I'm not too soon. I've been so looking forward to getting them that I didn't want to wait any longer in case they were all sold! We queued for such a long time last Christmas, only to be disappointed.'

'I'm sorry to hear that,' Ruth said.

'The fault was mine entirely for waiting until Christmas Eve,' the young woman told her. 'That's why I was determined to buy early this year.'

Ruth gave her another smile before hurrying to her father. 'There's someone here asking for sugar mice!' She almost squeaked herself she was so relieved and excited.

'Those are ready,' said her father, pointing to a wooden tray on the table. 'When you've served the customer, you can display the rest in the window.'

He sounded relieved and Ruth hurried back into the shop with the tray.

'How lovely!' cried the young woman. 'Give me a dozen – six pink and six white. Oh, how I love their little tails!' she exclaimed as Ruth packed them into a cardboard box. 'How much do I owe you?'

'They're a penny each.'

'A shilling then.' She took out a silk purse and found the silver coin. 'Thank you!' she said as Ruth hurried to hold the door open for her to leave. 'It's just not Christmas without sugar mice!'

Ruth closed the door behind her but was compelled to stand and watch as the woman walked up the street, box in hand, and her skirts swaying from side to side. Of course, it would be completely impractical to wear a crinoline in the shop. She wouldn't even be able to get behind the counter, but how she would love one for her Sunday best! As she took the mice from the tray to arrange them on a round glass dish in the window, she wondered if there would be any money for a new outfit this winter. She doubted it and decided that it would be kinder to her father not to ask for the money. She would make do with the things she already had. They weren't too shabby and now that she had finished growing there wasn't the problem of her clothes becoming too small. If her father was right and the American war finished soon, and they were back in the shop by the summer, she would ask for dress money then.

Chapter Six

Caroline walked back to Richmond Terrace feeling happy. She'd been determined to get some sugar mice this year.

She climbed the stone steps and rang the bell to be let in. Moments later Jenkins, whom her mother referred to as their butler, opened the door and inclined his head as she stepped into the hall.

'May I take your parcel, Miss Caroline?'

'Just put it on the table,' she instructed him. 'I'll attend to it when I've taken off my coat and hat.' She continued past him and up the stairs to her bedroom where she tossed her outdoor clothes onto the bed. The maid, Lottie, would hang them up for her later.

When she came back down, she picked up the box of confectionery and went into the parlour.

'Look what I got!' she exclaimed as she opened the lid and showed the sweets to her mother, hoping that they might meet with her approval.

'Oh, how lovely!' her mother responded. 'Shall we have one now? I've rung for Mrs Jenkins to bring me a pot of afternoon tea.'

Caroline had intended to keep the mice for Christmas Day, but she didn't argue. Her mother was in an amenable mood today and she knew better than to do anything that would try her temper.

'Which would you like? Pink or white?'

'Oh, a pink one, I think. Where did you get them?'

'The confectioner's shop on Queen Victoria Street. I thought it better to call early rather than be disappointed again.'

'Did you go yourself?' her mother asked after biting off the pink head. 'Ummm, delicious!' she declared. 'You should have sent Lottie,' she went on.

'I felt like a walk,' Caroline told her.

'Well, I must say that the atmosphere in the town is more pleasant since all those chimneys stopped belching their filth. It used to be so annoying to get those sooty spots on my white pelisse, but yesterday when I stepped out to the carriage there wasn't a mark on it. Long may it continue.'

'I'm not sure father would agree,' Caroline said.

'He rarely does agree with me,' replied her mother. 'I wish he would find some other business to amuse himself with – something less dirty. Your grandfather has invested money in the railways, but he doesn't feel the need to shovel the coal into the engines. And of course, Salesbury Hall is well away from the smog of the town. I don't know why your father insists we live here. I'm always telling him we need a country house, but he never listens to a word I say.'

'I'm sure he has his reasons,' Caroline replied, feeling that she ought to try to defend her father's decision. 'Maybe he can't afford another house.'

'What nonsense,' said her mother. 'I'm sure he can. It's just stubbornness.'

Caroline wasn't convinced. She'd seen how worried her father was by having to shut down the mill, but she didn't reply as Mrs Jenkins brought in the tray of tea and put it on the sideboard. She didn't want to spoil the afternoon by falling out with her mother. Instead, she selected a sugar mouse. She would have liked a pink one but took a white one so as not to spoil the symmetry of the box.

'Shall I take a cup of tea to father?' she asked.

'He's gone out. I don't know where. I hope he's back in good time for dinner. I get hungry if it's delayed too long and I refuse to sit down until everyone is here. It just isn't seemly.'

Caroline held up her mouse by its tail. It had a cute face and suddenly she was reluctant to bite into it. She put it down on her side plate and arranged its tail in a curl.

'I always wonder how they make these,' she said.

'Do you?' asked her mother. 'You are a curious girl.'

Caroline didn't respond. She was unsure in which way her mother regarded her as curious, but at a guess she would have interpreted it as odd rather than seeking knowledge. Not that her mother approved much of either. True, she'd been sent to school at Miss Parker's Academy on Church Street – a rather refined day and boarding school for young ladies, where she'd mixed with the daughters of some of the local gentry who considered themselves a cut above a girl whose father owned a mill. But most of what she had learnt there consisted of drawing, music, some needlepoint and a little French conversation. Nothing that would be inappropriate or tax the female brain or make her less desirable as a wife. Caroline knew that her mother's ambition for her was to marry well – someone more suitable than a mill owner she had stipulated once when the subject had come up with her father.

'I don't care who she marries as long as he's kind to her and she's happy,' her father had said. It had set off one of her mother's rages. She'd flounced out of the parlour and not spoken to him for three days.

'He doesn't care about you,' she'd complained to Caroline. 'He doesn't understand. I just want to prevent you from making the same mistakes I made.'

Caroline frowned as she recalled the conversation. She would be twenty on her next birthday in May and she knew that it wouldn't be long before her mother began to enquire about suitable gentlemen to introduce her to. An image of Sir Gilbert sprang to mind. Even though her mother had hated him, Caroline knew no such excuse would be accepted from her if someone similar was earmarked as a potential husband for her.

'Marry for money,' her mother always advised. 'Marrying for love will do you no good at all. Look at me.'

'Are you going to eat that?' her mother asked now, pointing to the sugar mouse.

'I think I'll save it after all,' she said, popping it back into the box with the others.

'Well now you've made me feel guilty about having one,' complained her mother.

'I didn't mean to do that. I'll have it now.'

Caroline retrieved the mouse and trying not to think of its endearing little face, she bit off its head. Her mouth filled with the sweet and sticky taste of pleasure, and she closed her eyes for a moment to savour it. For a moment she considered eating a second, but that would bring accusations of greed from her mother and warnings about having to pull her corset tighter if any man was to give her even passing consideration as a wife.

‘No one will marry a plump girl,’ her mother had remarked when the dressmaker, Mrs Anderton, had said that Caroline had grown since her last fitting.

She closed the lid on the box and put it to one side. As she did, the doorbell rang and she heard her father come in. He came into the parlour and glanced at the teapot.

‘It’s still warm,’ Caroline told him. ‘Shall I ring down for another cup?’

‘Run down to the kitchen and bring one up,’ he said. ‘I’m sure Mrs Jenkins will have her hands full cooking the dinner.’

‘It’s not Caroline’s place to go down to the kitchen!’ her mother told him.

‘I don’t mind,’ she said, thinking she’d be glad of an excuse to leave the tense atmosphere that had permeated the room as soon as her father came in. ‘I got sugar mice,’ she told him. ‘You can have one with your tea.’

He smiled. ‘Thank you,’ he said as he sat down opposite her mother. ‘It’s just what I need.’

He looked worn out, thought Caroline as she edged her way down the back stairs in her full skirt. He looked worn out and defeated. She wondered where he’d been. She guessed it was something to do with the supply of cotton, but she couldn’t ask him about it in front of her mother. Apparently, it wasn’t seemly for a woman to interest herself in business affairs.

Mrs Jenkins seemed surprised to see her, but didn’t protest as Caroline gathered a cup and saucer and took it back up, her crinoline brushing the sides of the narrow staircase. She poured tea for her father and offered him a sugar treat. He took a pink one. She’d known he would.

'You were lucky to get these,' he told her. 'Mr Hodgson is shutting up his shop after Christmas. He's going to be supervising the soup kitchen on Cleaver Street.'

'Soup kitchen?' exclaimed her mother, looking shocked. 'Why are they opening a soup kitchen?'

'To feed those who have no work,' he explained. 'It was Mayor Hutchinson's idea. We have a responsibility for the jobless. We can't just let them starve.'

Chapter Seven

'A soup kitchen. They're going to open a soup kitchen.' Sally could hear the disdain in her father's voice. 'They'd be better off making this government understand that they have a duty to do something about this deadlock at the American ports. It's cotton we need, not blasted charity!'

He slumped down on his chair, reached for his baccy tin and flung it aside when he remembered it was still empty.

'We don't want charity,' he continued. 'It's demeaning. I'll not queue up for a handout. I have some pride left.'

Sally and her mother exchanged a glance, and her mother shook her head slightly, warning Sally not to take him on. She put a cup of tea in her husband's hand.

'Drink that,' she told him. 'Getting cross won't help. And it's not our fault we're out of work. It's only right that the mill owners should help us out if they can't offer wages when we're willing to do our jobs.'

Sally watched her father gulp down his tea. 'I've been everywhere,' he said. 'There's no work. I'm wondering if we should just pack up and go.'

'Go where?' her mother asked, sounding astounded.

'Some folks are talking about going to America.'

'To fight?' asked her mother. 'You're not going to war,' she told him firmly. 'I'll not stand for that. What about us?'

'No! Not to fight. To work the cotton there,' he explained. 'They say there's jobs in weaving and spinning in the north. Perhaps we ought to go where the cotton is, rather than sitting here with nothing, waiting for it to come to us.'

'I don't know.' Her mother sounded bewildered. 'It's a long way. How would we get there?'

'By ship I imagine. I haven't looked into it properly, but Tom and Eli were talking at the Spread Eagle. Tom says there's been agents going around some of the mills looking for recruits and they both say they're determined to go.'

'You were in the Spread Eagle?' asked her mother.

'Aye. And there's no need to sound so disapproving. I only had a half.'

Sally saw that even the waste of a few pence had made her mother cross.

'It's no use us discussing what we can take to the pawn-shop to give us enough to pay this week's rent and then spending money in the pub,' she said.

'I'd been tramping all around the town looking for work,' replied her father. 'I was tired and thirsty.'

'Aye. And I've been cooking and cleaning here all day. I'm thirsty too,' her mother retorted, 'and there's only a few dregs left in the coffee tin and no tea at all now you've had the last cup. But I expect you think I'll make do with water.'

'Don't start, our Martha,' pleaded her father. 'Tha doesn't need to tell me how bad things are. That's why I'm suggesting we look into going to America.'

'And what will we use for money to get there?'

'We could sell up. We wouldn't be able to take any of this furniture and it would bring in a few bob – and the piano.'

'I worked hard to buy that piano,' she protested.

'I know. But we couldn't take it with us. I'll buy you another one when we get there. Tom says the wages are good and the housing is easy. They're all made from wood, not bricks like these and you can build them yourself. You order one and it's all ready and waiting when you arrive – on a decent plot of land too – with room for a kitchen garden. All you need's a screwdriver and you just put it together in no time at all.'

'That sounds like a right fairy tale,' her mother retorted.

'It's not. It's true. Tom said so and he's enquired into it.'

'Tom Dugdale's a fantasist!' she replied. 'Wood's good enough for a shed or a makeshift privy, but if I'm to live in a house I want a proper one made of bricks and mortar, not something that's likely to blow away in the first winter storm.'

'Well, summat'll have to be done,' her father told them. 'There's no jobs here and no prospect of any and I'd rather take my chances in a wooden house than sit here and starve to death.'

Sally wondered if her father was serious. Was there really work in America, or was Tom Dugdale making it up? She knew he had a reputation for storytelling, especially when he'd had a drink or two.

'I haven't heard of any American agents going around,' she said.

'Well, Tom says they're here and I've no reason to doubt him. If I see them, I'll go and make myself known to them and find out more about it.'

'I'm not going all that way!' declared her mother. 'It would be no better than being sent to New South Wales.'

'That's nonsense. We're not convicts! We're honest workers – and why shouldn't we go to work for masters who appreciate us? There's nothing left for us in this town. We need to move on.'

'But I've lived here all my life,' argued her mother. 'I have family here. I don't want to leave.'

'I'd like to go,' interrupted George. His eyes were shining at the prospect of an adventure and Sally found that she agreed with him. Why not take the opportunity to travel across the sea and visit another country? She knew people had gone before and done well. There were the Andertons for a start. Mrs Anderton's father had made a fortune in America they said, which was why his daughter lived in a big house on King Street with her American husband. And the idea of a big wooden house intrigued her. She wondered what it would look like. Would the roof slope, or be flat? Would it have windows? Would there be a chimney? And what if it caught fire? Surely a wooden house would easily burn. She'd be more afraid of that than of it blowing away.

'You'll do as you're told,' her mother reprimanded George, but Sally saw her father wink at his eldest son.

'We'll win her 'round,' he promised. 'We'll see if we can borrow a cart to take yon piano to the pop shop. Once that's gone, she'll have nowt to stay for.'

'You'll do no such thing!' said her mother. 'You'll touch that piano over my dead body!'

Her father laughed and her mother told them to get themselves up to the table because their tea was ready. She seemed to believe that the talk of going to America was over, but Sally saw that her father was serious about the idea and she doubted that he would let it go. It was exciting and frightening at the same time. She remembered the last visit they'd made to the seaside in the summer when the mills had been shut for the wakes weeks. She'd stood on the promenade and looked out at the sea that seemed to go on for ever. What would it be like to sail across it?

'They say this war will be over in a few more months anyway,' remarked her mother when they'd all begun to eat. She'd made butter pie even though it wasn't a Friday. Meat would be an occasional treat from now on, she'd told them. 'Things'll get back to normal then. We'll manage if we're careful,' she went on. 'I'm sure we will.'

Sally wasn't so certain. She'd seen the families who had been out of work for longer than them. The Irish who lived down around Butcher's Court were suffering, she knew. They hated to ask for help for fear of being sent back to Ireland and they were growing paler and thinner as the days passed, scavenging for anything they could find to keep themselves alive. And even the families, like themselves, who'd had a bit put by were falling on hard times. Even though her mother was determined not to part with her beloved piano, Sally had seen furniture being taken out of other houses and carried down to the pawn shop. She thought it wouldn't be much longer before the pawnbroker refused to take in anything more because there was no one left to buy it. Everyone wanted to scrape together a few shillings as best they could, but it was to spend on food and rent and not such luxuries as musical instruments and Sunday best clothing.

Chapter Eight

As Christmas approached, the sugar mice still sat on the plate in the window of the Hodgson's shop. Both Ruth and her father hoped that there would be a last-minute rush on the Monday, which was Christmas Eve, and although some customers did come, they were mostly the businessmen whose trade wasn't dependant on the mills – and in a town like Blackburn they were few.

Mrs Anderton, the dressmaker, came with her little daughter and bought some sweets.

'I feel guilty about getting them when so many can't afford any treats this Christmas,' she admitted when she'd chosen her pear drops and aniseed twists, some humbugs and four sugar mice.

'It has been quieter than usual,' Ruth admitted.

'I hear you're closing after today,' said Mrs Anderton.

'Yes. My father's going to be in charge of the soup kitchen.'

'So I heard. It's a sorry state of affairs,' went on Mrs Anderton. 'I've never known anything like it before. My mother says it's the first time she can recall that people have been out of work, and she's lived and worked here for nearly forty years.' She sighed and paid Ruth for her purchases.

A few other customers came – Mrs Sharples from the post office and her two daughters, then Mrs Tiplady whose husband ran the printing shop where Ruth's brother-in-law worked. At least Amos's job wasn't in the mill and her sister Naomi and her little nieces would be provided for. Her other sister Deborah had moved away to Manchester when she married and they didn't see as much of her. She'd written a week ago to say that her husband was still in work, but although the letter had been intended to sound optimistic, Ruth saw that her father had read between the lines and was concerned.

In the afternoon, as darkness began to fall her father told her to make a sign for the window reducing the sugar mice that were left to a farthing each. Ruth had seen the mill girl who'd come in asking for work looking into the window earlier, with her shawl pulled tight around her face, and she hoped that she might come back.

But by six o'clock the street was deserted and it was clear they would sell nothing more.

'Clear everything out of the window and pull the blinds down,' her father told her.

Ruth was taking out the plate of mice when she saw the mill girl again. She picked up the sign she'd made and held it up.

'Only a farthing each!' she called.

The girl hesitated then seemed to make up her mind. She pushed open the door and came in.

'Please may I have four?' she asked.

Ruth picked up the tongues and put two white and two pink into a paper cone. 'That'll be a penny, please.'

She watched as the girl struggled to get hold of the coin in her purse with fingers that looked numbed with cold.

'Happy Christmas!' called Ruth as she went out.

'Thank you! You too.'

'What shall I do with these that are left?' Ruth asked her father.

'Put them on the cold slab in the kitchen. Everything else will keep in the jars. They should be all right until we open again.'

When the shop had been tidied, the counter washed down and the floor mopped, Ruth turned the key in the door. Tomorrow would be Christmas Day. They would go to church in the morning and then come home to eat their dinner. In the afternoon they were to visit Naomi and Amos and have tea with them. Ruth had bought little gifts for her nieces, Hope and Nora – two rag dolls made with scraps of cloth and packed with sawdust. She knew that they would adore them.

In the kitchen her father was sitting by the fire reading the latest edition of the *Blackburn Standard* and frowning. Ruth checked on the chicken she'd bought for their dinner. It had seemed too rash to buy a goose when there were only two of them, but the plum pudding was simmering nicely and smelt so good that it made her mouth water.

'I've made a mutton pie and the vegetables are all ready to go in the pan,' Agatha said as she hung up her apron behind the door and reached for her shawl. 'I've put the ones for tomorrow in the pantry, so you'll only need to pop the chicken in the oven and then put the potatoes around it later.'

'Thank you, Agatha,' Ruth said. 'I hope you have a happy Christmas!'

'I will,' the maid replied. 'At least I have my job, so we'll not starve.'

'Has Bert been laid off?' asked Ruth's father.

'Aye. End of last week, so we still have his final wages, but it'll not be easy if things don't improve in the new year.' She hesitated and Ruth could see she was anxious. 'You will still need me, won't you?' she asked. 'I know you've shut up the shop, but…'

'Yes, of course. Don't worry. We'll still need you because Ruth and I will be out all day.'

Agatha smiled, relieved. 'Thank you,' she said. 'I'm sorry to ask, but I just wondered. Happy Christmas!' she called as she opened the door to let in a blast of icy air. A draught swept across the kitchen as she closed it behind her and the fire flickered and smoked.

'She needs her job,' Ruth observed as the maid's footsteps faded into the distance. 'But can we really afford to keep paying her?'

'How could I tell her any different?' her father asked. 'And how would we manage without her?'

'I could do her work,' Ruth offered. It wasn't a tempting option. It would mean being alone in the house all day, and the work was hard – especially the washing – but it was a less daunting prospect than the soup kitchen.

Her father shook his head. 'I've negotiated a wage for you at Cleaver Street,' he told her, 'and it's more than I pay Agatha so it wouldn't make any sense. I'll find the money from somewhere,' he promised. 'It won't be for long.'

Chapter Nine

Sally's parents had sat down with their children the week before Christmas and explained to them that this year things would be different.

'I know it's disappointing,' her mother had told them. 'But it would be imprudent to spend our money on expensive food and gifts when we don't know how long it's going to have to last us. We can still celebrate,' she went on, 'but there won't be any presents this year, and we won't be getting a goose or a plum pudding. We'll sit down to a dinner together, but it'll be something plain and wholesome – a hotpot perhaps. And we can still sing carols around the piano and play games like we always do. So, it's not as if we aren't having a Christmas at all.'

It was the younger ones who were the most disappointed. The twins looked stunned. They'd been promised a kaleidoscope months ago when they'd asked for one.

'If you're good, you can have it for Christmas,' their parents had told them. And now they were being told that they wouldn't get it after all.

Sally could see that they thought it wasn't fair. They were too young to understand that the things they'd always taken for granted in the past were no longer possible. Florrie and Ellen looked glum too. Even though they'd lost their jobs and had no money to hand to their mother at the end of the week, it was clear that they'd been expecting a present and the usual dinner.

'It's not the end of the world,' their father told them. 'Next year it will be different. We'll probably be in America by then!'

Sally saw her mother frown at him. She'd already told him not to raise the children's hopes until he was sure that it was the right thing to do. Tom Dugdale's talk of American manufacturers sending men to beg workers to emigrate seemed to have been a huge exaggeration. They may have visited Manchester, but none had been seen in Blackburn and Sally knew that her mother hoped they wouldn't come.

–

On Christmas Eve, Sally's mother sent her out to the market late in the afternoon when the stall holders began to reduce their prices. She didn't have much money to give her, but she was told to see what scrag ends of meat might be left to go into the hotpot.

Sally scoured the stalls for the best bargains and managed to get some lamb and some slices of bacon. She bought potatoes and oat cakes, but the apples were too expensive and treats such as mince pies out of the question. When all the money her mother had given her was spent, she knew she ought to head home, but she was tempted to walk back down Queen Victoria Street to Hodgson's. When she'd passed earlier, she'd seen that they had some sugar mice in the window – and she'd saved the penny of her own money since she'd lost her job at the mill, hoping to be able to afford a small treat at Christmas.

When the confectioner's daughter had called out to her that the sweets were reduced to a farthing each, she'd gone in and bought four. It had been a moment of madness, but the penny in her purse had weighed heavily and she'd been unable to resist buying one each for the twins and her little sisters. They had been so sad these past few days that she'd felt compelled to try to cheer them up on Christmas Day.

Wanting them to be a surprise for Christmas morning, she kept the mice hidden under her shawl when she got home until she had a chance to hide them behind the piano, inside four woollen stockings that she'd taken from the pile of clean clothes waiting to be put away.

'Bedtime,' her mother sighed later when the fire was almost out and the kitchen had grown too cold to sit in. Her mother picked up the one candle they'd allowed themselves in the kitchen and stood at the bottom of the stairs, shivering, as Sally's father checked the front door was locked. 'Are you coming up?' she asked Sally.

'Yes, I'll follow you,' she told her and watched as her mother began to mount the stairs, the low light from the guttering candle casting shadows with each step she took. She seemed sad and weary, and Sally wished she could have got a gift for her as well, as she usually did. Her mother deserved something nice, and Sally vowed that once she was back at work, she would save up to buy her mother a special present for her birthday later in the year.

Instead of following her parents up to the bedrooms, Sally waited until the light from the candle disappeared as her mother went into the room at the front where she and Sally's father slept. Sally was left in total darkness, but she'd lived in this house for all of her eighteen years and was so familiar with it that she could easily find her way. She felt behind the piano for the stockings and put them on the mantelpiece above the fireplace. Then she closed the parlour door quietly behind her and felt her way towards the foot of the stairs. One by one she crept up until she reached the room where she slept with her sisters. In the black silence she undressed and got into bed, glad that it was already warmed by Florrie's and Ellen's bodies.

-

When Christmas morning arrived, the house was quiet. There was none of the usual excitement. It was still dark when Sally got out of bed, but she could hear the church bells ringing to greet the day. She lit a precious candle to light her way down the steep stairs. In the kitchen her mother was kindling the fire with a few damp pieces of wood.

'The pump's frozen,' she announced. 'It's a good job I fetched some water in last night, but even that needs the ice breaking if you want to fill the kettle.'

With her teeth chattering and her hands numbed, Sally managed to get the kettle onto the hob where the fire was taking hold. She stood in front of it, rubbing her hands together to try to get them warm.

'Move thyself,' reprimanded her mother. 'You're blocking all the heat.'

Reluctantly, Sally moved away to see what other tasks needed to be done.

'Are we lighting a fire in the parlour?' she asked. 'It is Christmas Day.'

Her mother looked at the coal in the scuttle. 'Maybe after we've had our dinner,' she said. 'Just for an hour, whilst we sing some carols.'

Sally felt disappointed. One of the treats she always looked forward to at Christmas was the lighting of the fire in the parlour where they would spend the day sitting on the best chairs, rather than crowding into the kitchen as they normally did.

'Can you start peeling the potatoes?' her mother asked. 'I want to get the hotpot on to cook.'

Sally picked up the knife and wrapped a coarse apron over her clothes. She was already wearing two petticoats over her shift and stays, topped by a blouse and skirt, a jacket and her shawl pulled crossways and fastened behind her so as not to get in the way of her work. Even so she was freezing cold and struggled with her task.

By the time the vegetables were ready, the fire was blazing and the kitchen had warmed by a few degrees although the windows were still covered in a thick layer of ice. When Florrie came down, she put her mouth to the kitchen window and melted a small circle with her hot breath so that she could look outside.

'It's snowing,' she announced, although Sally could tell it held no excitement for her. It would be cold and wet outside and the storm meant they would need to stay in beside the fire if they were to keep comfortable.

The others came down one by one and huddled around the flames, pushing for position, although space was readily given up to her father when he came down and sat in his chair with his feet pushed up on the fender.

'Mam says that'll give you chilblains,' Ellen told him.

'Only when you come in from the cold,' Florrie told her.

'But it is cold in here,' she protested. 'Are we not going in the front parlour?'

'Later,' said her mother. 'Now, let me get near to check on this hotpot.'

Sally sat on a stool and looked at their sad faces. She wondered if she should tell them about their stockings, but decided she would wait until after dinner. She hoped the surprise would cheer them up.

When they'd eaten, her father took some of the blazing coals on a shovel and shouted at them all to clear a path as he carried them through to the grate in the front room.

'What's them stockings doing in there?' he asked his wife when he came back for more coal.

'Stockings? I know nowt about stockings,' she told him.

'It was me,' Sally said. 'I put them there after you'd gone to bed last night. There's one each for the little ones.'

'Stockings!' cried the twins, hurrying through to look. Sally followed them with her sisters close behind. Isaac and Esau were jumping up and down on the spot pointing at the small bulge in the toes of the grey woollen socks that she'd put on the mantelpiece.

'It isn't much,' she warned them, suddenly fearing that they were expecting a kaleidoscope after all. 'Just one each,' she said as she distributed the gifts. George looked hopeful. 'I'm sorry,' she told him. 'I only had enough money to buy four.'

He nodded, but as he watched his younger brothers and sisters exclaim in delight at the sugar mice, he was obviously disappointed and Sally wished she could have got one for him as well.

'Can we eat them now?' they asked when their mother came in. 'Please?'

'You shouldn't have wasted money,' she reprimanded Sally.

'It was my money.'

'Even so. We need every penny and you'll not be bringing in any more wages.'

'Please, let's not argue about it. Not today. I just wanted to do something nice for them.'

'You're a good lass,' said her mother giving her a hug. 'Go on,' she told the younger ones. 'Eat them if you must and then we'll do some singing.'

The children sat on the rug by the fire and savoured their sweet treats. Sally and George and their parents drank the last of the tea and afterwards her mother lifted the lid of the piano and played for them – *Silent Night, Holy Night*. They sang enthusiastically as the snow came down outside and settled on the street, muffling the town in an unaccustomed hush. Even the church bells had fallen silent and a blanket of white shrouded Blackburn as families in the houses all around tried to feel optimistic about the future – and failed.

Chapter Ten

Caroline Haworth had been woken on Christmas morning when Lottie came in with her early morning tea and pulled back the thick brocade curtains.

'Merry Christmas! It's snowing,' the maid told her. 'Would you like me to light your fire before I bring up the hot water? It feels very chilly in here.'

'Yes, please, Lottie. I'm not moving from here until you do,' Caroline replied as she pulled a thick bed jacket around her shoulders. She took a sip of the tea. It was strong and scalding hot, just the way she liked it.

'Which gown shall I get out?' asked Lottie.

'The thick blue one,' instructed Caroline. 'With the matching hat and the fur muff. Mother will insist we go to church and it'll be freezing cold in there. How deep is the snow?' she asked, suddenly hoping that it might be lying so thickly on the ground that her mother would decide it was too risky to send for the carriage.

'Don't worry. It's not sticking yet,' said Lottie and Caroline sighed. The chilly air and the hard pews of the parish church were not appealing.

Once Lottie had fetched up her washing water, the steam from it pluming in the chilly air, Caroline put aside her thick layers of blankets and eiderdown and lowered her feet to the rug by her bedside. She shivered. There was ice on the inside of the windowpane and she would have much preferred to stay longer in her warm bed.

But it was Christmas, Caroline reminded herself as she poured the hot water into the bowl, picked up her cloth and the scented soap and set about giving herself a thorough wash. She didn't dawdle. She washed her face, neck and ears, then under her arms and finally her private parts. Then Lottie helped her to dress before taking away the water and the pot from under the bed.

When Caroline reached the top of the stairs, she paused for a moment to admire the Christmas tree that had been brought inside and set up in the large hallway. It was decorated with ribbons and garlands and had candles attached to the branches that would be lit after dark that afternoon. Then, she and her parents would sit down around the huge oak table and there would be a cooked goose, with roasted potatoes, carrots, parsnips and other vegetables all laced with gravy, followed by a plum pudding.

When she went into the morning room her mother was already there with a cup of tea and a plate of eggs. She was opening some envelopes that had just been brought by the post boy.

'Christmas cards!' she announced, holding them up for Caroline to admire. 'So many people have sent them this year. I'm so glad I did the same or I would have looked unfashionable.'

The cards were beautiful, thought Caroline. Made from thick card and decorated with pictures of holly and mistletoe and rhyming verses wishing them well for the festive season.

'Christmas was quite dull when I was a child by comparison,' her mother told her. 'We received gifts on the Feast of the Epiphany, but the queen and Prince Albert have turned it into a delightful holiday with their traditions. Poor man,' she added in a whisper. 'I hear that he is quite unwell. We must remember him in our prayers.'

'Shall we display them?' Caroline asked, meaning the cards.

'Oh yes. I want any callers to see how many we have received! I think we should put them on the mantelpiece in the drawing room.'

Mrs Haworth always referred to the parlour as the drawing room. She liked to pretend that their house was much larger than it was, more like her father's house. Caroline's father always called it the parlour and it was yet another source of friction between her parents. She hoped that today, at least, they would be gracious to one another and that her mother wouldn't make a scene. Caroline had been counting down the days to this special celebration and she would hate to have it spoiled.

She spooned some of the scrambled eggs on to her own plate and took a slice of the fresh toast that Mrs Jenkins had just brought in.

'It's snowing,' she told her mother in case she hadn't noticed. 'Will we be going to church?'

'Of course! Everyone will be there. It wouldn't do to be absent. I've already sent for the carriage to be brought round, so eat that quickly. We mustn't be late.'

Caroline nodded as Mrs Jenkins poured her a cup of coffee. Attendance at church wasn't so much about worship as about being seen. Despite not being the most important lady in the town – that was reserved for Lady Feilden, the wife of Sir William Feilden – her mother regarded herself as the genuine daughter of the lord of the manor and better than most of the congregation. She considered the Fielden's not to be *proper* gentry having only recently received their titles. It could be embarrassing at times for Caroline who realised that the local inhabitants didn't regard her mother with the awe she expected. But the church service would have to be endured. It was only a couple of hours and then they could return home to a roaring log fire, a sumptuous dinner and maybe a glass of wine.

When she came down from her bedroom after putting on her hat and gloves, Caroline was surprised to see her father in the hallway wearing his coat with his Sunday best hat in his hand.

'Are you coming to church?' she asked him.

'Yes. To please your mother,' he added as if it was a penance he was forced to perform. 'She claims your grandparents will be there this morning and she doesn't want to be shown up by not having her husband at her side.'

'Will they be there?' Caroline asked. She knew they usually attended their local church to worship.

'I doubt it.' Her father glanced out of the window to where the snow was thickening in the sky. 'They'd be foolish to come into town in this weather,' he said. 'It's beginning to stick, and I wouldn't be surprised if there are drifts before the day's out.'

When the carriage came round from the stables the sounds of the hooves and wheels were muffled by the snow. Caroline saw that her father was concerned about the wisdom of setting out at all even though it was only a short journey.

'You and I could easily walk to the parish church,' he told her. 'But your mother refuses to go on foot because she thinks it makes her look like a peasant.'

Caroline tried not to laugh. What her father said was true. Her mother would walk nowhere except for a turn around the gardens at Salesbury Hall on a warm day.

'What are you waiting for?' demanded her mother as she descended the stairs wrapped in many layers of clothing to keep her warm.

Thankfully her father didn't respond but gave her his arm to escort her down the slippery steps and into the carriage. Caroline followed. The church bells had suddenly burst into song and her mother was fretting about being late as she wrapped a blanket around her knees. Caroline climbed in beside her, followed by her father who called to Simmons to set off. Her mother gasped as the wheels skidded on the slippery cobbles and her father frowned. Caroline hoped the weather wouldn't worsen too much whilst they were in the church. She dreaded having to trudge home through the snow with her mother complaining beside her.

The church was as cold as she'd anticipated, but it had been decorated for Christmas with greenery and candles and the singing of all the familiar carols soon warmed Caroline's mood. Afterwards, families greeted one another, wishing everyone a *Merry Christmas.* But there was a distinct damper on the festive spirit as some of the local businessmen gathered in groups and the talk inevitably turned to the cotton crisis.

'I wish your father wouldn't discuss business today,' her mother complained as they waited to greet the vicar before they left. 'It isn't seemly.'

'People are concerned,' Caroline reminded her.

'Your grandfather isn't concerned,' she replied. 'He says there's money to be made. But your father is too stubborn to listen.' Her expression was angry, but it changed in a moment as the vicar came into view and greeted her.

'A very nice sermon,' Mrs Haworth told him. 'Merry Christmas!'

'Merry Christmas to you, Mrs Haworth. It's always a pleasure to see you.'

'Come along,' said Caroline's mother once the vicar had moved on to speak to other parishioners. 'I'm sure Simmons will have the carriage waiting and we don't want to stand about here in the cold for too long.'

Caroline saw that her mother was anxious not to become surrounded by the worshippers who had come in their clogs and shawls to sit in the pews towards the back of the church. They were wishing one another a *Merry Christmas* too, but their voices were subdued and they stood as if they bore a heavy burden.

As her father excused himself from the conversation he'd been having with some of the other mill owners, Caroline saw him prepare to greet some of the familiar faces amongst his former employees, but they wilfully turned their backs as he approached and he looked perplexed and then hurt as they cold-shouldered him.

'They don't want to speak to me,' he told Caroline. 'They're people I've known for years. But I suppose I can't blame them,' he added. 'There'll not be much Christmas cheer in their homes this day.'

When they arrived back at Richmond Terrace and Caroline took off her damp outer coat and exchanged her wet boots for dainty slippers, she thought about the mill workers who were without jobs. They'd looked so sad and worried.

'Is there nothing more you can do for them?' she asked her father when she'd joined her parents in the dining room. 'I hate to think of them having no Christmas dinner.'

'I've done what I can. I paid them the wages they were owed, and I've given a donation to the soup kitchen that's opening in the new year. There's not much more I can do. It seems we're going to be living in straitened circumstances ourselves until this American war is over.'

Caroline saw her mother's face tighten.

'Let's not talk about that now,' she said. 'It's Christmas Day!'

Determined to avoid an argument, Caroline said nothing more. Perhaps she could speak to her father about it later, she thought, when her mother wasn't about. The sight of the workers refusing to speak to her father had upset her. It was so unusual. They would normally have touched their caps and greeted him in a friendly way, but their anger and resentment had been clear to see, and Caroline hoped there wasn't going to be trouble.

Her father carved the roasted goose and the plates were passed around. Caroline helped herself to the vegetables and gravy. It would have been a perfect day except for the incident with the workers at the church. It made her worried about the future and what it would mean for her personally if her father couldn't reopen his mill. The thought of living without everything that she'd always taken for granted frightened her, and although the food was delicious, she found she had little appetite for it when she thought about all those who would be going hungry today.

Chapter Eleven

Ruth had woken on Christmas morning to see the street outside covered by a thin layer of snow. It was even and unspoiled. No footprints or wheel tracks had marked it as there was no one about. She'd hurriedly washed and dressed herself and gone downstairs to light the fire and get her father's breakfast. He'd still been sleeping when she passed his room and she hadn't woken him. He'd looked so weary the previous evening that she'd thought the extra rest would do him good.

'Why didn't you call me?' he wanted to know when he came hurrying down a while later, fastening his collar as he came to warm himself in front of the flames.

'I thought you deserved a lie-in,' Ruth told him as she poured him a cup of tea.

'We mustn't be late for church,' he reminded her.

'There's plenty of time,' she said as she put bacon and eggs on his plate with a slice of bread and butter.

He sat down to eat and she went to get the chicken that she'd put in a dish with the potatoes and plenty of fat. It would go in the oven now and would be cooked by the time they came back from the service.

After the pots had been cleared away and washed, Ruth fetched her coat and bonnet and the muff that had been her mother's. Her mother had always worn it to go to church unless the weather was very warm, and it gave

Ruth some comfort to do the same – as if her mother were still close by. She missed her so much, especially when it was Christmas. Every year, she found herself thinking back to the time when both her sisters still lived at home with them. Her mother had always made Christmas so special, with lots of food and sweets and the house decorated with holly and other greenery. There had always been gifts hanging up in stockings on the fireplace – mostly small things like soaps or handkerchiefs and, of course, the sugar mice. It had been so special, so magical. Ruth wished she could rediscover that sense of wonder and happiness. She sometimes thought it was gone for ever and she would never feel such warm emotions again.

She stepped out into the cold street and waited as her father locked the door. The church bells were already ringing. Not only the parish church but every church in the town, and the sound brought a lump to her throat. Normally it would have thrilled her with the expectation of delights to come, but this year she kept thinking that the future was so uncertain and she was afraid of what it might bring.

They walked across the town calling season's greetings to all the people they saw, whether they knew them or not. People were crowding into the parish church as the time for the service drew near, hurrying to reach a pew in time and not have to endure the disapproving glances of those already seated if they arrived as the first hymn was being sung.

It all seemed so familiar – the decorations, the Christmas carols, the familiar readings from the bible about the birth of Jesus, yet Ruth sensed she was not alone in feeling that today things were different. After the service ended her father fell into conversation with some men outside the church – Mr Haworth the mill owner and several others who served on the town council. Despite it being Christmas their faces showed none of the joy that the day ought to have brought. They shook their heads and looked sad and worried as they spoke about the crisis. But worse were the faces of the mill workers as they straggled out from the pews at the back looking cold and daunted. They kept their faces averted and spoke to no one but hurried to their homes through the driving snow. Ruth wondered if they would have a Christmas dinner, or if they would have nothing to eat at all.

At home, she put the chicken and roast potatoes on the table and, as she listened to her father say grace, she thought again about the workers she'd seen.

'Do you think people will be going hungry today?' she asked her father as they filled their plates. 'Some of the people at church looked so sad and tired.'

'I fear they will go hungry,' he agreed, looking guiltily at the plentiful food on his plate.

'Maybe the soup kitchen should have opened before Christmas,' Ruth said. Even though she'd been fretting about helping to make the soup, the sight of the hungry workers that morning had made her realise that she was in a privileged position and ought to be glad that she could do something to help those less fortunate than herself.

'I think it probably should,' agreed her father. 'People are struggling to feed themselves and the news isn't good. Mr Haworth was telling me that bringing in cotton from other countries may not be as easy as some say.'

'Why's that?' she asked.

'For one thing there isn't much of it,' explained her father. 'The cotton grown in Egypt and India is mostly for their own use. There was always such a good supply of cheap cotton from America that it would have been pointless them trying to compete by growing crops for export. And even now they're saying that it may not be worth their while to plant more because they will suffer losses if the American cotton flows again. You can't blame them,' he added. 'The Americans have had a monopoly for years and although there are those who have warned of the dangers of depending on just one source, they haven't been listened to. The spinners and manufacturers wanted their raw material at the cheapest price possible and that has always been from America, and mostly the southern states. And even if it can be imported from India or Egypt it won't come straight away. It must be planted and grown and harvested first and that will take time.'

'So, we may not be opening our shop again in the spring?' Ruth asked, feeling sad.

'It seems not. It looks like this crisis may go on for much longer than was anticipated,' her father replied.

Chapter Twelve

It was a frosty morning, the day after the Feast of the Epiphany, when Ruth and her father walked to Cleaver Street. The snow that had fallen over Christmas had drifted along the roads and the way was slippery underfoot. Ruth had dressed in as many layers of clothes as she could manage because her father had warned her that the foundry would be cold. The fires would only be lit when the soup was ready to be cooked and today was to be about setting up the kitchen and deciding how best it could be run.

The door to the foundry was standing ajar when they arrived and Ruth followed her father inside where he joined a group of men that included Mr Hutchinson, the mayor, Mr Yates, the foundry owner, and a few other councillors who were also members of the soup kitchen sub-committee. The vats from their own kitchen had been carried down earlier by cart and were stacked near a huge fireplace that was empty and cold, although there were baskets of sticks and a few sacks of coal standing by ready to light the fire.

'What do you think, Mr Hodgson?' the mayor asked her father. 'Where's the best place for these tables?'

Ruth watched as her father assessed the space.

'Where will people be coming in?' he asked.

'Through the door here,' Mr Yates replied.

'So, they'll be coming in and going out through the same door?'

'Aye. I don't want them tramping the length of the foundry unsupervised.'

'Well, we'll need a table for them to be served and it can't be too far from the vats,' replied her father. 'We don't want to be carrying soup further than necessary. And once they're served, if they're not leaving, they'll be eating in here, so we need tables and benches, but not in the way of the flow of customers.'

'Hardly customers,' someone remarked.

'They'll be customers as far as I'm concerned and treated with respect,' her father corrected him. 'No one who comes here for food will be doing so through any fault of their own and they'll not be treated like beggars.'

'You're right, Mr Hodgson,' the mayor agreed. 'We need to keep the workers calm. We don't want any rioting or suchlike on our hands.'

'Rioting?' asked another councillor. 'Do you think that's a possibility?'

'Who knows?' said the mayor. 'People are angry and frustrated, and who can blame them? I fear it wouldn't take much to push them towards violence. We must do everything in our power to prevent it.'

Ruth watched as the men began to arrange the tables under the direction of her father. There was to be a long trestle where the soup would be served and shorter trestles with benches on either side where people could sit to eat. Behind the serving area and adjacent to the fireplace, wooden tables were arranged for the preparation of the food.

'The beef and vegetables should be arriving early tomorrow,' Mr Hutchinson said. 'We were hoping for them to come today, but the delivery's been held up by the weather.'

'How many will we be catering for?' her father asked as he inspected the range of sharp knives that had been collected for peeling and chopping.

'We've decided on 130 gallons,' Mr Hutchinson told him. 'We're getting barley, groats, turnips, peas, carrots and onions as well as the beef, and of course there's a sack or two of both salt and pepper for seasoning. It should make a tasty and nutritious meal. It'll be a pint a serving – free to those with tickets and a penny to everyone else.'

Her father nodded. 'And how many to prepare and serve it?' he asked.

'Enough. Mainly volunteers at the moment.'

'Wives?' asked her father dubiously. 'Or will they be sending their cooks?'

'Mrs Hutchinson has agreed to help,' bristled the mayor. 'How hard can it be to peel a few vegetables? I'm sure they'll manage.'

Ruth saw her father was worried, although he made no objections until they were on their way home later that day.

'It'll be a disaster. Mark my words,' he grumbled. 'It wouldn't surprise me if not one of the committee ladies who are coming to assist tomorrow has ever peeled a vegetable in their lives before.'

Ruth wondered if she should point out to her father that she'd rarely peeled a vegetable herself. True, she knew how to add the ingredients to a pot and keep it simmering and to stir it occasionally, but all the preparation had always been done by Agatha, and she wondered if it would be better after all for her father to take their maid to Cleaver Street and leave her at home. The prospect of being expected to make gallons and gallons of soup was so overwhelming that all she wanted to do was hide away.

When they reached Queen Victoria Street and went inside, Agatha had gone home, but she'd left a stew for their tea and it smelt delicious. Ruth lifted the lid and breathed in the aroma. She was hungry, as well as cold, and wanted nothing more than to eat and then sit beside the fire and try not to think about the next day. She feared that her father was going to be disappointed with her efforts. She dreaded letting him down and she'd hoped that despite his misgivings, there would be others who knew something about preparing vegetables who could guide her and show her what to do.

Chapter Thirteen

When the Christmas season was over, and the Grimes family were once again huddled around a meagre fire in the kitchen, Sally's father gave in to her mother's pleas to see sense and agreed to speak to the relief committee about getting some help.

With the snow still thick in the streets, Sally accompanied him to the town hall. As they crossed the empty market square and passed the shuttered market hall, they saw there was a queue of people who had come for the same reason. It snaked out of the front door, down the steps and all the way down the side of the building towards Penny Street.

'You go back home,' her father said. 'There's nowt to be gained by us both getting chilled to the marrow.'

'I'll wait with you,' Sally told him as she pulled her shawl more firmly around her shoulders. The sky was darkening again even though it had only just come light, and she saw the first few flakes of snow that presaged yet another storm. She knew that she would be soaked as well as frozen if she waited, but she hated to leave her father to suffer alone.

The line moved so slowly that at times it seemed to barely move at all, and those who came back down the town hall steps looked morose as they hurried away towards their homes.

'Don't expect much,' they warned those who were still waiting. 'It's an insult what they're offering. Sixpence a head for a week and that to be given in soup and bread. How do they expect us to manage on that? How do we pay the rent? How are we supposed to buy coal and candles, never mind clothe ourselves?'

They hurried off, heads down into the driving snow. Sally brushed the accumulation of flakes from her shoulders and turned to her father.

'It's next to nothing,' she said. 'Do you think it's worth the wait?'

He shrugged. 'I suppose it's better than nowt,' he replied. 'If it were just me then I'd be tempted to tell 'em what they can do with their soup. But it's the lasses and the twins that thy mother says we need to think of. We can't let them go hungry when there's summat on offer – no matter how frugal. And hopefully it won't be for long,' he said, trying to sound optimistic as he pulled his cap further down to keep the intensifying flakes of snow out of his eyes. 'Perhaps they'll come recruiting for workers to go to America like Tom said. You'd think they would be approaching folk in this queue. They'd get more workers here than they could possibly want.'

'I don't know about that,' interrupted the man who was waiting behind them. 'I got approached by one in the Sun coffee house before Christmas. But it wasn't work they were offering. They were after recruits to help fight their war. I told them to jog on.'

'If it brought their war to an end and sent us the cotton again, I might be tempted,' said another unemployed worker. 'At least I'd be fed and clothed and I'm beginning to doubt that will happen here.' He inclined his head towards the town hall door. It had been hours now and they'd only just reached the bottom of the steps. The snow was coming down harder and Sally had lost all feeling in her toes.

'You wouldn't go to fight, would you?' she asked her father. She was worried by the idea that he might be tempted to go away and leave them. How would they manage without him? They all depended on his reassuring presence. From her mother to the twins, they all needed him in their own way and the thought of him not being there was alarming.

'No,' he reassured her. 'If I go, I'll go to work. And we'll all go. I'll not see my family split up. There's no need to worry,' he told her, putting a cold arm around her and hugging her so that the wet snow soaked through her shawl and into her jacket. 'I'll not leave you,' he promised.

Dinner time had come and gone by the time they got inside the town hall and even then, they weren't near the front of the queue, but at least they were out of the snow. At last, it was their turn to be called through. Darkness was falling again and the lamps had been lit.

Some members of the relief committee were sitting behind a long oak table that was strewn with ledgers and pens. They looked as weary as the workers who had queued to see them, but at least they were dry and had a roaring fire in the grate at their backs, even though it was doing little to warm the lofty room.

'Name?' asked one. It was a question he must have repeated hundreds of times that day.

Sally listened as her father listed all the members of the family.

'We were good workers,' he told the committee. 'We had good wages, but it's all been taken from us. It isn't our fault. We want to work.'

The man nodded. He'd heard the same from everyone who had stood in front of the desk.

'I can give you sixpence a head for this week, but then it'll be tokens for bread and six pints of soup a day from the kitchen on Cleaver Street. It'll open tomorrow.' He paused and looked at Sally as if he'd only just noticed her standing there, shivering. 'There's work at the soup kitchen if you know how to prepare vegetables,' he told her. 'Go early tomorrow morning and ask for Mr Hodgson.'

'I'll take any work,' she told him.

'Paid?' interrupted her father. Sally was shocked. It had never occurred to her that she wouldn't be paid.

'Tuppence a day,' said the man. 'And it'll reduce the number of tokens I can give you,' he admitted.

'Hardly worth it then,' muttered her father.

'I'll do it. I'll go first thing,' Sally said. 'We'd rather work than rely on charity. Wouldn't we?' she asked her father.

'Aye,' he said. 'I'd rather you'd offered me work than tokens, but I don't suppose there's chance of that?'

'There may be something when the weather improves,' the man told them. 'The councillors are discussing it. There might be work in the stone quarries up at Shorrock's Delph.'

'Stone quarrying? I'm a weaver!' her father replied.

'There's no work for weavers. You know that,' replied the man irritably. The queue behind them was growing even more restless and he seemed eager to move them on now that the money had been handed over.

'There's work in America. Who do I talk to about that?' her father asked.

'I don't know,' he said. 'It's nothing to do with us. Move along now, please.'

Moments later they were back outside in the snow, trudging home in the twilight. Her father was angry and dispirited by the experience, but Sally felt optimistic. At least there would be work for her and although it didn't pay much it was better than hanging around the cold house with nothing to do.

'I wonder if there's anything else we can sell,' her mother said when she heard what they were being given to survive on. But when Sally looked around the bare kitchen it was clear that there wasn't much left that wasn't essential. Many of their belongings had already been taken to the pawn shop in the weeks before Christmas when her father and herself had been put on short time. The china tea set that used to be displayed on the dresser had gone. Her father's best Sunday suit and hat had gone. Her mother's best frock and her own blue skirt and jacket that she'd loved so much and the bonnet that matched it – all gone for a few shillings to buy food so that they wouldn't go hungry.

'We'll get them back when things look up,' her parents had promised. 'It's just to tide us over until the mills start up again.' Everyone had believed that the crisis would not continue for long. They had expected the government to intervene and send war ships to America to break the blockade. They'd believed that it would be put right, and quickly. It was unthinkable that cotton, the staple trade of the country, would simply disappear and the jobs and livelihoods of so many people along with it.

'There's the blankets,' suggested her father, still looking for anything of value.

'It's too cold to part with blankets in the middle of winter,' her mother told him. 'Maybe we can do without them when the warmer weather comes.'

'Surely we'll be back at work by the summer,' Sally said. 'It can't go on like this for so long, can it?'

'I don't know.' Her father sat down in his chair by the fire and stared at the embers. 'It doesn't bear thinking about – but if I get the chance to take us to America, that's where we'll go. I'll not stay here and try to survive on tokens!'

Chapter Fourteen

Ruth hardly slept the night before the soup kitchen opened. And when she did sleep for an hour or two, she was soon wakened by dreams of the soup being ruined and crowds of customers banging on the tables with their spoons to show their anger that there was nothing to eat after all.

She pushed the covers aside for a moment to cool her sweat-drenched body and steady her racing heartbeat. Then she began to shiver as the frosty night air struck her. She pulled the blankets back over herself and tried to get comfortable, willing herself to sleep, dreading the full day of work ahead of her when she was already tired out. It was still pitch black with no hint of dawn, but her father had said that they must be up early at six o'clock, before any sign of daylight. She had no idea how much longer she had left to try to snatch some sleep, and she despaired at her inability to stop fretting about what was to come.

Eventually she heard the creak of springs that alerted her to her father getting out of his bed. She heard the soft pad of his stockinged feet coming across thc landing to tap on her door to rouse her.

'I'm awake!' she called. She heard the catch in her voice that betrayed her anxiety, but her father said nothing more and she heard him going down the stairs.

Ruth got up, shivering. She washed her face in the icy water from the jug on the washstand and got dressed. Her father had told her to wear her oldest clothes and plenty of them.

'It won't be like working in the shop,' he'd warned her. 'You'll need something hardwearing that'll withstand a bit of mess.'

She turned back the blankets and the cotton sheet on her bed and left the damp bedclothes to air whilst she went down to see about some breakfast. It was too early for Agatha. Her father had given the maid a key so that she could let herself in after they'd gone.

'I've revived the fire and put the kettle on to boil,' he said. 'There's no time for anything cooked but there's bread and butter if you're hungry.'

Ruth didn't feel like eating. Butterflies were filling her stomach and making her feel slightly sick, but she didn't want to worry her father, so she managed to nibble a small portion of the bread and drink some tea before they set out through the dark, snowy morning towards the foundry.

The streetlights had been put out and her father carried an oil lamp to illuminate their way across town to Cleaver Street. Wrapped in a coat and a shawl with a bonnet tied around her head and her hands warmed by her mother's muff, Ruth trod in her father's footsteps as they walked through the silence. Now that the mills had shut down there were very few people about so early in the morning.

At least it wasn't snowing again. The sky had cleared and Ruth could see stars twinkling, more stars than there had ever been before now that the cloud and smog had cleared away. There appeared to be thousands of them up there, high above them in the vastness of space. Ruth paused a moment to stare up in wonder.

'Come along,' encouraged her father, glancing back at her. 'What are you looking at?'

'All the stars. I've never seen so many.'

Her father looked up too. 'I remember skies like this when I was a lad,' he told her. 'When I lived out in the countryside. There's usually such a lot of smoke hanging over the town that they're hidden.'

'They're beautiful,' said Ruth.

'Aye. That's the plough,' he told her pointing out the shape that resembled the implement the farmers used to furrow their fields. 'It points to the north.'

'Where do you think heaven is?' Ruth asked him, wondering if her mother was looking down and if she could see them, out so early in the morning, on their way to make soup. What would she make of it?

'Way beyond. Too far for us mortals to see,' her father replied. 'Come on,' he encouraged. 'We'll be frozen to the spot if we linger any longer.'

When they reached Cleaver Street the door they'd used before, the one which was to be the entrance and exit to the soup kitchen, was standing ajar and soft light was spilling out onto the compacted snow. When she followed her father inside, she saw Mr Yates lighting the gas lamps that hung from the ceiling. She could smell the lingering aroma of the gas and it made her queasy.

'Good morning!' called Mr Yates. 'It's a cold one. But I've set some of my men to start the fires, so it should warm up quickly.'

'Do you have anyone to clear a path at the front?' asked her father, stamping the snow from his boots. 'It'll make it easier when the deliveries come.'

'Aye. Freddy!' called Mr Yates to one of his workers. 'Take a shovel and clear a path before the wagons come with the meat and veggies. We don't want any accidents.'

'Come and get warm for a few minutes,' Ruth's father told her as the coal in the huge furnaces began to crackle and burn. 'The potatoes should be here any time and then we can make a start.' He glanced towards the outer door from where they could hear the steady scraping of Freddy's shovel as he moved the snow aside. 'There should be others coming soon to help,' he said expectantly.

'I told the relief committee to find some willing young lasses from the mills who know what hard work is,' Mr Yates remarked as he rubbed his cold hands together. 'I hope they heeded my words because if we have to rely on the likes of the mayor's wife there'll be no soup until teatime.'

The words were no sooner spoken than there was the sound of wheels and hooves outside and although they were anticipating a loaded cart, it was Mr Hutchinson and his wife who arrived. Mrs Hutchinson looked eager.

'What would you like me to do?' she asked Ruth's father.

'We're just waiting for the cart with the potatoes and turnips,' he said. 'Then you can make a start on the peeling and chopping. Meanwhile, we'll get water on to boil in the vats.'

Now that the room was slightly less freezing, Ruth put her mother's muff, her bonnet and her coat safely to one side and tied one of the coarse linen aprons that had been provided around herself. She began to fetch water in buckets from the pump and pour it into the vats that had been set over the fires. Once it was boiling the ingredients of the soup would be added and left to cook.

As she worked, she kept glancing towards the outer door, hoping that help would arrive soon. Several of the wives of the committee members had promised to come, but there was only the mayor's wife so far and Ruth could see that she knew no more about making soup than she did herself.

Before long there was a shout from one of the men that the cart had arrived and they began to carry in huge sacks filled with vegetables on their shoulders and put them down beside the tables set up for preparation. There were so many that Ruth could see it was an impossible task for just her and Mrs Hutchinson. But as she began to despair one or two committee ladies drifted in, remarking on the earliness of the hour.

'Right, ladies!' announced her father. 'We'll do potatoes at this table. Turnips there. Carrots and onions at the end, and some of you need to make a start on shelling the peas. Barley and groats should be arriving soon.'

The gathered ladies all stared about, unsure which task they should be taking on and, as her father hurried off to supervise the arrival of more sacks, it was left to Ruth to organise them. As she'd arrived before them and was wearing an apron and was clearly not one of them, they automatically turned to her for instruction.

Ruth quailed under their expectant faces. She'd never had to give anyone orders before and all these ladies were her superiors in social class. It seemed wrong to tell them what they must do, but she knew that if she didn't, the preparations for the soup would never get started. And she didn't want to let her father down.

'Perhaps you'd like to get an apron?' she suggested, pointing to the pile of linens with long strings attached.

'Oh, how charming,' Mrs Hutchinson said, picking one up and wrapping it around herself over what Ruth thought was an expensive frock. These women probably didn't have old clothes. Anything they no longer required would have been passed on to their maids either to wear or sell on at one of the second-hand stalls in the marketplace for ready cash.

The other women hung up their coats and hats and put on aprons as Ruth guided them to their places at the preparation tables. There was a definite preference for shelling peas which could be done sitting down and a reluctance to approach the onions. Ruth couldn't blame them. She would have liked to deal with the peas herself rather than the onions, but it was clear that the task would fall to her as most of the volunteers began the simpler jobs.

She picked up one of the sharp knives and sliced the first of the onions in half. The fierce aroma pricked her eyes and in moments the tears were streaming down her face as she attempted to peel and chop the offending vegetable. It was going to be a long and difficult morning, she thought, as she tried to wipe her eyes with her hand and only succeeded in making things worse as she touched the juice to her lids.

Chapter Fifteen

Sally was up at her usual time that morning, eager to go and ask about a job at the soup kitchen. And although her mother insisted she had some tea and bread before she went out into the cold, she ate and drank quickly.

It had stopped snowing overnight and there was a hint of faint sunlight when she went outside into the dawn. It was strange for the town to be so quiet. The noise of the mills usually reverberated everywhere on working days – a background to the sounds of carts and horses as they delivered raw cotton and collected woven cloth to be transported to Liverpool, from where it was sold all around the world. And on Sundays when the mills were silent, the church bells rang across the town calling the faithful to worship. The near silence now was strange and made Sally feel uneasy as she tramped through the inches of lying snow towards Cleaver Street.

The door to the foundry was open and there was a horse and cart outside. The breath from the horse's nostrils was clouding the freezing air as it waited impatiently, stamping its feet against the chill. Two men were hoisting sacks of vegetables onto their shoulders and carrying them in through an open doorway. Beyond it, Sally could see some women sitting or standing around wooden tables, some with knives in their hands, whilst a handful of men were opening the sacks and piling up the potatoes and other vegetables.

Sally took a deep breath to steady the sudden nerves that had set her stomach aflutter and walked determinedly towards the door. She had to step aside as one of the delivery men hurried out to the cart for another sack, but as soon as her way was clear she went into the foundry and looked about for Mr Hodgson. Although she didn't know him by sight, Sally knew that he was the confectioner from Queen Victoria Street and as she glanced around, she recognised his daughter, who had sold her the sugar mice. She was standing at one of the tables with an apron wrapped over a plain brown skirt and jacket and looked as if she was trying to organise the other women, who all looked older, and not the type of person that Sally had expected to find working here. They struck her as being gentry rather than unemployed mill workers and she hesitated, wondering if she had come to the right place.

Everyone was so busy that no one noticed her standing, hesitating, in the middle of the floor. Sally moved towards the tables where the women had begun their work. Some seemed to be looking at the potatoes and turnips with an air of puzzlement as if they weren't familiar with the raw vegetables and didn't quite know what to do with them. They held the knives awkwardly in their hands and in any other situation Sally might have laughed at their incompetence. If they didn't manage to get a shift on the soup would never be ready for dinner time.

A man approached her with a quizzical expression.

'I'm looking for Mr Hodgson,' she told him.

'That's me.'

'I've been sent by the relief committee,' she explained. 'They said there might be work for me here.'

'Thank goodness for that!' he exclaimed as if she was his salvation. But then his face clouded with anxiety once more. 'Are you the only one?' he asked, looking behind her as if he thought more help might suddenly materialise from the ether.

'I don't know if they're sending anyone else,' she admitted, surprised herself that there wasn't a crowd of mill girls clamouring for a job. Even if the wage was only tuppence a day it was better than nothing.

'Never mind,' he said. 'Let's hope more are on their way. I take it you know how to peel vegetables?'

'Yes. Of course.'

'Then let's get you started or we'll have a line of disappointed customers at twelve o' clock.'

He led her towards the trestle tables and introduced her to his daughter. 'Ruth,' he said, 'This is... I'm sorry, I didn't ask your name.'

'Sally. Sally Grimes.'

'Sally, this is Ruth. She'll show you what to do,' he said before hurrying off to answer some question that was being called to him across the room.

'Hello,' said Sally stretching out a hand in greeting. 'I remember you from the sweet shop. You sold me some sugar mice at a discounted price late on Christmas Eve.'

'Of course! I thought you looked familiar.' Ruth grasped her hand for a moment. She looked worried. 'I'm not really sure what I'm doing,' she admitted. 'It's my first morning and I'm totally out of my depth. I've never done anything like this before.'

She looked close to tears, although it might have been the half onion she was clutching in her other hand. Sally felt a wave of sympathy for her. 'Is there another apron?' she asked.

'Yes. There's a pile of them. I think Father was expecting more help. Are there more girls coming?' she asked hopefully.

'I don't know,' Sally told her as she fastened her shawl around her waist and put the apron on over it. 'To tell the truth, I expected some of the other mill girls to be here already. Maybe they'll come soon,' she added to try to reassure Ruth who looked increasingly overwhelmed by the task facing her. 'In the meantime, let's make a start,' she suggested as she unfastened the cuffs on her blouse and carefully rolled them back to keep them clean. It was freezing in the room despite the roaring fires and Sally hoped it would warm soon because her fingers still felt numb after her walk from home. It was a different prospect to the mill where the atmosphere had always been hot and muggy, even in the depths of winter.

She chose a sharp knife from the table and picked up a potato. Within a minute she'd peeled it and dropped it into the pail of cold water at her feet. She took up another and worked quickly to peel that as well.

It was a moment before she realised that the other women around the table were watching her in awe. Most of them had barely managed to peel one potato even though they'd been there longer – and the ones they had finished were still striped with peel and dirt and hadn't had the eyes removed. Even Ruth, beside her, wasn't very proficient and it was clear to Sally that none of them had much experience in the kitchen. She hoped that there would be reinforcements soon – and not more gentry and shop girls. There was a formidable pile of vegetables and many more in the sacks propped against the wall. It would take her a week to peel them all herself.

After about an hour, Ruth was called away to brew some tea for the workers. It came in a big urn with a splash of milk already added and some pewter mugs to drink out of. The other women seemed to think it was a good enough reason for a break and they downed their knives and found places to sit down, complaining that their legs and backs were aching. It made Sally want to shake her head in disbelief. They hadn't worked for much more than an hour and now they were shrieking about the mugs being too hot to hold when the tea had been poured into them. They were obviously more used to drinking tea from fragile china at tea parties in their fancy houses than doing real work. Drinking tea on the job was a treat she'd never encountered before and at barely nine o' clock in the morning she considered her shift had barely begun.

'Don't you want to sit down?' asked Ruth.

'I'm fine. I'm used to standing in the mill all day,' she replied as she took a mug of tea by its rim and managed a sip without burning either her lip or her tongue. It was well sugared, sweet and welcome. 'We're never going to have these veggies ready unless we press on,' she said. She could hear the water boiling in the great vats above the fires and she knew that the soup should have been put to cook by now.

The same worry was bothering Mr Hodgson.

'Ladies,' he cajoled. 'I think we need to get back to our work if the soup is to be ready on time.'

One or two of them looked at him as if they thought he had completely forgotten his place.

'Please?' he added with an air of desperation.

Reluctantly, the ladies took up their knives again, although Sally could hear some muttering under their breath that it wasn't what they'd expected and they were doing their best under difficult circumstances.

Sally remained tight-lipped and peeled potatoes one after the other until her fingers ached with the unaccustomed movement. Ruth, working beside her, was silent too although every so often she looked up despairingly at the slow progress of the work and Mr Hodgson kept walking anxiously around the tables obviously concerned about the time it was taking to prepare the soup.

Towards the middle of the morning, some more girls arrived, along with Mr Haworth from the mill. Sally recognised most of them and they exchanged brief greetings.

'I expected more of us,' she said to one named Elsie who came to work beside her.

'For tuppence a day?' Elsie asked. 'I'm only here because Mr Haworth pleaded with me to come. It's slave labour,' she complained. But she was a quick worker, as most of the other mill girls were, and gradually the piles of vegetables were diced and chopped and added to the vats along with some cuts of beef, barley and groats and plenty of salt and pepper.

Chapter Sixteen

Ruth relaxed a little as the aroma of the cooking soup began to drift out from the vats. After yet another tea break, the committee ladies were tasked with setting out dishes and spoons and she and the girl who'd been introduced as Sally turned their attention to slicing the loaves of fresh bread that had just been delivered, still warm from the ovens. Whether it would all be ready for twelve o' clock she doubted and the worried frown on her father's face betrayed that he thought it would be a close call.

'Folk are beginning to gather already,' he told her, coming in from yet another trip to the main door to peer out. 'How's the soup coming along?'

'It smells good.'

'Aye. But is it cooked. We can't offer up pink meat and half-raw, hard potatoes.'

He walked away to stir one of the vats with a huge ladle, frowning over the contents.

'Have you seen Mr Hutchinson?' he asked when he came back. 'We may have to delay the opening. It's far from being cooked and it's a quarter to already.'

'He's taken Mrs Hutchinson home,' one of the ladies told him. 'She came over quite faint. And I'm not surprised. None of us is used to this sort of work.'

'No. But we're all immensely grateful for your help,' Mr Hodgson assured her. 'We couldn't have done it without you.'

Ruth wasn't so sure. Given the number of committee women who had come, they hadn't achieved much. A few were competent – probably the ones who'd moved up in society with their marriages, but the rest, who'd expressed amazement that the potatoes came in such a variety of shapes and sizes, hadn't really been a lot of use. She couldn't help but wonder if they would come again the next day, and the day after that. She'd gained the impression that it hadn't been what they'd expected when they'd first offered their assistance.

Still, the morning had been saved by Sally Grimes and the other girls from Haworth's mill. If it hadn't been for them there would have been no soup at all and although it might be a little bit late it was simmering nicely and she thought that it would taste good.

Just before twelve, the mayor, Mr Hutchinson returned.

'Do you think we should have a ribbon or something – for the opening?' he asked. 'I have a speech ready,' he told them, fetching several sheets of folded paper out from his pocket.

Ruth exchanged a glance with her father, and she tried not to laugh as he raised his eyes heavenwards. Still, she thought, it might give the soup an extra twenty minutes to finish cooking if the mayor managed to get through all of his prepared oration before being heckled and pushed aside by hungry workers.

'Perhaps you could just say a few words,' her father suggested. 'Once the doors open, I doubt folk will want to wait. They've been queuing for quite a while and it's bitterly cold outside.'

It was clear that Mr Hutchinson wasn't keen to have his carefully written words cut short, but when he went to open the door and was greeted with the crowd eagerly jostling to come in, he appeared to see reason and contented himself with simply saying: 'I declare this soup kitchen open!' After which he had to move briskly aside to prevent himself being trampled by the rush.

Luckily, her father had foreseen that orderliness might not be as forthcoming as the committee members had expected. It was true that the workers were grateful, but they were starving and the smell of the soup had excited them. He'd asked Mr Yates to keep a few of the lads from the foundry on to act as monitors, to guide the customers towards the trestle where the soup would be served and then to the tables to sit down or back outside to take their meals home.

Even so, it was like bedlam after the doors were opened and Ruth was afraid of the situation becoming uncontrollable. The ladies beside her at the serving trestle gasped as the men pushed forwards, mostly ragged and unshaven with the gleam of finding satisfaction in their eyes.

'My goodness!' exclaimed one. 'How very rude you are! No!' she squealed as a man made a grab for the loaves. 'You can't take that much! You must show me your tickets!'

It wasn't like anything Ruth had experienced before. Her shop customers were always polite and respectful and although many of these men were quiet and thankful and touched their caps and expressed gratitude, there were many who thought it was their right to be fed and fed well.

'It's not our fault we're hungry!' one told the committee ladies. 'We're willing to work, but if your husbands throw us out on our ear with no wages what are we supposed to do? You owe us something!'

Ruth found that her hands were shaking as she ladled soup into bowls or poured it into dishes that the customers had brought. Many of them glared at her when the dishes weren't filled to the brim.

'It's a full pint,' she pointed out. 'Everyone gets a pint per token. I don't make the rules. I just do what I've been told.'

One man growled at her and she glanced backwards, looking for her father, and wondering if there was somewhere she could escape to if the man leapt over the table and tried to take what wasn't his. But one of the foundry lads named Freddy Fry saw what was happening and elbowed his way through the crowd.

'Move along,' he told the man. 'We won't stand for any unpleasantness. You'll be polite to these ladies if you know what's good for you.'

'Thank you,' Ruth said after the man had moved on.

'I'm sorry if he frightened you,' said Freddy. 'But he isn't a bad man. I know him slightly. He used to come into the Dun Horse before he lost his job. I'd never have believed he could behave so badly if I hadn't seen it with my own eyes.'

As the soup in the vats dwindled and the crowd kept on coming, Ruth began to worry that they hadn't made enough – or that the committee ladies had been bullied into giving away more than the fair share. She dreaded what might happen if those who had queued for hours in the ice and snow were turned away with nothing, but gradually the line at the tables diminished and by the time everyone had been served there was still some soup left over.

Ruth hoped she might be offered some. She was exhausted and hungry, as were all the helpers and some of the committee ladies looked almost dead on their feet, they were so tired.

'Well done, everyone!' her father congratulated them as the door was closed to anyone else coming in. 'I think there's a little left if anyone would like some.'

Sally Grimes and the other mill girls stepped forward eagerly even though the committee ladies thanked him politely but said that they thought they would prefer to go home and rest. And to see what their cooks had prepared, thought Ruth.

'You did well,' her father told her as he came to help himself to a bowl of the soup and a chunk of bread. 'I had my doubts earlier, but it all came together in the end. Tired?' he asked sympathetically when she did nothing more than nod. 'Get something to eat and sit down. It'll do no harm to rest a while before the clearing up begins.'

The clearing up! Ruth looked aghast at the dirty bowls, plates, spoons and jugs that all needed washing. There were the vats too. Then the tables to be scrubbed down. It would all have to be put in order so that they could do the same thing again tomorrow. The thought appalled her and this time it wasn't the onions that brought tears to her eyes, but pure exhaustion.

Chapter Seventeen

'It was like a mad house when I got there!' said Caroline's father that evening when they were sitting around the dining table in their house on Richmond Terrace. 'First there weren't enough women to prepare the soup. The committee ladies were next to useless, and that lass of Hodgson's wasn't much better. I don't think there would have been any soup at all without the lasses from the mill. I was proud of them. They deserved more than tuppence.'

'It's a nice bit of pocket money for them,' Caroline's mother remarked.

'It's not pocket money!' her father corrected his wife. 'It's wages. It'll go to their parents to buy food.'

Caroline held her breath as she watched her mother react to the words. Please don't let there be an argument, she prayed. She didn't think she had the strength or patience for any more shouting.

Her mother didn't reply, but turned her attention to her lamb chops, muttering that it was none of her business to know what the working classes did with their money.

'So, the soup was ready in time?' Caroline asked, pleased that it was girls from Haworth's who had saved the day.

'Just about,' he said. 'And a good job too. There was a crowd gathered outside – more of a mob than the orderly line of workers that the mayor was expecting. He thought he'd be opening up by cutting a fancy ribbon like it was a bazaar or something. He even had a lengthy speech ready, but he only managed a few words before they rushed him.' He laughed briefly at the memory. 'Luckily, there were a few of Yates's men on hand and it was a good job too. At one point I thought the women behind the tables were going to be overwhelmed.'

'It all sounds very sordid,' remarked Caroline's mother. 'You'd think they would be more grateful.'

'Aye. But empty bellies aren't good bedfellows with manners,' said her father. 'Something should have been done long since, before it got to this stage.'

Her mother didn't reply. It was clear that the affairs of the soup kitchen held little interest for her. 'My father has asked us to go for dinner on Sunday,' she said, changing the subject. 'He wants to talk to you – about business, I think. He has some advice to offer and I think you'd do well to listen.'

'What sort of advice?' asked Caroline's father with a frown.

Her mother shook her head dismissively. 'It'll be to do with the cotton. I think he knows how to get hold of some cheaply. And the Duttons will be there,' she added, with a glance at Caroline. 'You know their son, Thomas,' she reminded her. 'You met him at the ball just before Christmas.'

'Yes,' agreed Caroline. She did remember Thomas Dutton. He was a couple of years older than her – the son of the brewery owner and his wife. New money, her mother had referred to them scornfully when they had first been introduced. But it seemed that they had met with her grandfather's approval and Caroline was in no doubt about why they had been invited to Salesbury Hall.

She knew that her mother had taken the carriage earlier in response to a summons from her grandfather, and it seemed it was not only the future of Haworth's Mill that had been discussed. Caroline was well aware that now she had completed her studies at Miss Parker's Academy, her future, as far as her grandfather was concerned, held only marriage to a suitable husband.

It wasn't that Thomas Dutton was repulsive. Not like her mother's suitor, the odious Sir Gilbert. Thomas Dutton had been passably handsome with dark blue eyes and nondescript brown hair. He had been polite, but not overbearing. Assured, but not arrogant, and the family were wealthy, even though they were not gentry in the truest sense of the word. There wasn't much for her to object to, she realised – except that she was young and wanted more than the prospect of being a wife who sat on committees and invited acquaintances for tea parties. She wanted to experience life. To see things beyond the confines of the social sphere that her mother guarded so carefully. She found herself wondering about the mill girls who had put the committee ladies to shame by their ability to do something as simple as making soup. She had no idea how to make soup herself, she realised as she laid her knife and fork side by side on her plate for Lottie to clear away. She could embroider a sampler and play the piano and speak conversational French, but soup was a mystery to her and she decided that it was something she ought to learn about before she was married off to a man she had danced with only once.

–

'Is there anything I can do to help?' she asked her father later after her mother had retired to bed, saying that all the talk of starvation and hardship had worn her out.

'Help?' he asked looking puzzled.

'At the soup kitchen,' she told him. 'When you were talking earlier about what a shambles it had been today, I wondered if there was anything I could do.'

Her father looked doubtful. 'I don't know,' he said. 'I was hoping to persuade a few more of the girls from the mill to go along to help.'

'Are they not keen?' Caroline asked. 'I thought they would have been glad to be offered work.'

'They would if the wages were what they were used to, but tuppence a day is nothing, though it's all the relief committee is able to pay. Some of the girls I spoke to today said it was an insult. They don't really understand that it's all coming from charity and the funds are limited. It's not the same as selling cotton. Or not the same as it used to be when there was cotton to sell.'

He sighed and Caroline saw that the situation weighed heavily on his shoulders.

'Do you think grandfather can help?' she asked, remembering what her mother had said.

'No.' He shook his head. 'He'll lecture me about something or other, but the truth is that until this American war is resolved and the crops flow to the ports again there's nothing anyone can do except appeal to the government for assistance – either money to tide us over or an intervention with the Americans. But as things stand, they seem unwilling to do either. I think they grossly underestimate the hardship it's causing here in Lancashire. They don't see it for themselves so it's out of sight, out of mind for many of them in parliament. They'll not take it seriously until it affects them directly.'

'And will it?' Caroline asked.

'It will if it goes on for any length of time. The cotton trade is one of the main staples of the country whether those in London choose to acknowledge it or not.'

He sounded helpless and defeated and Caroline knew that she couldn't simply sit at home with her mother and do nothing.

'Let me help,' she asked him. 'Let me go to the soup kitchen tomorrow. I'm sure there's something I can do.'

'Can you peel potatoes?' he asked her directly. 'Can you chop onions? Do you know how many ounces of salt and pepper to add to a gallon of soup? No,' he said in response to her puzzled expression. 'Your grandfather has spent hundreds of pounds on your education, but you know nothing of those things. You've been prepared for a life of privilege and leisure. Your mother wants you to marry well. It's why we've been asked to dine with the Duttons on Sunday.'

'I realised that,' Caroline told him. 'But I'm not betrothed to anyone yet – and besides, you said that there are lots of committee ladies helping at the soup kitchen. It isn't as if I'd be completely out of my social circle.'

'You'll have to speak to your mother,' he told her. 'She'll have to give her permission because I'm far too busy to get into an argument with her about it. And if she says no, you must accept it and not keep badgering me.'

It wasn't what Caroline had wanted to hear. She'd hoped her father would agree without involving her mother because she had a feeling her mother would say no.

'But if she agrees, can I go?' she persisted.

'I suppose so. But be prepared to work hard,' he warned her. 'I won't be there tomorrow to protect you. I have a meeting in Manchester with my broker. It won't be easy and you'll be expected to learn quickly and turn your hand to anything you're asked to do.'

'I will,' she promised him, realising that he didn't want her to let him down. She wouldn't, she vowed. She'd prove that she was just as capable as his mill girls. How hard could it be?

–

Next morning she was already out of bed and had washed herself in the cold water from the previous evening when Lottie came in.

'Is everything all right, Miss Caroline?' the maid asked as she watched Caroline pushing aside the gowns that hung in her wardrobe.

'I'm going to help at the soup kitchen,' Caroline said, 'so I need to find something suitable to wear.'

Lottie came across and took out a striped navy-and-white skirt and a white blouse. 'You've had these a while,' she said. 'They might do.'

'Good. Help me put them on. Is my mother up yet?' she asked as Lottie did up the ties on the skirt.

'Not yet. But she was awake when I took her some tea about ten minutes ago.'

Caroline knew she would have to be quick if she was to leave before her mother saw her. She hurried down to the dining room and helped herself to a generous plate of scrambled eggs and bacon, then sent Lottie to fetch her coat and bonnet from her bedroom.

'Shall I send for Simmons to bring the carriage?' asked Lottie.

'No,' Caroline said firmly. 'I'll walk. It isn't far and it's fine today.'

'As you wish, Miss Caroline,' the maid said and opened the front door for her.

Caroline went down the front steps that had been cleared of snow and set off in the direction of Cleaver Street. It was true what her mother had said about the air being cleaner, she thought as she walked, as briskly as she dared on the icy paths, through the town centre. It was quite refreshing, and she was looking forward to doing something worthwhile with her day rather than sitting by the fire embroidering yet another handkerchief.

Chapter Eighteen

Ruth had been so tired after her first day at the soup kitchen that when she and her father arrived home, she blessed him for keeping Agatha on as their maid. The aroma of lamb hotpot keeping warm in the oven and the fresh bread and milk on the scullery shelf had been a welcome relief.

She'd eaten eagerly, surprised at her hunger even though she'd had a bowl of the soup earlier. Then she'd told her father that she was going to bed.

'You do look pale,' he'd sympathised. 'But I was proud of you today. I know it was demanding work and the committee ladies weren't a lot of help, but you did really well.'

'I was grateful to the mill girls,' she told him, thinking of Sally Grimes who had more or less taken over the organisation of the kitchen from her. 'We would never have managed without them. I hope they come again tomorrow. I know the tuppence they were paid wasn't much. Sally told me she was earning twelve shillings a week as a weaver at Haworth's mill.'

Her father had nodded. 'Everyone needs to pull together if we're to get through this,' he'd said. 'It isn't going to be easy.'

Ruth slept soundly that night, even though her body ached from the unaccustomed work, and she was still asleep when her father tapped on the door the next morning to say it was time to get up. She closed her eyes to have five more minutes under the warm bedclothes but was so afraid of falling back asleep that she couldn't really rest and soon got up to wash and dress for one more day at the kitchen. As she put on the jacket that smelt of the cooking of yesterday's soup – a mixed aroma of fatty meat and turnips – she wished she was dressing in the neat, printed frock and apron that she wore to serve in the shop. It would be a while before she was able to do that again, she realised, as she went down the stairs to the cold kitchen and a quick breakfast before leaving for Cleaver Street.

At the foundry she joined her father by the freshly lit fires to get warm after their icy walk. Her fingers and toes were numbed with the cold and she couldn't feel the buttons on her jacket to take it off or to tie on an apron to begin work.

She watched Freddy Fry bring in another sack of coal on his shoulder and put it down beside the furnace. He smiled at her as he turned to go and fetch another one and she shyly returned the smile. She wasn't used to being with men or boys and wasn't quite sure how she should respond. Of course, there had been gentleman who had come into the shop occasionally, although most of her customers had been women. But apart from them the only men she knew were her father and her two brothers-in-law.

Her hands began to tingle painfully as they warmed and as she shook them, she heard laughter behind her and the group of mill girls who had helped yesterday came in. She was glad to see them and greeted them warmly.

'Who's that?' Sally Grimes asked her, nodding towards Freddy who was coming back with more coal. 'Do you know his name?'

'Yes. He's Freddy Fry. He works for Mr Yates.'

She watched as Sally's eyes tracked the foundry worker as he took the coal to the fire and began to shovel it onto the growing flames.

One of the other mill girls nudged Sally, laughing.

'Don't be making moon eyes at him!' she warned her. 'You don't even know if he's spoken for!'

'Do you know?' Sally asked Ruth. 'Is he married, or courting?'

'I've no idea,' Ruth said as she watched the other girls with a sense of bewilderment. It was clear that Freddy was the object of their rapt attention as they watched him work with appreciative expressions until her father clapped his hands and called to them all to start fetching the jugs of water for the soup.

The mill girls sighed and turned their attention away from the foundry worker as they donned aprons and rolled up their sleeves.

'Are those committee women coming again?' Sally asked Ruth.

'I'm not sure. I think they said they would.'

'They weren't much use anyway,' remarked Sally. 'Mr Haworth has promised to try to persuade more of the weavers from the mill to come, but a lot aren't in the mood to do him any favours. Not that it's his fault,' she added. 'My father asked him about getting more cotton and he said there was none. He can't conjure it out of thin air, but some people want to blame him for being put out of work and don't see why they should help.'

‘My father says everyone needs to pull together,’ Ruth told her as they emptied the fresh water into the vats.

‘Aye,’ said Sally although she sounded doubtful. ‘But people are saying that cotton’s finished here. My father’s talking of taking us to America and getting work in the mills there.’

‘You’re not going, are you?’ asked Ruth, alarmed that she might lose her new friend and be left to cope alone.

‘I don’t know,’ Sally replied. ‘I’m not sure how serious he is. But the longer it goes on, the more people will consider going, and it might be better to go whilst there are still jobs on offer. The American mill owners are sending men over to recruit workers. They’ve been to Manchester, so it probably won’t be long before they come here.’

-

Later that morning, Ruth looked up from the vat of soup she was stirring as she heard whistling and shouting outside the door. She didn’t think it was anywhere near noon yet. At least she hoped it wasn’t because the potatoes still needed to soften and break down. But it was clear that a crowd had already gathered and something was going on. She hoped there wasn’t going to be any rioting. It was a prospect that was worrying her father.

‘What on earth is happening?’ he asked as he hurried towards the closed door to investigate the noise. ‘Good lord!’ he exclaimed a moment later. ‘I need some help here!’ he called.

Ruth put down the ladle she was holding and anxiously followed a few of the other girls to find out what the problem was, not knowing what she could do to help and feeling afraid that there might be some sort of violence.

'Please! Let the lady through!' her father appealed to the men and women who were waiting at the door. 'She's done nothing to hurt you!'

The door was wide open now and Ruth could see that a group of men had gathered around a well-dressed woman and were taunting her.

'Let me through,' said Freddy Fry, coming up behind them. He had his shirt sleeves rolled up and his waistcoat firmly buttoned across his ample chest and her father willingly stood aside as he burst out through the doors and roared at the men who had the woman surrounded. 'Move aside afore I move ye with my fists!' he shouted at them.

The men outside seem to realise that in their impoverished state they were no match for Freddy, and when he was joined by the other foundry workers they backed down and stood aside to allow the woman through.

She must be one of the committee ladies, thought Ruth at first, although she looked too young, and she certainly wasn't dressed for a day's work in her full crinoline skirt and fur-trimmed coat. Besides, if she had wanted to help peeling vegetables, she ought to have been here hours ago.

As the young woman reached the door, Ruth recognised her as the person who'd come to buy sugar mice before Christmas.

'It's Caroline Haworth!' exclaimed Sally.

'The mill owner's daughter?' Ruth asked.

'Yes. I wonder if she's come to help.'

'There's not much left to do,' observed Ruth. Nearly an hour had passed since the last of the vegetables had been peeled and the soup put on to cook. The mill girls had been enjoying a rest and a cup of tea before beginning to set out the jugs and basins on the trestles and the committee women had taken themselves into their own corner to chat before it was time for them to help serve the soup.

As she watched, Caroline Haworth looked around the room as if seeking someone she knew. Maybe she was looking for her father, but he'd only called in briefly earlier, so it was left to Ruth's father to approach her and ask what she wanted.

'I've come to help,' Ruth heard her say.

'It's mostly done,' Ruth's father told her. 'These girls have made the soup and put it on to cook – and we seem to have plenty of help to serve it out.'

'I should have come sooner,' Caroline replied. She looked disappointed and Ruth felt a bit sorry for her. She obviously meant well.

'There'll be plenty of washing up after dinner,' Sally said, speaking up. 'Perhaps Miss Haworth can help with that?'

'I will!' she said. 'I'll do whatever needs to be done. I want to help.'

'It'll be a shock to her,' Sally whispered to Ruth. 'I bet she's never washed so much as a teacup in her life!'

Ruth didn't reply. She thought Sally sounded mean. After all, Miss Haworth had come and offered to help them – and it wasn't her fault if she'd never washed up before. Like all of them, she'd come to do her best.

Chapter Nineteen

Caroline's heart was still racing in fear even though she was trying hard to seem composed. It had all been so unexpected. When she'd arrived in Cleaver Street and seen the men at the door, she'd assumed that they were waiting patiently and gratefully for some soup. But as she'd approached, she'd heard the murmuring of voices increase in tone and ferocity.

'She's the mill owner's daughter!' one had cried as she'd smiled and expected them to clear a way to let her through to the door. Instead, they'd gathered around her and she'd suddenly been wary and anxious about what they intended.

'It's thy father's fault we're standing here in the cold waiting for a handout,' one had told her.

'Aye. We were hoping he might have the gall to show his face, but we've seen nowt of him. Sitting by a roaring fire, is he? Has he sent thee in his place?'

'I've come to help,' Caroline had begun to explain. She'd thought they would thank her and let her through after that, but it had seemed to incense them even more.

'Come to play the lady bountiful,' she'd heard one remark. 'I bet you'll be getting more than a bit of thin soup for thy dinner.'

'I'm sorry,' Caroline told them, not really sure what she was apologising for, just hoping the words would pacify them. 'Please let me through.'

By now about half a dozen of the men were standing around her in a circle and their faces were fierce and angry. They seemed to blame her for their situation. One of them reached out to touch the fur on her coat.

'This must have cost a bit,' he said. 'I can see thy father isn't letting thee go without owt.'

'Well, she's a pretty lass,' said another as his face leered close to hers.

Caroline heard laughter and one of the men whistled the same whistle that she'd heard used in the street when the mill girls walked past the men who lingered outside the public houses.

It was then that she'd begun to panic as she realised that she'd put herself in a dangerous situation. She was glancing about in alarm, afraid to make eye contact with any of the men for fear of provoking them further, when she saw the door of the foundry open. A man looked out and assessed the situation but did nothing more than call for help. Desperately, Caroline hoped that help would come, because all she could see now were some girls about her own age peering out through the door, watching her predicament.

Then another man had appeared. He was tall and broad and dressed in only shirt sleeves and a waistcoat despite the cold weather. He strode out towards her, threatening the men with his fists if they didn't let her through.

Caroline was relieved when they began to move away, and she hurried towards her saviour to thank him.

'Come inside,' he said as he raised an arm as if to put it around her shoulders as a shield. She stopped in her tracks. It was unthinkable to allow a working man to touch her, no matter how dire the circumstances. He saw her reluctance and Caroline was grateful when he dropped his arm and gestured for her to go ahead of him to the door. She hurried across the slippery cobbles, terrified of falling and making an even bigger fool of herself, but she made it to the doorway without mishap and stepped inside where it was warm and the smell of cabbage was overwhelming.

'I've come to help,' she told the first man who had looked out of the door. 'Are you Mr Hodgson?'

Caroline was bewildered when his welcome was less enthusiastic than she'd expected. It seemed that the girls who were standing around, some of whom must be her father's mill hands, had already done most of the work and all that remained was the washing up.

'I'll do whatever needs to be done. I want to help,' she said, although the truth was that the prospect of washing up daunted her. She knew that Mrs Jenkins and Lottie washed up in the kitchen on Richmond Terrace. She'd seen Lottie at the sink once when she'd slipped down to the kitchen to ask Mrs Jenkins for more cake. Her forearms had been bare and she'd had them plunged into steaming water as she'd ferociously scrubbed at a pan with a stiff brush. Her hands had been red and the steam had made her hair hang in limp strands rather than the neat coils she usually wore. Caroline had thought then it looked an unpalatable chore and the thought of having to do something similar herself made her begin to regret coming.

But it was too late now, she told herself. She'd offered her help and it would look churlish to refuse to do what was asked.

'Just show me what needs to be done,' she said, trying to sound much more confident than she felt as she saw one of the girls whisper behind her hand to a companion. Caroline guessed that they were laughing at her, but she wouldn't be daunted, she decided. She'd show them that she was willing and capable. She had to prove herself, she realised, to them, to herself – and most of all to her father.

Mr Hodgson called to one of the girls. 'Ruth, will you show Miss Haworth where she can hang up her coat and hat and find her an apron?'

The girl came towards her with a smile and Caroline was glad she wasn't the one who had whispered. In fact, she thought that she looked familiar.

'I think we've already met,' she said as she took off her coat, trying to recall where she'd seen her. She didn't seem to be one of the committee ladies who were sitting apart watching her with interest. And Caroline didn't think she was a mill girl.

'We have,' replied the girl. 'You came into our shop to buy sugar mice before Christmas.'

'Of course!' exclaimed Caroline, realising that she was the confectioner's daughter. 'I knew I'd seen you before, but I couldn't think where. I'm Caroline Haworth,' she said, remembering her manners, but unsure how to correctly greet a shop assistant.

'I'm pleased to meet you,' Ruth said, then hesitated. 'Are you sure you want to help with the washing up?' she asked quietly. 'You're wearing such lovely clothes. It would be a shame to get them spoiled.'

Caroline looked down at the striped skirt and plain blouse. She was about to say that they were old and it didn't matter, but having seen what all the mill girls were wearing and realising that Ruth was wearing a frock that even Lottie would describe as shabby, she hesitated.

'I didn't have anything else,' she confessed after a moment, deciding it was best to be truthful. 'I don't have old clothes.'

'Well, here's an apron,' Ruth said, handing her a garment that looked constructed of pure sacking. Caroline took it and wasn't sure how to put it on.

'This bit goes over your head,' advised Ruth, 'then you need to pull these ties and fasten them tightly behind you.'

Caroline did as she was shown. She must look ridiculous, she thought, with the rough apron sticking out over the crinoline frame that held her skirts away from her legs. If she came again tomorrow, she would have to appeal to Lottie to try to find her something else to wear. No wonder the mill girls had laughed at her and the men outside had taunted her. It was clear that she had no idea what she was doing. But she was determined to do her bit and if that meant ruining her clothes, so be it. She wanted to show everyone that she cared.

Ruth led her to the back of the room where several large basins had been placed on stacks of bricks to serve as sinks. There were no taps, but there were some large jugs beside the sinks and buckets beneath them for the slops.

'You'll have to fill the jugs with water from the pump over there,' explained Ruth, 'and put it in the cauldrons over the fire to heat. Then you pour it into the sinks and add the soap. Once the customers have been served, the girls will start to clear the bowls and bring them across to be washed. Stack them on the board when they're clean. Some of them might be needed again today if it gets busy. Otherwise, they'll be ready for tomorrow. Can you manage that?'

'Yes, of course,' Caroline replied. Surely it couldn't be that difficult.

'You may want to roll up your sleeves,' Ruth suggested as she turned to go back to the trestle tables where the soup was being brought out for serving. At least she wouldn't be expected to face those men again, thought Caroline as she saw the committee ladies getting up from their stools to ladle out the soup. That would have been much more daunting than washing up.

When Ruth had gone, she picked up two of the jugs and took them to the pump. Of course she'd seen a pump before, but she'd never used one. She put one of the jugs down on the floor and placed the other on the slab where the water would gush out. Then she got hold of the handle and moved it up and down. Nothing happened.

'You'll have to pump harder than that,' one of the mill girls told her as she came up with more jugs. 'See, like this.' The girl grasped hold of the handle and thrust it up and down quickly many times in succession until the water began to flow. 'Take this one to be heated,' she told Caroline, handing her the filled jug. 'Then come back for another.'

Caroline picked it up. It was heavier than she expected and she carried it carefully across to where the fires were burning. The heat from them was fierce. They were much bigger and hotter than the fires she was used to at home. She hesitated, a little afraid to approach the blazing flames. But then she told herself that she was running the risk of being laughed at again if she didn't get on with it, so she strode up to the fire, feeling the searing heat on her face and began to pour the water from the jug into the cauldron that was hanging there on a makeshift chain.

As she did, she smelt a singeing aroma and wondered where it was coming from. It was only when she heard a man shout out in alarm that she realised her wide skirt was on fire.

She dropped the jug and stepped back in a panic as she saw the flames creeping upwards towards her hands. She grasped the fabric and shook it, trying to put out the fire but it seemed to encourage it as the flames spread up to the apron and gathered speed.

'Miss Haworth!'

She turned as someone called her name. She'd heard stories about maids who had been engulfed in flames as they tended fires and were burnt to death and she feared the same was about to happen to her. She began to scream as she desperately tried to free herself from the apron, but her fingers fumbled with the ties and she couldn't get them undone.

The cold water came as a shock as it hit her, making her gasp.

'Come away from the fire!' cried her rescuer as he grasped hold of her arm and tugged her out of harm's way. His other hand was patting down the last of the lingering flames and the aroma of burning fabric filled the air.

Caroline sobbed as she realised that the fire was out and she was safe, and then she began to shiver with a combination of the cold soaking and the shock of how close she had come to a catastrophe.

'Are you unharmed?' he asked and she saw that it was the same man who had rescued her earlier.

'I think so,' she managed to reply, still shocked by what had happened.

'Why on earth did you let your skirt get so close to the furnace?' he demanded, clearly angry with her for being so careless. 'It's a good job I saw what was happening. You could have been badly hurt!'

'I know. I'm sorry,' she whimpered. 'I didn't realise.'

As Mr Hodgson and the other women came rushing to see if she was harmed, her rescuer turned his anger on them.

'Who on earth let her go near the fire dressed like that?' he demanded. 'There was bound to be an accident.'

'I'm sorry. I'm so sorry,' gasped Ruth Hodgson. Caroline saw that she was in tears herself. 'I didn't think.'

Her rescuer seemed to regret his temper now that he was confronted with two sobbing women and he apologised for his outburst.

'I'm sorry to shout,' he said, looking ashamed of himself. 'But this is a dangerous place. You need to be more careful. You need to wear something less... less extravagant,' he told Caroline. 'This isn't a tea party.'

His rebuke stung and Caroline felt embarrassed. It was bad enough to have been rescued by him once, but twice in the same morning was more than she could bear as she looked down at the charred remains of her skirt and the pool of water around her feet.

'Miss Haworth,' said Mr Hodgson. 'Perhaps we should send for your carriage to take you home. You're wet through and you'll catch a chill. Ruth, find Miss Haworth's coat so she can put it around herself.'

He glanced down at her skirts and then quickly looked away, clearly perturbed. And when Caroline looked down herself, she saw that the remnants of the burnt cloth had dropped away, revealing the hoops of her crinoline and her stockinged legs beneath.

'We need to open the doors,' went on Mr Hodgson as he heard the men outside begin to shout and bang on them. 'It's gone noon. Back to work,' he chivvied the ladies. 'Freddy, will you let them in please, just a few at a time.'

His name was Freddy, thought Caroline as she watched him walk away from her. It was a nice name. She must thank him properly once she'd made herself decent again. She suspected that she might owe him her life, or at least being spared the scars of a bad burning.

Chapter Twenty

When the last of their customers had left and the committee women had gone home for a late lunch, and just the mill girls remained to attend to the last of the clearing up, Ruth saw her father sink onto one of the wooden benches at the tables. It had been a long, hard day for both of them – much harder than shop work and he looked tired out.

'Are you all right?' she asked him.

'Yes, of course I am. I'm just having five minutes,' he said, brushing aside her concern.

'Shall I make you a cup of tea?'

'No. No. I'm fine.' He waved the idea away with his hand. 'You have enough to do.'

Satisfied that there was no real need to worry, Ruth went to supervise the stacking up of the bowls ready for the next day, but when she glanced back across the foundry, she saw her father was still sitting down with his chin slumped to his chest. He didn't look right, she thought, and she hoped that it was just tiredness and nothing more sinister.

Her father wasn't a young man. He'd been a widower when he'd married her mother and although she would never have dared to ask him his age, his hair was thinner and greyer than the fathers of other girls around her age.

And it wasn't uncommon for people who didn't know them to assume that he was her grandfather.

As darkness fell at around four in the afternoon, they said goodbye to Mr Yates, who locked the foundry door behind them, and they began to walk back home to Queen Victoria Street. Ruth's father seemed short of breath as they plodded along through the remains of the snow that had partly melted in some earlier weak sunshine, but was now freezing solid again as the temperatures dropped.

'I'm sure Agatha will have left something good for our tea,' she said, trying to keep his spirits up. 'I'm grateful you kept her on. I'm that tired I don't think I would have been able to begin to cook for us.'

She glanced across at her father as he trudged along beside her. He looked grey and she hoped that he wasn't ill. She longed to ask him again if he was all right, but she knew he wouldn't admit to feeling unwell, even if he was. She just hoped that a hot meal and a good night's sleep would set him right, because they had it all to do again tomorrow.

'It all went quite well today, apart from the trouble with Caroline Haworth,' she said as they walked. 'The customers enjoyed the soup. I heard a lot of compliments about it. People said it was much nicer than they expected.'

She looked at him again. He seemed distracted as if something was worrying him.

'We're nearly there,' she said. 'You'll be able to sit by the fire when we get in.'

He nodded, but didn't reply. His breathing was laboured and Ruth hoped he hadn't caught a chill that was going to settle on his chest. She knew that bad chests were something to be feared in the elderly – and though she'd never considered her father to be elderly before, she thought that he resembled an old man this afternoon.

It was a relief when they arrived home and she got him inside. He sat down in his chair, still wearing his coat, whilst Ruth poked the fire into a warming blaze and then looked in the oven to see what Agatha had left for them.

'Stew,' she announced. 'Similar to yesterday, but I suppose it has to be something that will keep warm without spoiling. I'll get it out. Shall we sit at the table? Or do you want it on your knee?'

'I'm not hungry,' he replied.

'You have to eat,' she told him, feeling increasingly anxious. It was unlike him to refuse his food.

'I had some soup earlier.'

'I know. So did I. But I'm hungry again.' She studied him for a moment. He still looked pale. 'What's the matter?' she asked him. 'Are you ill? Shall I fetch the doctor?'

'No. No. It's nothing. It'll pass in a while.'

'What will pass?' she asked, going to him and kneeling beside his chair. She reached for his hand. It was icy cold. 'What is it?' she asked. 'Tell me what's wrong.'

'It's nothing,' he repeated.

'It's something!' she told him. 'I can see you're not well. There's no point trying to hide it.'

'There's nothing for you to worry about,' he said, squeezing her hand. 'It's happened before. I'll be right as rain in a while. You get your tea. Don't fret about me.'

'But what is it?' she persisted. 'I could see you were breathing hard when we were walking home. Is it your chest?'

'No, it's just a bit of indigestion,' he said. 'Don't worry about me.'

'But I am worried,' she protested as she held his hand with both of her own, trying to warm it. 'I hate to see you like this. I think I'll fetch the doctor.'

'No!' He shook his head emphatically. 'There's no need to trouble the doctor. It's happened before and it'll pass in a minute. Like I said, it's just indigestion.'

'Do you have a stomach ache? Are you in pain?' she quizzed him, trying to persuade him to tell her exactly what was troubling him.

'No. Just palpitations.'

'Palpitations?'

'My heart's racing a bit, but it'll settle in a minute.'

Ruth moved the fingers of one hand to his wrist to feel for his pulse and sure enough it was racing, but it wasn't a steady beat.

'Your heart feels like it's jumping about all over the place,' she told him, alarmed now, and wondering whether she dared to leave him alone whilst she ran across town to fetch Dr Skaife from his surgery on Union Street.

'It'll steady in a minute or two,' he said. 'It's happened before.'

'When? How often? Why have you been keeping this from me?' she asked, anger adding to her fear that he was seriously unwell and had chosen to hide it from her.

'I haven't been hiding it,' he replied. 'I didn't think it was important. But it's worse tonight,' he admitted. 'It's been a tiring day.'

'I'm going for the doctor,' Ruth announced as she stood up and began to put on her coat and bonnet again. 'There's something wrong. You can't just ignore it.'

'Don't fuss, Ruth,' he pleaded. But she took no notice of him. It was clear he needed help and she was determined that he should have it. She wasn't going to sit and watch him die because he was too stubborn to admit that there was something seriously wrong.

He sighed as she went to the door but didn't attempt to stop her. Ruth wondered if she should go for her sister to come and sit with him, but Naomi had Hope and Nora to care for and she would be back soon if she hurried.

The evening was fine and clear, but still very slippery underfoot on the crunchy, compacted snow. Ruth knew that she had to be quick, but the conditions were treacherous and as she was coming down past the parish church, she suddenly felt her feet slide from under her and she landed heavily on the hard ground. Shocked and hoping she hadn't broken anything, she began to get to her feet when someone came hurrying up behind her. It was Freddy Fry. She hoped that he would pass on by and not recognise her. She still felt embarrassed about the way he had told her off earlier for allowing Caroline Haworth to approach the fire at the foundry.

'Miss Hodgson. Please allow me to assist you,' he said, putting a hand under her arm to help her up. 'I saw you go down with a bit of a bump. Are you hurt?' he asked, looking at her with concern.

'No. I don't think so,' she said as she rubbed at her leg and tested her weight on the ankle that had buckled under her. She would have some huge bruises by morning, she suspected, but it wasn't her own health that was worrying her. As long as she could walk, she must hurry on for the doctor.

'It's very icy underfoot tonight,' Freddy said. 'You need to take care. Where are you off to?'

'I'm going for the doctor,' she told him. 'My father isn't well.'

'I'm sorry to hear that. I hope it wasn't the trouble we had earlier that's affected him.'

'I don't think so,' Ruth said, eager to get away from Freddy and go on her way. 'Thank you for helping me up, but I must hurry.' She was eager to reach Dr Skaife as soon as she could.

'Would you like me to walk with you? You could take my arm.'

'No,' Ruth told him, feeling uncomfortable. 'I can't impose on you.'

'I don't mind,' he replied. But she shook her head again. She felt shy and was slightly afraid of him. Besides, what if someone who knew her saw her arm in arm with a working man?

'There's really no need. It was just a tumble,' she told him.

'I can't just walk away and leave you,' Freddy protested. 'Please, take my arm.'

He was insistent and Ruth had little choice but to accept. She put her hand in the crook of his elbow and he guided her across the square, taking care to avoid the worst of the ice.

As they walked, she found that she was glad of his support. The fall had shocked her and she was afraid of slipping down again. And the awkwardness between them that she had feared didn't materialise as Freddy chatted away about the soup kitchen and asked more about her father's symptoms. She found that he was surprisingly easy to talk to.

'He seems very unwell,' she told Freddy. 'He's not a young man and I think he's been hiding his illness from me.'

'Well, I'm sure Dr Skaife will know what to do,' Freddy reassured her. 'He's a good doctor.'

'Thank you so much. I do appreciate your assistance,' Ruth told Freddy when they reached the heavy wooden door of the doctor's surgery.

'It was no trouble,' he replied. 'Would you like me to wait? I could see you safely home.'

'There's no need,' she told him. 'Dr Skaife will be with me and I mustn't delay you any longer.'

'Well. Goodnight then. I hope your father feels better soon.'

He touched his cap and turned to retrace his steps and Ruth hurried inside to find the benches around the waiting room filled with people – some coughing, some clutching at arms that looked like they might be broken and others with sickly infants on their knees. A spluttering fire burnt behind a guard at the far end of the room which was filled with a fug of unwashed bodies and the sharp notes of a disinfectant.

'There's a long wait,' one woman advised her. 'Take a seat,' she offered, making everyone on the nearest bench shove up to make room for Ruth.

'It's an emergency,' Ruth told her. 'I've come about my father.'

She heard a collective sigh echo around the room. 'We'll be here 'til mornin' if the doctor goes out on an emergency call,' grumbled an elderly man. 'I hope it's real serious.'

'It is,' Ruth assured him. 'It's his heart.'

There was some sympathetic nodding.

'Sounds like a hospital job,' remarked someone. 'I knew a woman with heart trouble. She dropped dead one morning – just like that.'

'Shush!' replied another patient. 'Tha doesn't want to be alarming yon lass!'

But the words had alarmed Ruth and by the time Dr Skaife came out to call his next patient she was in tears.

'It's my father. I think he's dying,' she sobbed. 'Please will you come?'

The doctor glanced around the crowded room. 'I'll be as quick as I can,' he told those who were waiting and then went to fetch his hat and coat and his medical bag to walk to Queen Victoria Street with Ruth.

The doctor asked her about her father's symptoms along the way and Ruth explained about the palpitations he was complaining of. Dr Skaife nodded but didn't increase his pace and Ruth was unsure whether to be reassured by his lack of urgency or whether it was simply the ice that was slowing him down.

It seemed an age before they arrived at the door. Ruth let them in and hurried to see how her father was. She found him still sitting by the fire, but the colour had returned to his cheeks and he had eaten most of the bowl of stew she'd put out for him.

'Dr Skaife,' he said when he saw the doctor come into the room behind his daughter. 'I'm sorry we've bothered you. Ruth was worried, but I'm feeling much better now. I'm afraid we've called you out for nothing. I'm so sorry.'

The doctor put his bag down on the table and pulled off his leather gloves. Ruth watched him take her father's wrist and feel his pulse. 'Your daughter said your heart was beating strangely.' He was silent for a moment. 'It seems steady enough now,' he pronounced.

'Like I said. I'm feeling better,' her father replied. 'I'm sorry we've bothered you.'

'It's no bother,' said the doctor. 'Has it happened before?'

'Now and again,' admitted her father. 'I usually sit down until it passes.'

The doctor nodded. 'Well, there's not much I can do now,' he said. 'But come and see me if it happens again.'

'What do you think it is, doctor?' her father asked. 'Should I be worried?'

'No,' he said reassuringly as he pulled his gloves back on. 'These things happen sometimes. I take it you're generally well? I heard you'd closed up your shop.'

'Just for the time being. I'm running the soup kitchen on Cleaver Street until things improve.'

'A worthy cause,' the doctor said. 'But try not to overdo things.'

'I won't,' said Ruth's father.

'Is he all right?' she whispered to the doctor as she showed him to the door. 'He really was very ill before. I can hardly believe the change in him.'

'His pulse is steady at the moment,' the doctor told her. 'But I think you've both had a scare. It was probably nothing more than tiredness given the circumstances. Take care of your father,' he advised. 'Don't let him do too much.'

'I won't,' promised Ruth, but when she'd closed and locked the front door and was walking back through the empty shop to the kitchen, she wondered how much the stress of the problems he'd had with the business had contributed to making him ill. She suspected that he'd been worried for a long time although, like his illness, he'd kept it to himself. And the trouble with Caroline Haworth wouldn't have helped either.

'I think you should get off to bed,' she told him as she began to clear the pots off the table to wash them up. She knew she could have left them for Agatha, but it seemed a selfish thing to do, even though she felt exhausted herself and her ankle was throbbing from her fall.

'I will,' he agreed. He stood up and kissed her on the cheek. 'Good night,' he said. 'Mind you cover the fire before you come up.'

'Good night,' Ruth replied and watched as he gave her a reassuring smile before going to the bottom of the stairs in the narrow lobby. She almost went to see him go up, wanting to make sure he reached the top safely, but she knew that he hated fuss. Instead, she listened to his steps and was relieved when she heard him climb up quickly as he normally did. Whatever had bothered him earlier seemed to have resolved, and the doctor hadn't seemed especially worried. Perhaps it would be all right. She hoped so. She had no idea how she would cope without him.

Chapter Twenty-One

After everything in the soup kitchen had been set straight for the next morning, Sally had said goodbye to her friends from the mill and walked home. It had certainly been an eventful day. First the trouble outside with Miss Haworth, and then her setting her skirt on fire. Thank goodness Freddy Fry had been there to save her not once, but twice. Sally smiled to herself at the memory of him. He'd been furious with Miss Haworth for being so careless and poor Ruth had taken some of the blame too. She'd been beside herself for the rest of the afternoon.

Still, the hungry families had eventually been fed and sent on their way, and Caroline Haworth had gone home in her father's carriage saying that her parents would probably be so angry with her that she might not be able to come again. She'd seemed regretful and Sally was impressed that she had at least tried to help with the washing up, which was more than any of the committee ladies had done. They had just stood at the trestles and doled out the soup as if it had been made with their own fair hands, when in fact the mill girls had done all the work. And the mill girls were banished to the sinks when the mayor and corporation came in to admire what had been achieved. Sally supposed she shouldn't have been surprised. There were always those who thought they were a cut above the rest.

When she got to the house, she went in, eager to regale the rest of the family with an account of her day, but when she pushed open the door to the back kitchen, she saw her father was home and was speaking animatedly to her mother who was wearing a worried frown.

He turned his head when he heard her.

'Sally!' he exclaimed. 'I'm glad you're here. Help me to convince your mother that we should go to America!'

'Has something happened?' she asked him, wondering what had got him so worked up.

'It has! I was in the Sun earlier and a couple of chaps came in looking for workers. I told them I was interested and gave them my details… well, details of the whole family… and they say there's work for us in Massachusetts. All we have to do is persuade your mother to agree and we can go! They said they'll sort out passage on the ship and everything we need to get settled. It's a great opportunity!' he went on excitedly. 'They told me there was nothing left for mill workers here. They said we should go to America. It's the land of opportunity!'

Sally looked at her mother and saw that she didn't agree.

'How do we even know what they say is true?' she asked. 'Why should we trust them?'

'Of course it's true!' exclaimed her father who was looking frustrated at his wife's lack of enthusiasm. 'There are cotton mills in America. Plenty of them – and they have cotton. Even if the ports weren't blockaded, you're not telling me that they aren't going to keep the best for themselves and just send us the scraps. Why should they export it when they can weave it themselves and make more money? Besides,' he went on, getting up from his chair and beginning to pace the small room. 'All the men who normally work in the mills have probably been conscripted into the army to fight. It's no wonder they need more hands.'

'And what will happen when those men come back and want their jobs?' pointed out her mother. 'It's bad enough being out of work here. I don't want to be out of work in a foreign country. They'd do nothing for us.'

'They're doing little enough for us here,' her father replied. 'A bit of soup on weekdays, but nothing on a Sunday because they're too busy with their religion. That isn't going to keep body and soul together. And they expect us to go cap in hand and be grateful when it's them that's put us out of work in the first place. We don't owe them owt!' he shouted, slapping his hand down on the table. 'We need to go where we can make summat of ourselves, somewhere that's not beholden to gentry, where the working man can rise by his own skill!'

Sally thought that what her father was saying made sense. And he was right about the gentry. Those committee women had looked down their noses at the folk who came into the kitchen for soup. They were willing to help, after a fashion, but they would never think of the workers as their equals.

'And the pay's good,' went on her father. 'It'll be in American dollars, but that's what their currency is. And we'll have a house – bigger than this,' he said, waving a hand around the cramped kitchen. 'All standing on its own too. Not in a row like these where you can hear every word that the neighbours say.'

'Wooden houses,' her mother reminded him. 'I don't want to live in a shed.'

'They're not sheds, our Martha,' argued her father. 'They're proper houses. This chap showed me a picture of one. It had steps up to the front door and a veranda to sit out on in the summertime.'

Sally could see that her mother still wasn't impressed, but her father's enthusiasm was infectious and she began to imagine the kind of life they might have in America. It looked much better than this smoky little northern town.

'I'd love to go,' she told her father. 'It sounds wonderful.'

'There you are,' he told his wife. 'And our George will want to go too. And Florrie and Ellen and the twins.'

'They'll only want to go because you're describing it like it'll be some sort of paradise,' grumbled her mother. 'You have no idea if this chap you've been speaking to is honest.'

'Well, it's true that some of the shipping companies are offering cheap passage,' her father responded. 'Joe Bracewell already has tickets for himself and his family. He showed them to me. They're to sail the week after next. If we don't get a move on all the jobs will be taken.'

'Let's just think about it,' pleaded her mother. 'Let's not do anything hasty that we might regret. If we do go, there'll be no coming back. It's a big decision.'

'All right,' conceded her father at last, sitting back down again. 'We'll think about it – but not for too long,' he warned.

–

When the others had come inside for their tea, George from a fruitless search for work, Florrie and Ellen from their classes at the school and the twins from a game on the street, their father began to talk about America again.

'We'll have more to eat than this,' he told them as their mother shared out the jugs of soup that Sally had brought home.

After her brothers and sisters had eaten what was in their bowls and realised there weren't going to be any second helpings, they looked eagerly at their father, waiting to hear more about the wonderful country he was promising to take them to. Sally saw that her mother was still doubtful, but she was outnumbered and would probably have to agree in the end. It was true that there was nothing for them here. No work, no food, no future. Surely it was for the best to try to improve their situation? Besides, the more her father talked about mills with endless supplies of cotton, big houses and plentiful meals, the more she felt the anticipation grow in her.

'I know you're worried about leaving everything you know,' she told her mother as they cleared away the pots later. 'But I think we should listen to what Dad says.'

'You're young,' her mother replied. 'It's easier for you to uproot yourself and go all that way. It's different for me. This is all I've ever known. I'm too old to be starting again somewhere new.'

'You're not that old!' she told her mother. 'And Dad says he'll buy you another piano when we get there, if that's what's worrying you. It might have to be sold anyway.'

'Or broken up for firewood,' interrupted her father as he overheard the conversation.

'Never!' Her mother looked scandalised.

'What else will we do to keep warm when the coal's gone?' he asked. 'There'll be no more handouts until next week.'

'We still have more soup tickets,' Sally pointed out.

'Aye, but nowt to burn other than yon piano. Besides,' he went on. 'It's shameful. I'd rather have work. And there's work in America. I think we should go, Martha,' he said to his wife.

Sally could see that her mother was softening, and she went to bed, not dreading another day in the soup kitchen, but with her head filled with the wonders of a far-off country that would be their new home.

Chapter Twenty-Two

Caroline had been dreading facing her parents, but when the carriage drew up outside the house, she had no choice but to get out and go up the steps, no matter how reluctantly. Her mother was waiting for her in the hallway. She was clearly furious.

'What in heaven's name did you think you were playing at?' she demanded. 'You've brought shame on us all!'

There were no words of comfort for her narrow escape, noticed Caroline. Although she wasn't surprised. The only thing that was concerning her mother was how the affair reflected on her – and she had taken the view that it reflected very badly indeed.

'I went to help those worse off than myself,' Caroline tried to explain.

'Your grandfather didn't pay for you to have a good education so that you could work in a soup kitchen!' replied her mother. 'What on earth will people think? What will the Duttons say if they hear about it? And they surely will. Those common people are full of gossip. They'll tell everyone about you. You'll be lucky to live it down.'

Caroline bit back an acerbic reply. To hear her mother talk anyone would think she'd gone out to sell her body on the streets. But she also kept silent because she knew that if she tried to defend herself, she would cry. She'd been badly frightened by the sight of the flames licking at her skirt and it was only the hoop of her crinoline that had kept her legs from being burnt. What she really craved was some sympathy, a hug and some reassurance.

'I need to change my clothes,' she said. She heard her voice trembling as she spoke and she wished that Mrs Jenkins would come to take care of her. The housekeeper had been more of a mother to her than her real mother for as long as Caroline could remember. When she'd been a child and she'd scraped a knee or trapped a finger it was always Mrs Jenkins she'd run to for it to be rubbed better or cured with a dollop of the ointment she kept on the kitchen table.

'That skirt is ruined,' observed her mother. 'I can see your legs! What must Simmons have thought when he came to collect you? Go and make yourself decent. We'll see what your father has to say when he gets home.'

As she climbed the stairs to her bedroom, Caroline worried more about what her father would say than her mother's anger. She'd disobeyed him by not getting her mother's permission to go to the soup kitchen, and she'd let him down by proving so useless that she'd set herself alight. He would be angry too. But his anger would touch her in a way that her mother's never could.

Upstairs, alone in her room, she didn't ring for Lottie to come and help her. With trembling fingers, she fumbled at the ties that held her ruined skirt. It was charred and blackened and smelt of the fire. She threw it into a corner where she wouldn't have to look at it then unfastened the crinoline frame and stepped out of it. She took off her blouse and her stays and her stockings and when she was wearing nothing more than her shift, she threw herself onto the bed and wept, not ladylike tears but great gulping sobs as the events of the day played out again and again in her memory. From the jeering faces of the unemployed millhands to the sight of the flames beginning to engulf her, Caroline had never known fear like it in her life and she wondered if she was capable of living in the world she'd been allowed a glimpse of today.

But as she recalled all the horrible things that had happened to her, the memory of Freddy Fry also loomed large – the feel of his hand on her arm as he'd pulled her away from the fire. She could still see him on his knees, beating out the flames that threatened to engulf her, and she couldn't forget the anger in his eyes as he'd shouted at her for being so careless. His anger hadn't been the same as that of the millhands though. It had been fuelled by his concern for her and she wished that she'd taken the trouble to thank him properly for saving her both times. He must think that she was snobbish and ungrateful. She hadn't even asked if he'd burnt his hands whilst putting out her skirt. She must seek him out tomorrow and thank him properly, she decided. And despite everything that had happened and her reluctance to return to the soup kitchen the next day, she found that she was looking forward to seeing him again.

It was silly, of course. He lived in a completely different social circle from her and any attraction she felt towards him must be quickly quelled. Besides, he would have no interest in someone like her. She was beyond his reach. But he was handsome, and his intense blue eyes had drilled into her soul as he'd spoken masterfully to her about staying away from the open fire. It had ignited a different sort of flame inside her. Something she couldn't quite explain, and as well as making her feel ashamed, it had kindled a feeling of wanting to know him better.

Drying her face on an embroidered cotton handkerchief, she sat up and leant back against the pillows. She was cold and shivering now. There was no fire in her room and she was wearing next to nothing. She turned back her covers and slipped between the sheets as if she was an invalid. She was so tired, she realised. She would just close her eyes and rest for a while before she went back downstairs to face her parents.

'Miss Caroline. Miss Caroline!'

She woke to the sound of Lottie's anxious voice. She was standing by the bed with a candle in her hand. It was dark outside the window where the curtains had not been drawn and the room was freezing cold.

'Miss Caroline? Are you unwell?'

'No.' Caroline sat up quickly, realising that she had fallen asleep. 'I was just tired,' she said. 'What time is it?'

'Six o' clock,' Lottie said as she put the candle holder down on the bedside table and went to close the curtains. 'I thought you were still out. I would have come up sooner if I'd known you were here.' She went around lighting the other candles and the room flickered into view. 'What's this?' she asked when she noticed the skirt that Caroline had thrown down. 'It's been burnt!'

'I had a small accident at the soup kitchen. It's nothing,' Caroline added as she saw the look of horror on Lottie's face. 'You can cut it up for dusters or put it out for the rag gatherers. It's beyond mending. And will you light a fire, please? It's very cold in here.'

'Are you sure you want a fire?' asked Lottie. She sounded doubtful as if Caroline might not be trusted to take care of herself.

'Yes,' Caroline told her, still hugging the blankets around her. 'I'll wait for the bedroom to warm up before I get up and dress for dinner. There's plenty of time.'

'Very well, Miss,' said Lottie. 'I'll fetch some hot water as well. Unless you'd like me to fill a bath?'

'No. There's no need,' Caroline told her, knowing how much work it would entail. 'A good wash down will be sufficient. Thank you,' she added.

–

Later, when she was washed and decently dressed in a fresh gown, Caroline went downstairs to the parlour where she found her mother and father waiting for her.

Her father looked at her anxiously. 'Are you all right?' he asked in a worried tone. 'I heard about what happened to you at the soup kitchen.'

'It was nothing,' Caroline told him. 'Just a small mishap.'

'Your mother says she knew nothing about you going,' he said. He glanced from his daughter to his wife and back again. 'I told you that you must ask her permission,' he went on, as if he was asking her to confirm it. It was clear that there had already been words about what she'd done and her father had, as usual, been blamed. 'Did you not ask her?' he persisted.

'No,' admitted Caroline. She knew she must tell the truth for her father's sake.

'Why not?'

'I was afraid she would say no.'

'I most certainly would have said no,' her mother told her. 'And I would have been right to do so. Look at what happened. You could have been badly burnt. Thomas

Dutton wouldn't have wanted a wife with scars on her body.'

Caroline almost snapped back at her mother to ask if that was all she cared about, but her father shook his head to warn her not to retaliate.

'Well, she won't go again,' he told his wife.

'Do I have no say in this?' Caroline asked.

Her father looked puzzled. 'Surely you don't want to go again?' he asked. 'Not after everything you've been through.' He gave her a hard look and Caroline realised that he'd learnt everything about her day, from her escape from the crowd, to her treatment by the mill girls as well as the accident with the fire.

'I do,' she told him. 'I know I wasn't a lot of help today, but I can learn. I can work hard. It showed me how much people are struggling and I'd feel guilty if I sat about and did nothing.'

Her mother gave her a look of disgust. 'You really are your father's daughter,' she accused her. 'A real lady would never involve herself with such common people.'

Her father's gaze shifted to his wife and Caroline saw the anger on his face.

'She's a brave girl, and a caring one too,' he told her. 'She doesn't think the workers are beneath her like you do. She can see that they are as good as you are, if not better. They've always worked hard at the mill to earn their wages to keep their families and it isn't their fault there's no cotton. At least she wants to help them and not just blame them for something beyond their control!'

Caroline held her breath. She knew that her father had gone too far this time. It was because he was tired and worried that he'd snapped back at his wife.

Her mother looked shocked for a moment. Then she composed herself.

'How dare you speak to me like that?' she demanded. 'The worst thing I ever did in my life was to allow you to charm your way into my bed. My mother warned me. My father too, but I wouldn't listen. And now I'm paying the price.' Then she turned her wrath on Caroline. 'Do as you please,' she told her. 'But don't blame me if you end up in a situation like this. Trapped with a man who cares nothing for you and doesn't even have the money to support you. I've a good mind to call for the carriage and go to Salesbury Hall!' she threatened her husband. 'Although I don't suppose you would even care if I left you!'

'Try it,' responded Caroline's father. 'You know your father will send you back. You know he told you when you married me that it was your choice, but it was a choice you would have to live with. He won't take you in.'

Tears welled in her mother's eyes and it shocked Caroline more than her dramatic outbursts ever had. For a few moments there was a tense silence. Then her mother swept out of the room without a word and her father sank onto the sofa with an air of defeat.

'I'm sorry,' whispered Caroline as she sat down too.

'It's not your fault,' replied her father. 'None of it is your fault. Never think that it is.'

Caroline wanted to know if he would allow her to go to the soup kitchen again the next day, but she knew better than to raise the subject now. She would wait until morning and hope that tempers had cooled before she asked again.

Chapter Twenty-Three

Ruth woke early the next morning. In fact, she'd hardly slept at all, waking several times in the night because she'd thought she heard her father calling for her. But every time she'd slipped out of bed and tiptoed across the landing to the door of his room, he'd been sleeping, seemingly peacefully and she'd told herself that she was worrying about nothing.

She reached out to the small table beside her bed and felt for the box of matches to light the candle. Then anxiously she carried it, guarding the flame against draughts with her hand, to her father's door.

'Are you awake?' she whispered.

'What time is it?' he asked.

'I'm not certain.' She carried the candle over to his bedside table where he kept his pocket watch overnight. 'Just before six,' she told him. 'How do you feel? Are you well enough to get up?'

Ruth hoped he would say yes because if he didn't, she knew she would have to go to the soup kitchen alone and take on the task of organising the workers. The thought terrified her.

'I'm all right. There's no need for you to fuss,' he replied. 'Go on downstairs. I'll be down in a minute.'

'I'll just get dressed first,' she told him and hurried back to her own room to pull on her clothes and brush her hair.

She would have to wash her hands and face at the kitchen sink. She'd forgotten to bring a jug of water upstairs last night; she'd been so distracted by her father's illness.

In the kitchen she lit the lamp and it cast shadows as she poked at the fire, trying to coax a blaze from the coals she'd banked up the night before. When the flames began to take hold, she broke the ice on the top of the pail in the scullery and filled the kettle before putting it on to the hob to boil.

She rubbed her hands together vigorously to warm them before she picked up the bread knife and cut into the loaf on the table. The butter was so hard that it wouldn't spread, so she had to add a few small lumps here and there and then spread treacle over the top.

By the time her father came down she had the tea brewed and the breakfast was ready. She studied him apprehensively for any signs of his being unwell, but as he sat down to drink his tea and eat the bread, he seemed the same as he was every morning, and she relaxed and ate her own meal before clearing the table and putting on her coat and bonnet. As she put her hands into the warm fur muff and glanced about the kitchen to make sure everything had been left in good order for Agatha, Ruth longed to ask her father again if he felt strong enough to go to work, but she already knew what his answer would be. He'd put on his own coat and hat and was adding more coal to the fire before putting the guard in front of it to prevent any burning coals falling out of the grate and spoiling the mat that covered the floor in front of the hearth. She thought that maybe he was moving more slowly than usual and that he seemed tired, but she told herself that it could just be her imagination.

They set off down the street and Ruth was relieved that he didn't seem breathless as he walked along beside her through the darkness, the lantern swinging in time to each step. He didn't say much though and she sensed that he didn't want to discuss what had happened the day before.

When they reached Cleaver Street, the door was ajar and inside the foundry the lads had the fires going. Freddy Fry smiled when he saw them.

'Are you better, sir?' he asked her father.

'I'm perfectly well,' he replied. 'Why do you ask?'

'I bumped into Miss Hodgson yesterday evening on her way to fetch the doctor. She said you weren't well.'

'It was nothing,' her father replied. 'My daughter was being over cautious.'

'Only because I worry about you,' Ruth said as Mr Yates came hurrying across.

'Mr Hodgson,' he said, sounding surprised to see him. 'We didn't think you'd be coming today. Freddy here said you'd been taken poorly.'

'It was just a bit of indigestion.'

'Not the soup I hope?'

Ruth saw her father frown. 'Of course not,' he replied. 'I'm all right now.'

'Good. Good to hear it,' Mr Yates said. 'We were worried about managing without you.' He glanced at Ruth, but she said nothing. She didn't want to reassure him that she could have taken her father's place, because she doubted that she could.

Soon the mill girls began to flock in and take off their coats and tie on their aprons. They were obviously used to hard work and didn't take much organising as they picked up the knives and peelers and began to get the fresh vegetables ready for the soup pot. They chatted away as they worked, but Ruth didn't join in. They all knew one another already, and she felt awkward about expressing her own opinions as the talk drifted from the coldness of the weather to the ingredients of the soup and then to the problem of the missing cotton.

'I just wish the cotton would come again so that we could get back to normal,' said a girl named Ellen. 'I'd much rather be working at my looms than peeling turnips.'

'Aye, and the pay's better,' agreed another.

'Still, it has it's compensations,' remarked Sally as they paused to watch Freddy Fry come past with a heavy sack resting across his shoulders. 'Old Albert at t' mill doesn't provide the same eyeful as that,' she remarked as her eyes tracked the foundry worker all the way to the furnaces where he began to shovel coal.

Ruth thought that she ought to chivvy them back to their tasks, but she didn't want to get on the wrong side of them. Sally, especially, had been such a help to her yesterday and she'd been grateful. But the way they kept looking at Freddy and grinning at one another made her feel uncomfortable. It might have been inconsequential behaviour for them, but she was worried that he would see them and that he might be offended. He had been such a gentleman the previous evening and it had surprised her how caring he was. She didn't think it was fair of them to be so focused on his appearance. It demeaned him.

Soon, though, they turned their attention back to the vegetables and the talk returned to the cotton famine and their lost jobs. As they talked and worked, Ruth looked around for her father. She felt a rush of alarm when she saw him sat down at one of the tables set out for the customers to eat their soup. She excused herself quietly and went over to speak to him.

'Are you feeling ill again?' she asked when she reached him.

'I'm just having five minutes before the rush begins,' he told her, although it was only about eight o'clock and it would be hours before the doors were opened for the soup to be served. He looked obviously tired and Ruth wondered if she should insist that he went home to rest properly. The soup kitchen was hard work and she was worried that it was going to prove too much for her father.

'I'm worried that you've taken on too much,' she told him. 'Perhaps you ought to have stayed at home and rested today.'

'I can't afford to lose this job!' Almost immediately he looked sorry that he'd snapped at her. 'You mustn't worry,' he added, taking her hand in his. 'There's nothing to fret about.'

But the way he'd said it made her wonder if there was a need for her to be concerned. She'd just been listening to the mill girls talk about how hard their families were finding it to manage and she'd been feeling guilty that the famine hadn't affected her family so badly. Now, though, she wondered if her father's finances were worse than she'd thought. The idea struck her with horror. He'd told her that they could manage. He'd said they would reopen the shop in a few months. He'd even kept Agatha on to look after the house for them. But what if he wasn't being honest with her? He kept telling her not to worry, but what if he was just trying to protect her by not wanting her to know about their financial situation and his health?

She was about to ask him to be truthful with her about how much money he had lost over the past few months, but before she could say anything she heard a silence fall across the foundry as Caroline Haworth came in, followed by her father.

Chapter Twenty-Four

Caroline was aware of every pair of eyes in the soup kitchen being turned on her. It was clear that they were all surprised to see her again. She was even slightly surprised herself. When she'd gone to bed the previous night, she hadn't had much hope of her parents agreeing to let her come.

Even so, she'd asked Lottie to wake her early and even begged a plain skirt and blouse from her, telling her that she would give her some money to buy herself new clothes.

'Are you sure you want to wear these?' Lottie had asked earlier that morning when she'd brought Caroline a cup of tea in her room.

'As long as you don't mind,' Caroline had told her.

'No,' said the maid. 'Your mother remarked only the other day that these were looking a bit shabby. She doesn't like me answering the door in them. Says it gives the wrong impression.'

Caroline had fingered the coarse cotton weave of the white blouse, wondering if it might prove to be uncomfortable, although she had no intention of complaining. It had sleeves that could easily be rolled up for work and even if the collar was worn and the fabric turning slightly yellow, she knew it was far more suitable for working in the soup kitchen than her outfit the previous day.

Luckily, she and Lottie were a similar size and when she put it on, she found the blouse fitted her quite well. The skirt was a bit tight, but not so much that it couldn't be fastened. It was made of a thick woollen material that would keep her warm and more importantly it hung neatly around her legs rather than swaying over a crinoline. Caroline knew it made her look unfashionable and poor, but there was less risk of having another accident if she was around the open flames.

When she'd gone into the morning room where the breakfast was served her father hadn't commented on her clothes. She doubted that he'd even noticed she was wearing Lottie's castoffs.

'I want to go to help at the soup kitchen again today,' she'd told him. He'd put down the morning paper with a sigh.

'You know your mother doesn't want you to.'

'I know. But I think she's wrong. I want to help.'

He'd given the barest of shrugs. It was clear that he too disagreed with her mother.

'Will you be there today?' she'd asked him.

'Yes. I'm going in five minutes,' he'd told her. 'I'm walking.'

'Then I'll walk with you,' Caroline had told him before she began to quickly push scrambled eggs into her mouth so that she would be ready and he wouldn't have an excuse to set off without her.

But now, as the silence of the foundry echoed in her ears, she wondered if she'd made the right choice. She wondered if she was welcome.

'Good morning, Mr Haworth,' said Freddy Fry before fixing his gaze on Caroline. 'Miss Haworth,' he greeted her. 'I hope you're recovered?'

'I am. Thank you.'

She stood, almost transfixed, under his gaze as he appraised her.

'I didn't think you'd come back,' remarked Freddy, still watching her. 'Not after what happened.'

'I never thanked you properly for coming to my rescue yesterday,' Caroline said. 'You must think I'm very ungrateful.'

He shrugged his shoulders. 'I wouldn't have liked to see you go up in flames.'

'But you must have hurt your hands. Were they badly burnt?'

'They're tough,' he replied, holding out one of his calloused palms for her inspection. 'They have to be to work in a foundry.'

Caroline stared at his hand. It was ingrained with dirt from handling the coal, and the nails were broken and dirty.

Freddy seemed embarrassed by her scrutiny and folded his arms. Caroline felt mortified at his reaction. She hadn't been judging him for his unclean hands as he obviously thought. She'd been wondering what it might feel like if he took her hand in his, or even touched her face – or even her body. It had been a silly daydream and she regretted it. No matter how attractive he was she knew that there could never be any relationship of that sort between them and she must keep a check on her imagination.

He gave her a nod and went on his way to collect another sack of coal. Unable to help herself, Caroline watched him go.

'Wait for me to walk home with you at the end of the day,' her father said, interrupting her contemplation of the foundry worker.

'I will,' she promised. Whether it was because he thought the streets were dangerous or because he thought it would be better if they faced the wrath of her mother together, Caroline wasn't sure, but she'd been glad of his protection this morning even though it was still too early for the unemployed to be gathered at the door.

Caroline hung up her coat and bonnet and picked up an apron from the freshly laundered pile. As she put it on, Ruth Hodgson came up to her.

'I'm pleased to see you,' she said.

'Well, I wasn't going to let setting myself on fire deter me,' she joked. Ruth smiled politely as if she wasn't sure whether or not to laugh. She was a quiet little thing, thought Caroline. A few years younger than herself and obviously shy even though she'd worked as a shop assistant for her father. She appeared to be as far out of her depth at she felt herself and Caroline was keen to make a friend and ally of her. She suspected by the way the mill girls were eyeing her up and down that she wasn't going to be in for an easy time.

'What would you like me to do today?' she asked.

'You could shell some peas,' Ruth suggested. 'Not so many of the committee ladies come this early,' she added.

Caroline nodded. The table where the sack of peas was waiting was empty and she would have to sit alone, but at least she would be doing something useful and it meant she could keep her distance from the mill girls.

Chapter Twenty-Five

At the end of the day, Ruth found her father looking pale and exhausted, sitting on a stool at the preparation tables. Mr Yates came across to them, jangling his keys in his hand, ready to lock up.

'You look tired, Mr Hodgson,' he observed.

'It's been a long day,' her father replied as he stood up, putting a hand out to steady himself.

'Aye.' The foundry owner looked concerned. 'It's not an easy task organising this kitchen.'

'It'll get easier,' her father told him. 'I think it went better today, now that we're getting more organised, and the soup was ready on time.'

'Aye. Those coming through seemed less set on trouble today,' agreed Mr Yates. 'Anyway, I'll let you get off,' he went on, clearly keen to secure the building and go home himself.

Ruth followed her father out into the freezing night. The stars were bright again and he paused to look up at them.

'Are you all right?' she asked him.

'Tired, that's all.' Ruth was surprised that he had admitted it. She thought it was the first time she'd ever heard him say he was tired.

'Pa, you would say if it's too much for you, wouldn't you?' she asked him as they walked home.

'It's not too much for me,' he replied.

'But you were ill yesterday.'

'And today I'm well.'

'But you are tired. And Mr Yates wasn't expecting you to come this morning. Maybe you should have taken a day off to rest,' she persisted. 'Maybe you should take tomorrow off. Like you said, things are organised now. I'm sure we could manage without you for one day.'

'No, Ruth,' he told her. 'I was asked to do this job and do it I will. I'll not be accused of being unreliable or too…' He hesitated. 'Too old,' he finished, sounding sad.

'You're not old,' she replied, although the truth was that as he walked slowly at her side, he did seem old tonight and it frightened her. But he turned and smiled to reassure her.

'You don't need to worry about me,' he told her once more. It was the way he kept repeating it that made Ruth wonder if she did have cause to worry.

She was glad when they got home to Queen Victoria Street. She hung up their coats, revived the fire and took the meal Agatha had left them out of the oven. After they'd got warm and eaten her father seemed better, even though his yawns betrayed how weary he was.

'There's a council meeting tonight,' he said as he finished his cup of tea and consulted his pocket watch. 'I really should attend.'

'I'm sure they won't mind if you miss it this time,' said Ruth, sincerely hoping he wasn't serious about going out again. 'I think an early night would do us both good,' she persisted. 'I'm tired out myself.'

'You go up then,' he said, and Ruth was tempted. Her legs ached with the unaccustomed standing, but she hadn't wanted to sit on a stool all day like the committee ladies.

She wanted the mill girls to regard her as one of them – the real workers.

'I'll go in half an hour,' she said, picking up her book to read, worried that her father might try to sneak out if she wasn't there to stop him.

He yawned again and leant back in his chair. At least he hadn't complained about the palpitations again or been breathless, but it was clear that the episode the day before, combined with his new job, had worn him out. It was so different from his usual work where he was his own boss and could pace himself. Ruth knew that he sometimes sat down for an hour after his dinner before he went back to the sweet making. She'd thought nothing of it in the past, but now she wondered if it was because he'd been unwell for some time.

It was hard to broach the subject with him though. She knew that if she asked, he would simply repeat his instruction to her not to worry. She loved him for wanting to protect her, but it didn't reassure her. She wanted to help him, and she couldn't do that unless he was honest with her.

She had begun to wonder why he'd taken on the job at the soup kitchen. He must have realised what hard work it was going to be. She closed the book and looked across at him.

'Not interesting?' he asked.

'I can't concentrate,' she confessed.

'Too tired?'

'Partly. But I am worried about you. I know you keep telling me not to, but I do worry. This job at the kitchen. Is there no one else who could do it?' she asked. 'I'm sure we could manage. I could carry on working there,' she suggested. 'But it seems silly to do a job that leaves you so worn out at the end of the day.'

'It's only because it's different from what I'm used to. I'll acclimatise to it,' he said, stifling another yawn behind his hand.

'Don't go tomorrow,' Ruth pleaded. 'Stay at home and rest.'

'I can't do that. They need me. There's a lot to be done.'

'Tell them you made a mistake,' she asked him. 'Say it's not what you expected. Tell them that it's too much. I'm sure they'll understand. With so many men out of work I'm sure they can easily find someone else to do it.'

'No.' He shook his head.

'Why not?' she asked, anxious about why he was being so stubborn. 'We'll be opening the shop again in a few months, won't we? Surely we can manage until then?'

Ruth was horrified as she saw her father wipe tears from his eyes. She'd never seen him cry before. She didn't think he was capable.

'What is it? What's wrong?' she asked as the book fell to the floor and she rushed to kneel beside him and comfort him. 'Are you ill again?'

'No. No, it's not that.'

'Then what?'

He met her frantic gaze and then looked away. He seemed ashamed and humiliated.

'I need the wages,' he confessed.

'Why do you need those wages?' she demanded, determined to get to the truth. 'I thought we had plenty put by in savings. We have savings, don't we? We have enough to tide us over until we can open the shop again? Don't we?' she asked. But she saw from his expression what the answer was, and a cold shiver ran through her as she realised her worst fears were being confirmed.

'I'm sorry, Ruth,' he said, reaching to grasp her hand. 'I didn't want you to know. But the shop has been doing badly for a while. Ever since the cotton stopped coming and folk began to make economies. Perhaps I shouldn't have kept it from you, but we've been struggling, and I've been dipping into savings to pay bills and buy food. I thought it would soon get better. I thought things would improve. And I didn't want you to be worried.'

Ruth clasped both her hands around his as tears rolled down his cheeks.

'I'm sorry,' he said again. 'Please forgive me. I was just trying to protect you.'

Ruth buried her head in his lap, knowing that he was embarrassed by his tears. She didn't want to make it worse by crying herself, but it was a struggle. Despite wondering if things were worse than he had pretended, the news was a huge shock to her. She'd never suspected that things were so bad that he'd spent their savings. But one thing was clear, the burden had become too much for her father to bear alone and it was up to her to step up and take some responsibility. It was time for him to stop treating her like a child and allow her to help him. How she could do that she wasn't sure, but she would find a way. She had to. There was no other choice.

Chapter Twenty-Six

When Sally had watched Ruth allocate the task of shelling peas to the mill owner's daughter, her first thought had been that at least it would keep her well away from the fire, even though Caroline had been dressed in clothes that looked borrowed from her maid. There was not a crinoline in sight as she'd settled on to a stool and reached for the first pea pod. Sally had to give her credit for turning up again. She was the last person she'd expected to walk in through the door after yesterday's accident. Maybe Caroline was made of stronger stuff than she'd thought.

Walking home, she felt more optimistic. The soup making had gone well and the men and women who'd come to eat today had mostly been polite and grateful. Her father hadn't come in to eat with them, but her mother had brought her brothers and sisters rather than waiting for Sally to carry soup home at the end of the day, and she'd been thankful to see the younger ones seated at the table with a bowl of soup and a chunk of bread in front of them. When she'd asked about her father, worried that he was deliberately going hungry rather than face what he considered the shame of taking charity, her mother had told her that he'd been offered some work although she wasn't sure what it was. It had seemed good news to Sally and she hoped he'd been taken on at one of the mills that were still running. If he could bring in a decent wage then, with the addition of her daily earnings, they might just be able to manage until the arrangements were finalised for their move to America.

When she reached home, she pushed open the door and stamped off the remains of snow and ice that were clinging to her boots before she stepped inside and wiped her feet on the mat.

Voices were coming from the kitchen and she hurried to the door ready to hear good news. But her father's face was grim as he sat by the fire warming his hands.

'Hello,' she said, unsure what was wrong. 'Mam said you'd been offered a job.'

'Aye,' he agreed. 'At yon stone quarry.'

'At the stone quarry? Doing what?'

'What do you think?' he snapped at her. 'Quarrying the stone.'

'He can't be doing that,' her mother told her. 'I've told him to refuse it. He's a trained weaver. He can't be going up Shorrock's Delph breaking up stones. It's filthy work. Dangerous too. You tell him,' she pleaded with Sally. 'Tell him to turn it down.'

Sally looked to her father who was staring at his hands. 'Do you want to do it?' she asked him.

'Of course not! But I've no choice, have I? If I don't accept it then we'll starve.'

'Surely they wouldn't allow that?' argued her mother. 'Not when we have children.'

'They would,' Sally's father told her. 'Anyone who refuses work loses their relief payments.'

'Could we manage until we get the tickets for the boat?' asked Sally. 'How long did they say it would take?'

Her father shrugged his shoulders. 'Two weeks. Three. I'm not certain. The chap I spoke to said he would sort it out and then come back to let me know the day we're going to sail. He couldn't give a date until he'd spoken to the steamer company. He said it depended on available places. I'll have to take this work,' he said gloomily. 'Whether I want to or not.'

'But it won't be for long,' Sally pointed out to comfort both him and her mother. 'Just until we can sail,' she told her mother, hoping that the turn of events would increase her enthusiasm for their emigration. 'When do you start?' she asked her father.

'Tomorrow,' he told her. 'I've to be up there for eight o' clock in the morning. A shilling a day. It's going to be damned cold.'

–

Her mother had managed to buy some potatoes from the market, but they were very green and full of eyes and by the time she'd taken all the bad bits out there wasn't much left, but she'd cooked them up and they ate them with salt and gravy that she'd made from some scraps of vegetables. At least they'd had soup earlier, thought Sally as they sat around the table.

'Do you think there might be work for me at the quarry?' asked George, breaking the silence as they ate.

'No!' said her mother. 'I'll not let you go up there as well.'

'Why not? I'm capable. I'm not a child any more,' he complained. 'I hate messing about all day doing nowt. I want to work.'

'Wait until we get to America,' advised her father. 'There'll be proper work there. Not made-up work like this.'

'What do you mean *made-up work*?' asked Sally.

'They want us to dig out rock to make a new path in yon park,' he explained. 'As if it hasn't got enough paths already.'

Sally's father was always scathing when he spoke about the new Corporation Park that had been built on the hillside where the reservoirs were. It had been open land before where he'd enjoyed walking and the formality of the green lawns and flower beds and artificial fountains irritated him. 'Waste of money,' he would say when anyone asked him about it. 'Should have left it like it was instead of spending all that cash. No one will use it anyway.'

'Who's paying for that?' her mother asked him, meaning the new path.

'The mayor and corporation by all accounts, but it'll be coming out of our rates. Next thing they'll be complaining that the rates aren't being paid. Probably don't understand that folk need food, not paths to walk on.'

'I heard they asked for money from the government to help us,' said Sally. 'Some of the committee ladies were talking about it today. Some of their husbands have sent letters to the newspapers saying that more needs to be done.'

'Well, that's right enough,' her father replied. 'Though it's cotton that's wanted. But it's clear they'll do nowt about that. Those in London have never valued the work we do here. It'll be different in America.'

Chapter Twenty-Seven

When Ruth went to wake her father the next morning, it was clear that he wasn't going to be capable of a day's work. He tried to get out of bed, but his legs seemed weak and he was having trouble standing up.

'Get back into bed,' she told him, as she took his arm to steady him. 'You can't go to Cleaver Street like this.'

'I'll be all right in a minute,' he grumbled, but his words seemed slurred like the drunks in the town centre on a Friday night even though he never allowed a drop of alcohol to pass his lips.

'You're exhausted,' Ruth told him. 'Stay there. I'll make you a cup of tea and then I'll go and explain that you're not well today. They'll understand,' she reassured him.

'Who'll get everything organised? They can't manage without me.'

'I'll do it,' she told him, trying to sound more confident than she felt. In truth, the idea of having to boss people about made her quail inside. She feared that no one would take any notice of her and the kitchen would descend into chaos. But there was nothing else she could do. She doubted her father could get down the stairs, never mind walk to the other side of town.

She hurried to put the kettle on. At least she wouldn't have to leave him on his own for long. Agatha would be coming later and she would look after him and make sure that he rested.

Ruth carried a cup of tea and some slices of buttered bread up to her father's room. It was bitterly cold in there and she fetched a blanket from her own bed to wrap around his shoulders.

'Ask Agatha to light a fire in here when she comes,' she instructed him. 'I'd do it myself, but I must get to the kitchen.'

'Tell them I'm on my way,' he instructed her.

'No. You must stay at home for today,' she reprimanded him. 'Please don't even try to get up until Agatha comes.'

Still worried about him, Ruth set off across town on her own. She couldn't wear the muff because she had to carry the lantern, but she'd pulled on some old woollen gloves that were her father's. They were too big, but at least they kept her hands from freezing. As she walked, she wondered if she ought to go for the doctor again, but she needed to explain to them at the soup kitchen that her father wasn't coming and she didn't want to delay. If he was no better by the time she arrived home that afternoon she would go then, she decided, although she kept telling herself that it was probably just tiredness and he would be better soon.

Fine snow began to fall as she walked and she was glad to arrive at the foundry and get inside. Mr Yates looked round when he saw her.

'On your own?' he asked.

'My father's still poorly. He wanted to come, but I made him rest. I'll take over this morning,' she announced as she pulled off the gloves.

Mr Yates exchanged a glance with Freddy Fry, who'd paused in his coal shovelling to hear what she had to say.

'You?' he asked her, sounding incredulous.

'Yes,' she replied even though she heard the doubt in her own voice. 'Can we get those fires started, please?' she asked Freddy. 'The vegetables will be here soon.'

'Yes, miss!' He grinned and Ruth was afraid that he was making fun of her. She felt herself blush, so she turned away to hang up her coat and get an apron. It was less than clean, she noticed. She would have to be brave later and take the laundry woman to task over it.

Soon the mill girls began to arrive and Ruth asked them to begin fetching the pails of water for the vats.

'Where's your father this morning?' Sally Grimes asked her.

'He's not well.'

'I'm sorry to hear that.'

'I need to do the organising today,' explained Ruth. 'I won't have time to help peel the vegetables I'm afraid.'

'Don't you worry,' Sally told her as she fastened the strings on her apron. 'Would you like me to sort out the preparation tables?'

'Would you?' asked Ruth, grateful for the offer of help.

'Of course. We can all pull together,' she said as she saw Freddy bringing in a sack of potatoes. 'Put them down there,' she told him with a voice of authority. 'And we'll need the turnips next.'

Freddy raised an eyebrow and smiled. 'I can see I need to watch my step this morning,' he said and winked at Sally as he turned to go to the waiting cart for another sack. Ruth was relieved to see the colour heighten on Sally's face as well. She was glad it wasn't just her that Freddy was teasing. But Sally was quicker to recover her wits.

'Less of your cheek!' she called after him, but from the smile on her face, Ruth realised that Sally Grimes had a genuine affection for Freddy Fry, and she was surprised that it made her feel jealous.

–

Ruth's tasks turned out to be not so onerous as she'd feared. Her father had done his preparations well and most of the workers were already clear what their tasks were. Before long the vegetables were being peeled, the water was boiling in the vats and the plates and bowls were being set out ready on the tables.

'I hope your father feels better soon,' Caroline said when Ruth went to check on the progress of the peas and carrots. 'It must be a worry for you.'

'It is. Thank you,' Ruth said, glad of Caroline's acknowledgement of her troubles. Despite what some of the mill girls had said about her, Caroline had turned up and worked just as hard as they had – and for someone who'd never podded a pea in her life before, Ruth was envious of the speed that she was working her way through the huge pile in front of her. 'If there's anything I can do, I'd be glad to help,' Caroline went on. 'Has he seen a doctor?'

'He has. Dr Skaife came the day before yesterday, but he wasn't concerned. He said it was just tiredness.'

'Well, your father's not a young man,' Caroline told her. 'Perhaps he needs to take more care. Does he need this job? Would he not be better opening his shop again? I'd love to buy some sweets,' she confessed with a smile.

'He wants to help,' Ruth told her. She didn't want to betray her father's confidence about their financial situation.

'That's nice,' agreed Caroline. 'My father wants to help, and I do too. That's why I'm here. But don't be afraid to ask if you need anything,' she repeated.

Ruth nodded and thanked her again. She seemed a nice person and it was good of her to be concerned, but there wasn't a lot she could do. Ruth doubted that even Caroline Haworth could make the cotton flow again.

As she walked across to check the tables once more, she saw Agatha in the doorway.

'We're not open yet!' Mr Yates called across to her as she stood, looking around.

'It's all right. She's our housekeeper. She must want me,' Ruth told him, a feeling of foreboding gnawing at her. If Agatha had come to look for her then it could only be because her father had worsened.

'He's not at all well,' Agatha replied when Ruth asked about her father. 'I think you need to fetch the doctor.' She seemed unsure, as if there was something she was holding back.

'What is it? Tell me!' said Ruth, growing alarmed.

'I think he might have had some sort of a fit,' Agatha told her. 'He's having trouble moving his arm and his face is drooping a bit on the side. I've seen it before,' she went on. 'I had an uncle that was the same.' She hesitated again, clearly unwilling to be the bearer of such bad news. 'He never got the use back properly,' she said. 'But the doctor might be able to do something if he comes now. You really need to run and get him,' she implored Ruth.

'Go,' said Mr Yates who had come up behind her to hear most of the conversation. 'Everything's under control here. We don't need you for the rest of the day. I'll make sure everything's done before I lock up.'

'Thank you,' Ruth told him, gratefully. She hurried towards the door with Agatha.

'Your coat and hat!' he called after her.

Ruth ran to get them.

'Is it your father?' Sally asked. 'I hope he's going to be all right.'

'Thanks.' Ruth fumbled with her coat and Sally put down her knife and wiped her hands before coming to help her put it on. She fastened the buttons that Ruth's trembling fingers couldn't manage and handed her bonnet to her.

'Fetch the doctor,' she said. 'He'll know what to do.'

The cold of the morning struck Ruth with its full force as soon as she stepped out of the door. It was snowing hard now.

'Go to Randal Street and fetch my sister, Naomi,' she told Agatha. 'It's number twenty-two. She has two little girls but I'm sure she'll come to help you. She needs to know. Tell her I've gone for the doctor and that I won't be long.'

Ruth hurried in the direction of Union Street, not daring to run and still afraid of falling, but knowing that there was no time to waste. When she pushed open the door of the doctor's surgery, she saw the waiting room was as full as it had been the last time she'd come.

'It's an emergency,' she told the woman who acted as the doctor's assistant. 'My father has had a fit. He needs the doctor.'

'Sit down,' said the woman, not unkindly. 'Dr Skaife is with a patient, but I'll tell him in a moment.'

Ruth perched on the end of the bench and she heard the patients mumbling about having to wait even longer. She felt sorry for them, but her father's health was her priority and she hoped the doctor would come straight away.

'Miss Hodgson,' he said when he came out. 'What's happened?'

Ruth repeated what Agatha had told her. 'Please will you come?' she implored him.

'I will,' he said, 'as soon as I've finished my surgery. Try not to worry,' he added. 'You go home and I'll come along very soon.'

Ruth glanced round the room. There must be a dozen or more people waiting and she knew that more would probably come in before the doors were closed at twelve o' clock. It would be hours before Dr Skaife came. She wanted to plead with him to come now, but he'd already called in his next patient and there was nothing more she could do except go home to care for her father and wait.

She stepped back out into the snowstorm and battled, head down, against the fierce flakes that the wind was driving into her eyes as she picked her way carefully through the gathering drifts to Queen Victoria Street.

Once home she stamped the snow from her boots and went in. Welcome warmth met her as she opened the kitchen door and Agatha looked up expectantly from the table where she was rolling out pastry with Hope and Naomi.

'Is the doctor with you?' she asked.

Ruth shook her head. 'Dr Skaife said he would come after morning surgery,' she replied. 'How is he?' she asked about her father.

'Much the same. Your sister's with him.'

'I'll go up,' said Ruth and after she'd hung her wet bonnet and coat on a peg, she climbed the narrow stairs with trepidation. She took a moment outside her father's bedroom door to compose herself. She didn't want to alarm him.

He was awake and sitting up in bed with the blanket still draped around his shoulders, but the room was warm now from the fire blazing in the grate. Her sister was sitting on a stool by the bed, with a bowl in her hand trying to feed him some broth. Ruth studied him closely. It had been dark when she'd left him that morning, but now she could see what Agatha had noticed. There was an odd look to the side of his face. One eye was barely open and a trickle of the broth was running from the corner of his mouth.

'What are you doing back?' he asked her. His speech still sounded slurred. 'Naomi's come to look after me. There's no need for you as well.'

'I came to see how you were. Agatha came to the soup kitchen to find me. She was worried.'

'She fusses,' he said, waving his good hand.

'She wanted me to go for the doctor.'

'I hope you didn't bother him.'

'I did,' confessed Ruth. 'He's coming in a while.' She exchanged a glance with her sister who looked relieved at the news.

'He'll be cross to have his time wasted again,' her father grumbled.

'We'll see,' Ruth said.

'Is everything all right at the soup kitchen?' he asked. 'Are they managing without me?'

'Yes. It's all fine,' she reassured him. 'Mr Yates said he will lock up later. There's no need for you to fret.'

'I need to get up,' he said.

'Stay there,' advised Ruth. 'It's snowing again outside and it feels cosy in here now with the fire going.'

She reached to straighten the bedclothes, not knowing what else to say to him. It was obvious to her that he had suffered some sort of a fit, but she wasn't sure if he was unaware of it or if he was trying to be brave. But one thing was clear. It was going to be some time before he was well enough to work again and Ruth realised that it would be up to her to try to keep his job for him in the meantime. No matter how daunted she was by the prospect, she needed to continue as the manager of the soup kitchen until her father was better.

Chapter Twenty-Eight

When Sally arrived home and saw her father, she was shocked. He was slumped in the chair by the fire, and he was filthy – covered from head to toe in a fine white dust that even the blizzard on the way home had not washed off.

'Did they make you work in this?' she asked, taking in his fingers, white at the tips with the cold and scratched and torn from the hard labour.

'Aye,' he breathed. 'It was bitter. I'm only just getting the feeling back in my hands and feet.'

'He can't do this,' Sally told her mother when he'd gone down the path to the privy. 'We can't let him go again tomorrow.'

'I've already told him,' she agreed. 'I've said that we'll manage somehow, but he'll not listen. And it's true that if he refuses to work, they will take the relief off us. I asked about it today when I went to collect the soup tokens.'

'It isn't fair,' said Sally as she wondered if it would be possible for her to put some soup to one side for them, even if they weren't given tokens. She knew it would be wrong and that she could be accused of stealing if she was found out, but she couldn't bear to see her father reduced to this. He had always been so proud of his work at the mill. He was a good weaver, and she knew that Mr

Haworth had valued his skill at the looms. To see his hands all bloodied and torn broke her heart. It wasn't fair.

'Is there no news about the tickets to America?' she asked.

'I've heard nothing,' her mother said. 'But the trains didn't run today because of the weather, so the man who said he'd get them for us wouldn't have been able to get here.'

'What are you talking about?' asked her father coming back in. He went to wash his hands at the stone sink and grimaced as the soap stung at the cuts on his skin.

'I was asking Mam about the tickets for America.'

'They can't come soon enough,' he told them, and Sally agreed. From what she'd overheard at the soup kitchen that morning, the mill owners were doubtful that any cotton would come for a long time. The mayor and the relief committee were keen to spread the opinion that these hard times would soon be over, but Sally set more store by the likes of Mr Haworth and Mr Yates who thought they were in for a summer of famine to follow the hard winter. In fact, she wondered if things would ever be the same again. It was amazing how quickly life could change, she reflected as she helped her mother dish out the meagre tea of bread sliced as thinly as possible and spread with lard, followed by weak coffee with just a dash of blue-labelled milk. This time last year, food had been plentiful and they'd had a warm and happy home with a bright future to look forward to for all of them. And now, because of something happening thousands of miles away they were suffering in such poverty as she'd never have imagined.

Still, it wouldn't be for ever. If only they could hang on, then surely it wouldn't be long before they could get on that boat? And even if they had to walk all the way to the docks at Liverpool carrying what belongings they could, as her father had warned they might, then they would do it and they would wave goodbye to this place and begin again somewhere better.

She'd be sorry to leave her friends, of course, although one or two other families were also talking of emigrating. And she'd be sorry to leave Freddy Fry behind. Sally pictured him shovelling coal, the muscles in his arms and shoulders taut and strong. He was certainly handsome and she'd loved the way that he'd winked at her earlier. Maybe he could be persuaded to sail across the sea as well. He wasn't a cotton worker, but where there was cotton there was always a need for machinery, so they must have foundries in America and surely there would be work in those?

She was roused from her daydream by her mother asking her to put the twins to bed. She laughed at herself for letting her imagination run away with her, but there was little else to do other than dream of better things on a night like this when the snow kept on falling and her brothers complained that they were still hungry and the bedsheets were damp and cold.

'When we get to America the sun will shine every day,' she told them. 'We'll have a big house with roaring fires in every room and outside there'll be a garden filled with apple trees and you'll eat so many that they'll give you a tummy ache and then you will have something to complain about!'

'Is it true?' asked Isaac.

'Of course it's true!' Sally told them as she kissed them and pulled the blankets up around their ears wishing that they had more to pile on top rather than having to make do by adding their outside coats, which were still wet from their walk home from school.

Downstairs she found George arguing with their father about going to work in the stone quarry.

'If you can do it, so can I,' he was saying.

'Look at my hands,' replied their father, holding them out. 'I'll not let you go, and don't let the relief committee send you. Tell them it's mill work or nothing.'

'But you went,' he replied.

'Aye, because this is my family and I'll support it the best way I can. But I'll not allow a child of mine to be taken advantage of, because it's slave labour. That's all it is. Slave labour just to build a silly, bloody path!'

'Mr Hodgson didn't come today,' Sally told them, changing the subject as they huddled round the fire waiting for bedtime, all of them reluctant to leave the paltry flames and go up to the freezing cold bedrooms. 'They're saying he's had a stroke.'

'Poor man,' said her mother. 'He's another victim of this mess we're in. I bet it wouldn't have happened if he'd been able to keep his shop open. What about his daughter?'

'Ruth came to take his place, but then she was called home. I don't know if she'll come again tomorrow. You wouldn't think that a shopkeeper would need the money, but I suppose they haven't been selling many sweets these past months. It's not just the mill workers who're being affected.'

'Did Caroline Haworth come again?' asked her father.

'She did. She worked hard as well and she's not as stuck-up as you might imagine.'

'Well her father's a decent sort, even if her mother thinks she's gentry. I'm glad Caroline's prepared to do her bit. What have they had her doing?'

'Shelling peas. She has no idea how to peel a potato.'

'Doesn't surprise me,' her father replied. 'And I've no room to talk. I was useless in that quarry compared to the lads who're used to working there. And talking of work, I suppose we'd all best get off to bed. At least it seems to have stopped snowing,' he observed. 'It should make it easier tomorrow.'

Chapter Twenty-Nine

It had been late when Dr Skaife eventually knocked on the door of Queen Victoria Street. Agatha had gone home and Ruth opened the door to find the doctor caked in a layer of snow and ice.

'Please, come in,' she said, moving aside to let him step, dripping, into the passageway. Behind her, Naomi waited at the foot of the stairs to show the doctor up. She'd taken Hope and Nora home to bed and made sure that her husband Amos had got his tea, but despite Ruth's assurance that she could manage and there was nothing more her sister could do, Naomi had walked back through the snow.

'He's had a stroke. I'm sure the doctor will confirm it,' she'd told Ruth earlier. 'I just hope he doesn't want to send him to the hospital. We must nurse him at home if we possibly can.'

Ruth watched as Dr Skaife followed Naomi up the stairs, then she went up herself even though there was no space for her in her father's bedroom and she had to stand in the doorway.

The doctor greeted her father jovially. 'Now then, Mr Hodgson, what's troubling you tonight?' he asked. He took his wrist to feel his pulse. 'Nice and steady,' he pronounced. 'Any pain?'

'I'm all right, doctor,' her father told him. 'I'm only sorry you've been dragged out again in this weather, but these girls insisted.'

'And right they were,' pronounced the doctor. 'It looks like you've had a bit of a turn. I doubt there's any permanent harm done, but you'll have to rest.'

He packed his equipment into his black holdall and indicated to Ruth and Naomi that they should follow him downstairs.

'It looks like he's had a small stroke,' he confirmed when they were in the kitchen and their father couldn't overhear. 'It's clear he has some paralysis down his right side. It may improve. It's hard to tell, but he's going to need careful nursing. I'll leave a prescription with you,' he said, taking out a pen from an inside pocket and writing on a pad of paper from his bag. He left it on the table. 'The chemist will be closed now but you can get it first thing tomorrow. It'll help him to be more comfortable. I'll call by in a day or two to see how he is,' he promised. Then he settled his hat onto his head, drew on his gloves and Ruth showed him out into the night.

'I told you,' said Naomi when she went back to the kitchen. 'I'm surprised you didn't see it yourself before you left him alone this morning.'

It sounded like an accusation and Ruth responded to defend herself.

'It was dark. He said he was all right and I knew Agatha was coming. I had to get to the soup kitchen,' she explained.

'Well, you'll have to give that up,' Naomi said as if she thought it was an indulgence. 'Pa's going to need care now and I've got the girls to look after. I can't be here all the time. You'll have to stay at home and nurse him.'

'I can't,' Ruth told her.

'Of course you can! He's your father. You must put him first.'

'You don't understand,' Ruth told her sister. 'We need the money I'll earn. He's spent everything trying to keep the shop going. All our savings have gone. The money for working at the soup kitchen is all we have.'

Naomi stared at her as if she didn't know what to make of it. 'Are you sure?' she asked after a moment. 'I thought there was plenty. I thought he'd taken the job to help out not because he needed to.'

'He's kept it from us,' Ruth told her. 'But when he wasn't well yesterday, he suddenly got upset and it all came out. I was shocked too. But the truth is that I need to try to do the work because if they find someone else and we have nothing coming in, I don't know how we'll manage.'

'No, you must be mistaken. You must have misunderstood,' replied Naomi. 'He's kept Agatha on. He wouldn't have done that if he couldn't afford to pay her.'

'He hadn't the heart to sack her,' explained Ruth.

'Well, if what you say is true, she'll have to be sacked,' Naomi said.

'But who'll do the housework?'

'You'll have to do it.'

'But I've told you, I need to do the work at the soup kitchen. And if Agatha's here she can care for Pa whilst I'm out.'

Ruth sank down onto a chair feeling tired out and defeated. She suspected that her sister didn't believe what she was telling her. It wasn't surprising. She could barely believe it herself.

'Go up and ask him if you don't believe me,' she said to her sister. Naomi hesitated then shook her head.

'Not now. He's tired. And he hasn't been making much sense all day. I think it's the stroke that's confused him. I'm sure we'll find you're mistaken. He can't have spent everything. He's always been so careful.'

Ruth didn't argue, but Naomi couldn't possibly know that what their father had said wasn't true. What she did know was that tomorrow she must trust Agatha to look after him and she must go to the soup kitchen to explain that she was taking on her father's role whilst he was ill. She just hoped that she could manage the work, because she feared what the alternative might be.

-

Next morning, she was up early after another restless night. She'd woken time and time again to check on her father, who was restless and distressed. She wished that she'd been able to get the medicine that the doctor had prescribed, but Naomi had promised that she would get it as soon as the chemist opened his shop, and would check in on their father to make sure that Agatha was happy to nurse him until Ruth came home.

'I'll stay with him for a while,' she'd promised, 'but it's difficult when I have the girls. They don't like to sit still for long and I don't like to ask Amos's mother to mind them. She isn't well herself.'

Ruth knew that Naomi was doing her best and she was thankful to have Agatha coming, but she still felt a huge burden had fallen on to her. She'd always relied on her father, especially since her mother had died and the idea of him being so ill, and maybe never entirely recovering, frightened her. What would she do if he couldn't work? What would happen to the shop? If all their savings really had been spent and there was no money coming in, how would they manage?

Ruth couldn't get the worries out of her head as she dressed herself and went downstairs to make her father a hot drink and something to eat before she left. Outside the weather was still bad. The streets would be treacherous underfoot again. Part of her wanted to stay at home and look after her father. She was his daughter and it didn't seem right to leave his care to Agatha, no matter that they had known her for years and she was trustworthy and caring. But Ruth knew she had no choice if they were to be able to pay their bills.

As she brewed tea, she acknowledged to herself that another part of the reason she would have preferred to stay at home was because she was afraid of what would happen at the soup kitchen. What if they wouldn't allow her to take on her father's job? What if they sent her home? How would she manage then?

She took the tea and some bread and butter up to her father. There wasn't much food left in the house and she needed to go shopping, but she wasn't sure when she would have the opportunity – and neither was she sure how much money there was. Her father kept it somewhere in his bedroom, but she wasn't certain where. She thought that he kept enough back from the takings each week to buy food, before he took the rest to the bank, but it wasn't something she'd ever had to deal with. He had always taken care of it.

Her father was awake when she went in.

'I've brought you some breakfast,' she said. 'Do you want me to help you sit up?'

'I need to use the chamber pot,' he told her. 'Will you help me?'

Ruth faltered. She wasn't sure that she could manage and it was embarrassing for her. She hated the thought of having to assist her father with such intimate bodily functions. It didn't seem right. But then she realised that it would have to be done. She couldn't refuse him.

'Of course,' she said as she reached for the white enamelled pot that was kept under the bed. She put an arm around her father as he struggled to sit. He tried to swing his legs over the edge of the bed, but the right one was very weak and Ruth had to take most of his weight. She was thankful that he was only lightly built or she would never have managed. At last, they arranged the pot so he could use it, and Ruth tried not to look as the stream of warm urine filled it. She knew that when she'd got him back into bed, she would have to take it down to the privy to empty it – and that would be another difficult task because he hadn't had the opportunity to clear a proper path and she dreaded slipping and spilling the contents.

At last, when everything was set ready for Agatha in the kitchen and her father had finished his breakfast and was settled in bed, Ruth put on her coat and hat and went out to face the next challenge of the morning.

All the way to Cleaver Street, she tried to rehearse in her head what she would say when she got there. She knew that she had to seem confident and capable. They wouldn't let her take over from her father if she seemed unable to step up to the task.

When she arrived, she paused for a moment at the door to straighten her shoulders and lift her chin. She had to do this well.

'Where's thy father? Is he still poorly?' asked Mr Yates when she went in.

'He can't come again today, I'm afraid,' Ruth replied, setting down the lantern. 'He's asked me to take over for the time being.'

Mr Yates looked doubtful. 'Can tha manage it?' he asked.

'Yes,' she replied. 'Most of the hard work is done and I managed it yesterday,' she reminded him.

'Aye,' he replied. 'It's a big task for a lass though. Still, it's not for me to say whether it's all right or not. It's up to the committee. They appointed thy father. They might want to bring in someone else if he can't do the job.'

It was what Ruth was afraid of.

'I'm sure that won't be necessary,' she said as she took off her coat and hung it up. 'Have the vegetables come yet?'

Mr Yates shrugged his shoulders. 'Not yet,' he said, indicating the empty space beneath the tables. It had been a stupid question, Ruth realised. She must do better than this if she was to be taken seriously.

'Let's get the fires going then,' she said.

Mr Yates nodded. Freddy Fry and the other foundry lads were already carrying in the coal and soon the furnaces had been kindled into life and the horse and cart arrived with the first delivery of potatoes and turnips. Before long the mill girls came in and settled quickly to their tasks.

'Is your father no better?' Sally asked her.

'No. He's not coming today. I'm taking over from him.'

'I see.' She looked doubtful as well, but it made Ruth even more determined to succeed. Not that she would have any problem with the mill girls. They were all hard workers, despite their tendency to pause whenever Freddy Fry went past. It was the committee ladies who worried her. She was hesitant to try to be the boss of her elders and betters, but the ladies tended to work at their own pace and in their own way, and Ruth knew that if she didn't try to organise them better, the jobs would never get done.

Soon Caroline Haworth arrived with her father. She greeted Ruth warmly and said she was sorry that her father was still unwell.

'Will he be back tomorrow?' Mr Haworth asked her.

Ruth wasn't sure how to reply. But after a moment she decided it was best to be honest.

'No,' she told him. 'Dr Skaife thinks he's had a slight stroke. It could be a week or two before he's strong enough to come back.'

'A stroke?' repeated Mr Haworth. 'I am sorry. That's not good news. Have you let the committee know?'

Ruth shook her head. 'I can take on his job until he's better,' she said.

'I'm not sure you can just take over,' he warned her. 'It's up to the committee who they have running the kitchen and you're…' He didn't finish what he was going to say. He had no need. Ruth knew what he was thinking. She was too young – and she was a woman. The committee would never have appointed a woman to such an important role.

'You'd better speak to Mayor Hutchinson when he comes,' Mr Haworth told her. 'See what he says.'

'I will,' she promised, 'but until then someone has to organise this soup.' She hurried away and called to the girls to start adding the vegetables because the water was boiling. She stood and supervised the addition of the salt and pepper – enough to make the soup tasty, but not so much as to be wasteful. Then, from somewhere, she found the courage to ask the committee ladies to finish their tea break and get on with shelling the peas. Some of them looked a little affronted, but most had now heard the news about her father and were sympathetic.

'Don't worry,' said one. 'I'm sure the mayor will find someone capable to take over and then you can stay at home and look after your father. He'll need you now,' she warned. 'You really should be with him.'

Ruth smiled but said nothing. She was worried that it was what everyone would tell her – that her place was beside her father, nursing him, not here at the soup kitchen. And part of her agreed with them. She knew it was what was expected of her. Folk would be scandalised by her continuing to work and leaving the care of her father to the daily maid. What they didn't know was that she desperately needed his wages.

-

The customers had come in and some were seated around the tables, eating, when Mayor Hutchinson arrived with a worried expression. It was clear he'd heard about her father's illness, thought Ruth as he glanced about, warily, as if he expected there to be a disaster. When he saw that everything was progressing well, he seemed to relax slightly, but his brow was still furrowed as he came across to speak to her.

'I've been told your father's had a stroke. Is it true?' he demanded.

'A slight stroke,' she confirmed.

'He's not in any fit state to run the soup kitchen then,' the mayor said. 'I was hoping it wasn't true.'

'I can do it,' Ruth told him.

'Do what?' He clearly hadn't understood her and Ruth quailed at having to make herself clearer. She was afraid of his response.

'I can run the soup kitchen for my father,' she said, trying to sound confident.

'What?' He seemed stunned. 'No. No,' he went on. 'That will never do. We'll have to find a man to do it. We'll have to find someone suitable.'

'But who is there?' asked Ruth, surprising herself by her audacity. 'All the unemployed are mill workers.'

'There's Mr Yates,' said the mayor. 'He'll have to do it.'

'But I'm here and I know what's required. I was here when my father set everything up,' she reminded him. 'I know what needs to be done.'

'But you'll have to be at home looking after him.'

'My sister can care for him, along with our daily maid. I'm not needed at home,' she told him.

The mayor shook his head. 'It's very irregular,' he told her. 'Although you do seem to have got things done today.'

'And yesterday,' she reminded him. 'Everything has gone like clockwork.'

'Well,' he conceded. 'That's true. I was worried about what I'd find when I heard. But it can't be a permanent arrangement,' he warned her. 'You can come again on Monday if we haven't found anyone else before then, but it's not a solution. We can't put a lass in charge,' he said.

Ruth wanted to ask him why not. But she knew the answer. It was because she wasn't a man. The best she could hope for was that the committee wouldn't be able to find anyone else willing to do the job and they would be forced to keep her on.

'And you'll pay me my father's wages?' she asked as the mayor began to turn away.

'Goodness me. No!' he burst out. 'You can have the wages you're entitled to. The ones that we agreed with your father, but we can't pay you a man's wages! Whatever made you ask such a thing?'

Ruth felt the hot flush creep up her cheeks. Whether it was shame or anger she wasn't certain. But she did know that it was unfair. She also knew that she needed the money the committee had agreed to pay her father, although she doubted that the mayor would change his mind. She might as well have asked for the moon as for a fair day's pay.

Chapter Thirty

Caroline thought that she'd never been so tired in her life. She had a newfound respect for the mill girls who were used to working much longer hours and considered the soup kitchen to be only part-time employment. When she put on her coat and hat at the end of the day, feeling worn out and aching from head to toe with the unaccustomed physical exertion, they hurried out as if they were fresh from their beds, talking about what they would do for the rest of the afternoon. Meanwhile she stumbled to the carriage, in which her father insisted she travel to and from Cleaver Street after the incident with the hostile crowd at the door, and rode home to hand her outer clothing to Jenkins and call for Lottie to bring her a cup of tea in her bedroom.

It was a relief that this morning was Sunday. The kitchen was to be closed on Sundays, although how the unemployed were expected to feed themselves whilst the committee members and their wives attended church, Caroline was unsure. It seemed wrong that whilst the gentry were sitting down to a roast dinner and pudding, those who had no income were denied even the soup and plain bread that had sustained them throughout the week.

Caroline closed her eyes and allowed herself to doze in the warm bed. There would be no church this morning. Simmons had made it clear last night that the roads were too icy and Caroline knew her mother would never contemplate walking. She was hoping that the bad weather might also reprieve her from the visit to Salesbury Hall, but as she lay in bed, she heard the steady drip of melting snow from the eaves of the house and realised it was thawing.

Moments later there was a knock at her door. Annoyed that she could get no peace, Caroline pulled the blankets up around her face and tried to feign sleep, but Lottie crept in anyway and began to draw back the curtains.

'Leave them closed. I'm having a lie-in,' she grumbled. 'If you knock and I don't answer then you should go away, not just barge in!'

'I'm sorry, Miss Caroline, but your mother sent me. She says you're to get dressed in the blue with the white flower design ready to go to your grandfather's.'

'Are the roads passable?' Caroline asked. 'Simmons said there was no question of getting the carriage out.'

'The weather's improving,' Lottie confirmed. 'The carriage will be at the door for twelve thirty and your mother expects you to be ready.'

'What time is it now?'

'Almost eleven.'

'What!' Caroline couldn't believe that she'd slept for so long. She had thought it was only about eight, or nine at the latest. No wonder her mother had sent Lottie to rouse her.

'You've missed breakfast,' the maid informed her as she flung open the wardrobe doors to find the gown Caroline was to wear. 'Mrs Jenkins has cleared it all away.' She turned with a sympathetic look. 'I can bring you some coffee and toast,' she offered.

'Would you?' Caroline said as she sat up and rubbed her eyes.

Lottie took the gown down from its hanger and put it over the end of the bed. 'I'll be back in a minute,' she said.

Caroline thanked her. She knew that she ought to appreciate Lottie more. She worked long hours and never complained. It was something she'd previously taken for granted, but as she pulled a shawl around her shoulders to keep warm it occurred to her that Lottie never got to have a lie-in and she must think her spoiled and lazy to be in bed so late in the morning.

Lottie came back with the coffee and toast on a tray. It was all hot and Caroline suspected Mrs Jenkins had made it especially. She thanked the maid again, and once more when she returned with the jug of hot water for her to wash in and added coal to the fire so that the room would be warmer. It seemed to amuse Lottie and Caroline felt embarrassed. She liked Lottie, although she realised that she didn't really know her at all. Their discussions were always about clothing and hairstyles and what Caroline wanted. But since she'd listened to the mill girls talking at the soup kitchen, she'd realised that Lottie must have her own thoughts and opinions about things too. She wondered what the maid really thought of her, and her father and mother. She wondered if Lottie and Mr and Mrs Jenkins talked about them down in the kitchen in the way that the mill girls had discussed her father when they weren't aware that she was listening.

As she pushed back the covers and got out of bed to warm herself in front of the fire, she reflected that the events of the week had thrown her life into disarray. The position that had been carved out for her in the sphere of society to which she belonged suddenly seemed ridiculous. The only reason she was here in this warm and sumptuous bedroom with as many different gowns as she wanted, and a maid to attend to her, was an accident of birth. She'd done nothing to deserve it. The mill girls and the maids worked far harder than she had ever done.

She frowned as she poured the hot water into the bowl, rubbed her facecloth with the soap and began to wash herself down. She'd been tempted to give up going to the soup kitchen after the first couple of days because she'd been so tired and lonely. There'd been no one there to talk to and she'd been jealous of the mill girls chatting and laughing amongst themselves. She would have loved to join in, but they fell silent when she approached. Caroline couldn't blame them, but she'd been made painfully aware that she wasn't one of them. Even though one or two, like Sally Grimes, had been friendly enough, it had come with a degree of wariness that proved they thought she was quite different.

She could have conversed with the committee ladies. She already knew some of them from her mother's parties. But they were much older than her and seemed scandalised that she was sitting with the mill girls podding peas. *Fish out of water*, she thought as she retrieved the slippery soap from the bowl. She knew what it meant now.

When she was dressed and Lottie had helped her with her hair, Caroline put on her coat and best Sunday bonnet and went downstairs with her kid gloves and her little reticule in her hand. The clock in the hallway had struck noon some time ago and she saw that Simmons was already at the door with the carriage. Her mother, ready to leave, came out of the sitting room, followed by her father wearing his best suit and a reluctant expression. She didn't need to ask what they'd been discussing. She knew her mother would have been giving him instructions on how to behave and what to say to her grandfather.

Outside, the thaw was well underway. A thin drizzle was turning the snow to slush and Caroline stepped carefully to avoid the puddles. Her father handed her into the coach after her mother, then climbed up and closed the door. He called to Simmons and they set off through the quiet streets and out into the countryside.

Her mother grew perceptibly more cheerful as they approached her childhood home. It was where she considered herself to belong, not in a terrace in the middle of town. The old hall had stood here for centuries and been home to generations of the de Lacy family. Built from the grey local stone it resembled a fortress and the central tower had once been the safe retreat of her ancestors from invasions by the Scots. The tower had been added to over time and the wings of the house that now stretched out on either side of it were a jumble of chimneys, pinnacles and mismatched windows. It wasn't particularly pretty, but it was impressive and what had once been the medieval hall was now turned into a passageway to the stable block. It was where Simmons drew up the carriage so they could get down in the dry.

They handed their outdoor clothes to a sombre servant dressed all in black and then her mother preceded Caroline and her father up the wide stairs to the huge sitting room where the windows looked out over the driveway at one side and the formal knot gardens at the other.

Caroline saw that the Duttons had already arrived and were sitting around the roaring log fire in the hearth that had been built large enough to roast a hog. Mr Dutton and Thomas stood up to greet them as they entered.

'You know Mr and Mrs Dutton?' her grandfather enquired of her father.

'I do,' he said as he shook the brewery owner's outstretched hand and nodded to Thomas. 'We've met on a number of occasions.'

'And this is Caroline!' Her grandfather drew her forward with an arm around her shoulders. He smelt of wine and she saw that the Duttons' glasses were already filled. She smiled politely. She had also met them before, but would have been hard pressed to pick them out from a dozen other couples who had recently come into money through their businesses. The mother was thin and fair-haired, dressed in a silvery grey, whilst her husband by contrast was ample, with a paunch that looked fit to burst out from beneath his colourful silk waistcoat. Thomas, of course, she did recall. He was much as she remembered him – a plain-looking young man, neither handsome nor repulsive. Nondescript was the best word Caroline could find to describe him.

He smiled at her eagerly and she responded coolly. If her grandfather thought this matchmaking was going to be easy, Caroline was determined to prove him wrong.

They'd barely sat down when the butler came to announce that luncheon was served and her grandfather offered Mrs Dutton his arm to escort her to the dining room. Looking embarrassed, Mr Dutton allowed her grandmother to take his arm and, followed by her parents they began to process down the long wooden-panelled corridor. Thomas met her eyes, seeming unsure what to do. The family were obviously unused to her grandparents' formal rituals and for a moment she felt sorry for him.

Caroline knew he was supposed to offer her his arm, but she decided not to embarrass him and walked ahead of him through the doorway.

'It's a magnificent house,' he said as he walked beside her.

'It's been in the family for generations,' Caroline told him. 'It looks imposing, but in truth it's draughty and damp and when it rains the servants have to put out buckets in the places where the rain drips through.' Thomas Dutton looked unsure how to respond. 'I'm sure the new house your father has built at Yew Tree is water-tight even if it's not so large,' she told him.

By this time they'd reached the dining room and as expected, she had been given a chair next to Thomas. He sat down looking awkward and stared at the array of glasses and cutlery set out in front of him. Her grandparents had set out to impress their guests, but Caroline saw that they were intimidated by the splendour.

The first course was soup and she noticed that Thomas waited for her to begin before reaching for his own spoon. Whether it was his good manners or because he'd waited to see which piece of cutlery she would pick up, she didn't know.

A week or so ago she might have felt superior to him. She guessed that her mother still did and Caroline was surprised that she would even contemplate the thought of these people marrying into the family. But unlike her mother, she wasn't the daughter of a gentleman, she reasoned. She suspected that her grandfather considered her to be inferior too, which was why Thomas Dutton was seen as good enough for her.

'I'm sick of the sight and smell of soup,' Caroline confessed to Thomas.

'This is very good!' he protested.

'I suppose so. It seems rather thin. I've become used to the more substantial offering at the soup kitchen on Cleaver Street.'

He paused, spoon midway to his mouth and stared at her. Caroline tried not to laugh although it was the reaction she had hoped for.

'I… I had no idea,' he stuttered.

She did laugh then. 'I'm sorry,' she apologised. 'I should have explained. My father hasn't fallen on such hard times that we're forced to visit the soup kitchen for our dinner. I'm helping out there.'

'Really? Doing what?' he asked.

'Shelling peas, mostly. I tried peeling potatoes, but I wasn't much use.'

'Still, it's commendable of you to give it a go,' he replied. It was Caroline's turn to be unsure how to respond. She'd hoped that he would be scandalised. She'd hoped it would put him off considering her as a potential wife. In truth, she'd hoped to provoke an argument with him, but all she saw was admiration.

'The mill girls do most of the work,' she said. 'I'm really not much help.'

'Even so. I'm impressed,' he told her.

Damn, she thought. Impressing him was exactly what she didn't want to do. She turned her attention back to the soup, thinking that he wouldn't be so amazed if she told him how she'd set her skirts on fire. She didn't mention it though. She found herself reluctant to talk to him about Freddy Fry – about how he'd pulled her away from danger and beaten out the flames with his own hands, caring nothing for himself. She relived the feel of his hand on her arm and the fierceness of his blue eyes as he'd shouted at her for her carelessness. She couldn't imagine Thomas Dutton speaking to her like that and she knew she ought to be scandalised at Freddy's familiar behaviour, but when she compared the two men, it was Freddy she wished was sitting beside her now.

-

When the meal ended, Caroline's grandmother led her and her mother and Mrs Dutton to the drawing room where they made inconsequential small talk until the men joined them. Her mother had whispered fiercely to her as they left the dining room that she must not mention the soup kitchen to either her grandmother or Mrs Dutton. Caroline wondered if her mother had overheard what she'd said to Thomas. She hoped not. She would never forgive her if she knew. So, the talk was of the weather, the latest fashions and tea parties. No mention was made of the cotton crisis. It was not a suitable topic for polite conversation.

When her father came to join them, Caroline guessed that cotton had been on the men's agenda. Her father looked angry and she wondered what had been said. She hoped there hadn't been a row because it would only make things worse between her parents and she would have to deal with the consequences. But when her grandfather came in and filled his glass with brandy it was obvious from his flushed face that harsh words had been exchanged.

'I've been telling your husband that there's plenty of cotton in the warehouses in Liverpool,' he said to Caroline's mother. 'But he tells me it isn't suitable.' He glared at her father. 'Cotton is cotton, I say.'

Caroline's father had come to sit beside her and she put a hand on his arm to warn him to keep quiet. Her grandfather always thought he knew better in matters of business and any disagreement with him was never well received.

'Now look at the Duttons here,' went on her grandfather. 'They aren't complaining. Business is good for you, isn't it, Mr Dutton?'

'I can't grumble,' agreed Mr Dutton. 'It hasn't hit the breweries as badly as the mills.'

'You chose the wrong business to get into,' went on her grandfather, waving his glass at Caroline's father. 'You ought to have gone into brewing. There's no shortage of hops and grain because they're grown in this country. It doesn't do to trust these foreigners,' he went on.

Her father didn't reply and Caroline wished that they could leave before things became even more uncomfortable.

'It's beginning to snow again,' she ventured. 'Maybe we should think about setting off back to Blackburn. We don't want to leave it too late and be stranded here.'

Thankfully, a few light flurries were falling and her mother reluctantly agreed with her. Their coats and hats were brought and Caroline dutifully kissed her grandparents goodbye.

'So,' said her mother, as soon as they were in the carriage. 'What did you think of Thomas Dutton? Your grandfather thinks it would be a good match.'

Caroline didn't reply straight away. She knew that this was a path she must tread carefully.

'Well?' asked her mother.

'He was very polite,' conceded Caroline. 'But I didn't have much time to converse with him. I would need to know him better before I could say if I find him suitable.'

'Don't start getting ideas about needing to fall in love with someone,' her mother warned her. 'No good comes of that.' She glared at Caroline's father who was sitting in the corner of the carriage looking irritated and cross. 'It's better to be guided by those who know more than you about such matters. Thomas Dutton is a respectable young man and your grandfather is willing to settle a sizeable amount of money on him if he agrees to marry you.'

So that was it, thought Caroline. It was about money.

'It isn't that he's not wealthy himself,' went on her mother. 'His father has done well in trade and he's the only son. But of course, he'll have to wait to inherit that money, and in the meantime your grandfather wants you to live in a decent house when you're married. You ought to be grateful,' went on her mother. 'If it was left to your father goodness only knows who you might end up being married to.'

Freddy Fry, Caroline thought. What might it be like to marry him? Of course, there would be no money from her grandfather if she took up with a foundry worker.

'I don't know what you find so amusing,' reprimanded her mother. Caroline had been unaware that her daydream had put a smile on her face and she took a moment to rearrange her features. 'Marrying well is so important,' she reminded her. 'Don't make the same mistake I did.'

'Oh, give it a rest, Amelia,' pleaded her father. 'Let the girl decide for herself.'

'It did mc no good!' she retaliated.

'You could have done worse,' he told her. 'Much worse. I've never cheated on you. I've never beaten you. There are women amongst your acquaintances who would be grateful for that.'

‘Who?’ she demanded. ‘Tell me who? You can’t, can you? It was a stupid thing to say!’

It was, agreed Caroline. Her father ought to know better than to provoke an argument with her mother even if he was angry because of what her grandfather had said. Still, it had distracted her mother from her talk about Thomas Dutton and for that at least Caroline was grateful.

Chapter Thirty-One

Sally had appreciated the lie-in on Sunday morning. It was nice not to have to get up early for work, but she knew that she and her family would miss the soup and bread today.

As well as the food tokens, her father had been allowed two buckets of coal, but they had to last them for the week, and when she went downstairs Sally found that her mother had delayed lighting the fire.

'I've left your father in bed,' she said. 'He's exhausted. I'll light it when he and the little ones get up. We'll manage until then.'

Sally didn't disagree, but it was bitingly cold in the kitchen and the one oatcake that she ate didn't do much to fill her. She longed to sit in front of a roaring fire, eating fried bacon and buttered bread with a cup of strong tea – her usual Sunday morning breakfast. It was months since she'd enjoyed that, and she missed it.

Outside, she could hear the steady drip of melting snow. She hoped it might signal the end of the cold spell. Even though there were still months of winter to endure until the respite of springtime came, it would make everyone's life easier if the freezing temperatures rose even by a few degrees.

Before long, her father came down and he set light to the kindling in the grate and added a few lumps of coal.

Then he huddled beside the flames, looking despondent as the coal began to burn and the kitchen began to warm up.

Her mother set the kettle to boil and Sally looked forward to a hot drink.

'If they heated yon church even I might be tempted to go this morning,' remarked her father as the bells rang out for morning prayer.

Sally doubted he would. The only times he'd been in the church were for his wedding, the baptisms of his children and when they'd buried her grandmother last winter. She'd been sad when her grandmother had died. She missed her wisdom and humour. But now she thought that it had been a blessing that she wasn't forced to endure this hardship. And how could they have considered going to America if she'd still been living? She would never have agreed to the long journey, and they couldn't have left her alone.

Her thoughts were interrupted by somebody knocking on the door.

'Whoever can that be?' asked her mother, looking alarmed. Not many people knocked. Friends and neighbours mostly walked straight in with a greeting. A knock on the door often meant trouble.

Her father went through the front parlour to see who it was and Sally heard him greet someone amicably and invite them in.

The man who appeared in the kitchen doorway was a stranger. He was well-dressed and held his hat in his hand.

'This is my wife,' her father said, making the introductions, 'and this is my daughter, Sally.'

The man held out a hand to her mother. 'I'm real pleased to make your acquaintance, ma'am,' he said.

'This is Mr Grady, the agent who's arranging our tickets,' explained her father.

Having wiped her palms on her apron, Sally's mother shook the visitor's hand, invited him to sit on the best chair by the fire and offered him a cup of tea.

'Thank you, ma'am,' he said and seated himself. 'I have the tickets with me,' he told her father as he reached into an inside pocket. 'They're for the *Alexander Marshall*. She sails on the twenty-fourth, out of Liverpool, so that should give you ample time to pack up your belongings and travel to the docks. There's a cabin onboard for you and your family and all meals are arranged, but you'll need to take bedding, if you have any, as well as personal belongings.' He hesitated. 'I'm afraid I can't help with travel on the boat train to Liverpool,' he said. 'But that will be your only expense. Someone will meet you at the other end. Once you've cleared immigration at Castle Garden ask for Mr Wolfe, and he'll take you onwards to Fall River where there's accommodation and jobs waiting for you.'

'We'll get ourselves to Liverpool,' her father assured him. 'We have a few things to sell that are too big to take. My wife's piano,' he explained. 'She's reluctant to see it go, but I've promised her a new one when we get there. They do have pianos in America, don't they?' he asked.

'They sure do, Mr Grimes. It'll be no problem at all to purchase one once you have your new home set up. I'm sure you'll love it, ma'am,' he told her mother. 'I can see what you're reduced to here, and I can tell you that you've made the right decision to come and work for us in Massachusetts. You won't regret it.'

At that moment, George came hurrying down the stairs, aware that he was missing something exciting. He stared at the man in his fancy clothes who was sitting by their hearth.

'Are you the American?' he asked, gazing at him in wonder.

'I sure am. You must be George.'

The man stood up and shook Sally's brother by the hand. Sally could see that George was impressed.

'Mr Grady has brought our tickets,' said their father. 'We sail on the twenty-fourth!'

The younger children crept into the kitchen one by one and looked at the man who was now drinking a cup of tea and waving away their mother's apologies that she couldn't offer him anything to eat.

'It sure grieves me to see you folks living like this,' he told them. 'But it won't be for long. There are better times coming for you,' he promised. 'You'll not go hungry in America.'

He stayed until he'd drained his teacup and then, after shaking hands with them again, he went out into the cold morning saying he had a few more visits to make.

'That's it then!' declared Sally's father when he'd seen him out. 'Only another couple of weeks to endure this and we'll be off. Time to get that piano sold, old girl,' he told her mother. 'Go and ask at the pawn shop tomorrow.'

It was as if the troubles of the last few months had suddenly been lifted from his shoulders. He was suddenly the father that Sally remembered, smiling and confident with a future to look forward to. And although her mother still looked doubtful about what was to come, she said nothing to burst his bubble and agreed that the piano could be sold.

Chapter Thirty-Two

Agatha didn't come on a Sunday and it was left to Ruth to care for her father. Thankfully, she thought he was a little bit better. His speech was clearer and his leg didn't seem as weak. He wanted to get up and come down the stairs, but Ruth persuaded him to stay in his room until Amos and Naomi called in after church. She was afraid that he might stumble and fall if she tried to help him down alone.

She lit a fire for him and carried up some breakfast.

'I'm sorry,' he told her as she helped him to drink, wiping his mouth with a cloth where the tea dribbled out.

'What for?' she asked.

'For this. For being a burden,' he said.

'You're not a burden. You can't help being poorly.'

'Perhaps I should have seen Dr Skaife sooner,' he said. 'I kept dismissing those palpitations as nothing, but now I wonder if they caused this. I can't help thinking it might have been prevented if I'd gone to see him earlier.'

'It's no good thinking like that,' Ruth told him. 'There's probably no connection. The only thing we need to think about now is getting you better.'

'I've made a mess of everything,' he told her. 'I'm worried about how you're going to manage.'

'I'll manage,' she said. 'I'm sure they'll let me take over at the soup kitchen in your place.'

'Did they say you could?' He seemed surprised.

'Mayor Hutchinson said I was to go in tomorrow. The committee need to meet to agree it, but why wouldn't they? I've helped you with it from the beginning.'

'You're a willing lass, Ruth,' he told her, squeezing her hand. 'But don't set your hopes on it. I know those men. They'll be reluctant to have you in charge.'

'Would you rather I didn't go?' she asked him.

He didn't reply straight away. 'I would prefer to have you here,' he admitted after a moment. 'Agatha's kind, but she's not family. And…'

'And what?' Ruth asked him.

'It's not a job for a lass, having to be responsible for all the workers and the soup making. I'm worried it'll be too hard for you.'

'I can do it,' she told him. Even though she had her own doubts she didn't want to admit to them. She didn't want him to have to worry about losing his wages.

Just before dinner time, her sister and brother-in-law came with her nieces. After they'd all been up to see Ruth's father he asked to speak with Amos alone. Ruth thought it must be something he was too embarrassed to ask his daughters for help with, so they left the men alone and came back downstairs.

'We prayed for him at church,' Naomi told her. The news disturbed Ruth. The vicar tended to pray only for those he considered seriously ill. 'Are you still going to the soup kitchen tomorrow?' she asked.

'Yes. I need to,' Ruth told her.

'I'm sure he hasn't spent all his money. Have you asked him again, now that he seems brighter?' her sister said.

'No. I don't want to make him feel uncomfortable if it's true,' she replied. 'Money isn't something he would normally discuss with me.'

'Are you talking about money?' Amos asked, overhearing them as he came down from the bedroom. He looked concerned.

'Yes. What's wrong?' Naomi asked him. 'Has he said something to you about it?'

'He has,' Amos replied. 'It isn't good news. He said that he didn't know how to tell you, so he decided to confess to me. It seems he's got himself into debt trying to keep the shop open.'

'Debt?' Ruth asked. That was worse than the savings all being spent. She'd never have dreamt that her father would borrow money. It was something he always warned against. *Neither a lender nor a borrower be* was one of his favourite expressions. He'd always shaken his head when he'd seen workers coming out of the pawnshop counting their money. *They'll live to regret it*, he'd often commented.

'It can't be true!' Naomi exclaimed. She started for the stairs, but Amos put out a hand to stop her.

'Leave him for a moment,' he advised. 'He's very upset. Let him gather himself before you go up.'

'How bad is it?' Ruth asked her brother-in-law. 'Does he owe a lot? Who has he borrowed from?'

'He's borrowed from the bank, so it's not like it's a loan shark. But they'll still expect the payments to be made, and now that there's no money coming in, he's beside himself worrying about how he'll manage it. He was talking about going back to the soup kitchen himself tomorrow, but I told him it's out of the question. He can barely stand never mind do a day's work.'

'How much has he borrowed?' Naomi asked. 'Did he say?'

'Not exactly. But it's set against the house.'

'What does that mean?' Ruth asked him.

'It means that if the payments aren't met, the bank is entitled to sell the house to cover the debt,' he explained.

'Sell the house?' asked Ruth. 'But where would we live? What about the shop? He was talking about opening again in the spring when things are better.' She could barely understand the seriousness of what she was being told.

'You'd have to move out. The business would be closed for good,' Amos told her. 'I'm sorry to have to tell you this. It should have come from your father really, but he couldn't face telling you himself.'

Ruth stared at her brother-in-law trying to make sense of what he was saying. She'd suspected that things were bad from what her father had revealed to her earlier, but she hadn't thought they were this bad. Amos was telling her that she might lose everything – her home, the confectionery business, all the security that she'd always taken for granted.

'Where would we go? Where would we live?' she asked.

'I don't know,' Amos said. 'It's a shock for me as well. I never would have imagined things would come to this.'

He sat down at the table as if lost in thought. Even Hope and Nora were quiet, not understanding what was being said but realising that something was wrong.

'What are we going to do?' asked Naomi. 'There isn't enough room for them to come and live with us. Do you think Deborah would take them in?'

'We might not have to sell up,' Ruth told them. 'Father will be better soon and if I keep working at the soup kitchen, we'll manage. Won't we?' she asked sounding forlorn.

'I'm not sure,' admitted Amos. 'Your father didn't give me much detail.'

'He won't have borrowed much,' said Naomi. 'I'm sure we'll find it's not as bad as you think. He's just confused with being unwell.'

'I hope you're right,' Amos replied. 'I really do. But it might be better if you let the maid go,' he suggested to Ruth. 'I don't think your father can afford her wages now.'

'But how will I manage without her?' gasped Ruth.

'Perhaps you should give up the soup kitchen,' suggested Naomi.

'But then there would be no wage at all coming in,' Ruth pointed out. 'If I can do father's job and be paid his wages, we'd be better off keeping Agatha on to nurse father and do the housework.'

'Does he need nursing all the time?' Naomi asked. 'I don't mind coming in for an hour or so to help out even if I can't be here all day.'

'Well, he is a little better,' Ruth agreed, grateful for her sister's offer. Much as she relied on Agatha, her wages were almost as much as she was earning at the moment and if things were as bad as Amos seemed to think they were, it was obvious that the maid was a luxury they could no longer afford if she couldn't persuade the mayor and committee to keep her on in her father's place.

–

Ruth arrived early at Cleaver Street the next morning. She was determined not to give the committee any reason to decide that she wasn't capable of doing her father's job because it was imperative that she earned enough money to tide them over until the shop was open again.

Freddy was already there and he smiled at her warmly and asked after her father.

'He's a little better,' she said.

'And how are you?' he asked.

The question surprised Ruth and she saw from his expression that he was genuinely interested in her welfare.

'I'm coping,' she told him, fighting down the tears that had taken her by surprise in response to his unexpected kindness.

'If there's anything I can do to help, you only need to ask,' he told her, and although others had made the same offer, Ruth felt that Freddy really meant it and she was grateful, as well as surprised that he should take the time to single her out when there were so many other girls clamouring for his attention.

'How's your father?' asked Mr Yates when he came in.

'He's improving,' she replied. 'I'm sure there's no reason to look for a replacement for him. I can organise the kitchen until he's well enough to come back.'

'So, he will be able to take up his role again?' Mr Yates sounded doubtful.

'I'm sure he will,' Ruth reassured him, although the truth was that she feared it would be a long time before her father was well enough to work again. But she reasoned that if she could prevent the committee giving his job to someone else straight away, it would give her time to prove herself and show that it wasn't necessary to bring in another man.

She was hanging up her coat, ready to begin work when she saw Caroline Haworth come in. She was wearing her expensive fur-trimmed coat and a matching bonnet, but when she took them off, Ruth saw that underneath she had on the plain blouse and skirt that she'd worn the previous week, although they looked freshly laundered.

'I was determined to be here sooner this week,' she told Ruth. 'I asked my maid Lottie to call me as soon as she got out of bed herself. I've never left the house before my father in my life before,' she confided as she tied on an apron. 'I'm sorry,' she went on. 'I'm prattling on about myself when I should be asking about your father.'

Ruth reassured her that he was getting better.

'That's good to hear. Give him my best wishes. Will you be taking charge again?' she asked.

'If they let me,' Ruth said. 'Mayor Hutchinson agreed to let me do it today, but I need to convince the committee. They may want to get a man in.'

'A man? What nonsense. You're perfectly capable.'

'I hope I am,' Ruth replied as she saw Sally Grimes coming through the door. It was a relief to see the mill girl. She'd been such a help last week that Ruth had found herself relying on her to organise the vegetable preparation. She looked different this morning though. Ruth was puzzled by the change in her, but when Sally greeted her enthusiastically she thought it was because she seemed happy – though why she would be happy to be peeling potatoes in the foundry at this time of the morning she couldn't imagine.

Sally enquired after her father as well and it warmed Ruth to think that these other girls truly cared about him when they barely knew him.

'I hope he's back soon,' Sally said. 'Not that I don't think you can do his job,' she added to Ruth. 'I'd just like to know he's better before we go.'

'Go? Go where?' asked Ruth, her heart sinking. She really hoped Sally wasn't going away.

'We have our tickets for America!' Sally told them. 'The agent came with them yesterday and told us we sail on the twenty-fourth. My mother's dashing about like someone possessed trying to find bags to pack our things and this morning she has to persuade the pawn broker to give us enough for the piano to pay our fares on the train to Liverpool.' She sounded excited.

'My father will be sorry to lose you and Mr Grimes,' Caroline told her. 'He always speaks very highly of him.'

'That's nice to know,' replied Sally. 'But we need to go where the work is.'

'I appreciate that,' said Caroline. 'I don't blame you. It sounds such a brave thing to do, to pack up all you own and sail to the New World.'

'It's not so new,' Sally replied. 'A lot of people have already gone and more will emigrate because of this crisis. It stands to reason to go where the cotton is.'

Caroline nodded, but Ruth could see that the thought of losing skilled workers from her father's mill worried her. It made her realise that it wasn't just the millworkers who were being brought low by the cotton famine. It was affecting everyone from the workers to the employers, as well as the shopkeepers.

'Right!' she said, as she saw the mayor and his wife arrive, followed by a couple more members of the relief committee. 'Let's get to work. I can see Freddy Fry bringing in the sacks of turnips. We'll start with those.'

'Can we speak with you, Miss Hodgson?' asked the mayor a few minutes later when Ruth had made sure the fires were lit, the water was on to boil, and the vegetables were being chopped.

She followed him across to one of the tables set out for the workers to eat at. Mr Yates and the other committee members were sitting around it. They looked concerned as she approached.

'How is your father?' they asked, and once again Ruth answered positively that he was making good progress.

'It isn't what I heard,' Mr Airey told her. 'I was speaking with Dr Skaife at church yesterday and he says your father has paralysis down one side. He isn't sure if he'll ever be fit to come back to work.'

Ruth frowned. Dr Skaife had no business discussing her father's health.

'He's much improved since the doctor saw him,' she explained. 'And until he is well enough to return, I'm willing to do his work.'

Mr Airey looked doubtful. 'I think it would be too much for you,' he said, although Ruth could see that he meant it kindly. 'You should be at home nursing your father, not worrying about the soup kitchen. I think it's better if we find someone else to take over. Don't you think so, gentlemen?'

The others nodded in agreement.

'I know you want to continue to help,' Mr Yates told her, sympathetically, 'and you are managing well – I'll grant you that. But it could never be a long-term solution.'

Ruth felt both angry and disappointed. She wasn't sure what to say, but after a moment she decided to be honest.

'My father needs his wages,' she confessed. 'He has no other income since he closed down the shop.'

'I appreciate that,' said Mayor Hutchinson. 'But you must tell him not to worry. He needs to concentrate on getting better. I'm sure he has a little bit put by to tide him over. I know what a sensible and prudent man he is.'

Ruth wanted to explain that he had nothing, that he was in debt to the bank, but she knew her father would be mortified if she told these men that he'd made bad decisions about his money. Ruth knew that he would hate to lose their respect. Besides, her father's financial affairs were none of their business. If he'd wanted them to know, then surely he would have been honest with them about why he was taking the job in the first place.

'But can I continue for the time being?' she asked, hating to plead. 'My sister is going to help to nurse my father, so I'd be more use here than at home.' She wanted to mention the money again, but she didn't like to press the point. She knew how much men hated to discuss the subject with women. They were afraid it was too taxing for the female brain.

'Maybe for a day or so, until we arrange a replacement?' Mr Yates asked the other committee members. 'Miss Hodgson does know what needs to be done. We might struggle without her.'

'Could you not do it?' asked Mayor Hutchinson.

'You know I can't take it on,' Mr Yates told him. 'I have other commitments. I need to try to save my own business from ruin,' he went on. 'And I suspect if I was in charge here, the motivation to find a permanent replacement for Mr Hodgson might be diminished. I know you're all busy men.'

The committee members nodded in agreement and eventually conceded that Ruth should manage the soup kitchen until a better arrangement could be made.

'And my father's wages?' she asked hopefully.

'Well, obviously we can't pay him whilst he's off ill,' explained the mayor as if it was something he wouldn't expect Ruth to understand. 'We can pay you your wages of course.'

Ruth wanted to argue that it wasn't fair. Her wages were not for such an important role with responsibilities. But the men seemed satisfied that the matter was settled, for the time being at least and the conversation amongst them turned to other subjects as she was left in no doubt that it was time for her to go and get on with the work she had been allotted.

'What did they want with you?' Caroline asked when she got back to the soup preparation tables. 'It all looked very intense.'

Ruth briefly explained what the committee members had agreed.

'Well, that's hardly fair!' Caroline exclaimed. 'They should have agreed to pay you extra.'

Ruth was pleased that she agreed, but she was at a loss to know how to convince the men of the unfairness of what they were proposing.

'Don't worry,' Caroline told her. 'I'll speak to my father about it. I'm sure he'll agree that it's wrong. I'll ask him to speak to those men on your behalf. I'm sure they'll listen to him.'

'Would you?' Ruth asked, feeling surprised and grateful. Caroline Haworth was the last person she would have expected to come to her rescue, and she was genuinely moved that someone like her could be so affronted on her behalf.

'Yes. Leave it with me,' Caroline told her. 'I'll make sure you get paid properly. You deserve it.'

Chapter Thirty-Three

Caroline shelled the last of the peas and added them to the vats of soup that were bubbling away over the fires, taking care to keep her skirt out of the way of the flames.

'I'm glad to see you're remembering to take care,' said a voice behind her and she turned to see that Freddy Fry was watching her. She smiled. Despite everything, his approval mattered to her and she glowed in his approbation. But she knew she must keep her feelings in check. Back at the preparation tables, as she struggled clumsily to take the peel off a potato, she tried to turn her thoughts to Thomas Dutton instead. How she wished that he had the same effect on her that Freddy Fry did. Talk of marriage would be an easy decision then. But although he was pleasant and there was nothing about him that she could reasonably object to, her reaction to him just wasn't the same – and she had no idea why.

'Try angling it the other way, like this,' said Sally Grimes. Caroline realised that the mill girl had been watching her poor attempts to deal with the potato. Sally took the knife and the vegetable from her and showed her a better way to peel it. It looked so simple and she felt foolish for the desperate way she'd been hacking at it. 'Now you have a go,' Sally said.

'No one has ever shown me what to do before,' Caroline told her gratefully as she managed quite a long piece of thin peel. 'That's much easier. I don't know why I didn't think of it myself. Thank you.'

'You'll soon get the hang of it,' said Sally.

'I'll need to,' replied Caroline. 'There's a whole sackful there, and who'll do them when you leave us?'

'Well, you have a couple of weeks to hone your skills,' laughed Sally.

'Are you looking forward to it? Going to America?' Caroline asked her.

'Yes, of course I am. We've been promised good wages and a big house. I may even get a bed to myself.'

'Don't overestimate the pleasure of that,' interrupted Ruth as she walked past and overheard the conversation. 'I have a bed to myself and it's been so cold these past few nights that I'd have welcomed another body to warm me up.'

'Well, I suppose it depends on the body.' Sally grinned and pointed a knife in the direction of the furnaces. 'I wouldn't mind sharing a bed with Freddy Fry.'

Caroline burst out laughing at the audacity and also at the scandalised look on Ruth's face. The truth was that even though her own bed was warmed for her, she quite liked the idea of Freddy Fry as well.

'I think you've shocked Ruth,' Caroline told Sally.

'But not you,' she observed. 'I expected you to be much too ladylike to laugh like that.'

Caroline smiled. It was the first time she felt as if at least one of the mill girls might accept her as a friend.

'We're not that different,' she replied.

'Do you find him attractive then? Freddy, I mean?' asked Sally curiously.

'He's good-looking,' agreed Caroline, glancing towards Freddy who seemed aware that they were discussing him.

'He's one thing I'll be sorry to leave behind,' Sally said. 'But seeing as I'm going, you could try setting your cap at him. Unless your father has someone better lined up for you.'

'I think my grandfather has.' Caroline sighed. 'I'm expected to marry someone he's chosen,' she explained. 'My mother says that love doesn't matter. Money and status are the elements I should be considering.'

'I wouldn't rule out marrying for money, if a man had plenty of it,' Sally said thoughtfully. 'But not if he was hideous though. I'd draw the line at ugly.'

Caroline nodded. She almost began to talk about her own mother doing the same, but she remembered herself in time. It was pleasant to be on more friendly terms with Sally Grimes, but she mustn't forget herself and begin to gossip like a common fishwife. She had to remember who she was because one day, hopefully before long, this soup kitchen wouldn't be needed and she would go back to being the mill owner's daughter. And it wouldn't do for the workers to be familiar with her then, or to know her family's secrets.

-

Later, when the soup had been eaten and the pots washed, Caroline travelled home in the carriage to be greeted by a hot drink and a warm fire, and Lottie's insistence that she change out of the old clothes she was wearing into something more fitting.

As she washed her hands with the scented soap and scrubbed her nails with a brush, she found she was still thinking about Freddy Fry. It was true what Sally had said. He was as far from her social sphere as Thomas Dutton was from Sally's. Even if she did want to marry for love, and Sally opted for wealth, it could never be. They each must keep to their place in society. That's how the world was.

The thought led her on to remember what Ruth had told her about the committee being reluctant to pay her fairly for running the soup kitchen. There was a promise she'd made that she must keep concerning that.

She dried her hands and rubbed some rose-scented ointment into them, before going down to see if her father had come home. He was in his study, still frowning over the numbers he had written on various pieces of paper, as if they might offer him some solution if he stared at them for long enough.

He smiled indulgently when he saw her in the doorway and beckoned her in.

'I heard you laughing with some of the mill girls earlier,' he said.

'You don't mind, do you?' Caroline asked, worried that he was about to reprimand her.

'No. Of course not. I was pleased to see you chatting with them. I was worried last week that you seemed rather lonely at Cleaver Street.'

'I was,' she agreed, gratified that he'd noticed. 'It was all very strange at first, and I think they were wary of me. But things seemed easier today. Sally Grimes showed me how to peel potatoes.'

It was his turn to laugh. 'Don't tell your mother,' he warned.

'It's probably best not to,' agreed Caroline, enjoying having the secret with him. 'I think she imagines I'm just using my superiority to make the soup.'

Her father laughed and Caroline was glad to see him look his old self, if only for a moment. She knew he was desperately worried about the mill and she wished there was more she could do to help than peel a few vegetables.

'So, did you want to ask me something?' her father enquired.

'I did,' Caroline replied, sitting down on the chair he kept for guests. 'I wanted to ask you about Ruth Hodgson.'

'She did well today,' he said. 'I wasn't sure about her at first, but I think she's surprised everyone by how well she's stepped into her father's shoes and kept the kitchen running.'

'She is capable,' confirmed Caroline. 'She's very quiet, and at first I thought she was too shy to give out orders, but she understands how everything needs to be organised and although she doesn't shout or make a fuss, she makes sure things get done.'

'So, there's no problem,' her father said.

'Well, there is,' Caroline told him. 'The thing is that although the committee are happy for her do the job for the time being, they won't pay her what they were paying her father – and it seems unfair.'

'But she's only a lass. She can't expect a man's wage.'

'But she's doing the same job,' Caroline argued. 'And between us, I think she needs the money.'

'What makes you say that?' he asked. 'What has she told you?'

'She hasn't told me anything. It's just something I sense,' Caroline replied. 'She seemed a bit desperate after they told her they'd only pay her the wage she'd been promised for helping.'

Her father frowned. 'I wouldn't have thought Mr Hodgson would be short of money. He's always been very generous to those worse off, and he gave a generous donation to the relief effort not long ago. I saw the figures. I remember because it made me feel uncomfortable about what I could afford to give.'

'Maybe he didn't envisage things getting this bad. He has shut his shop,' Caroline reminded her father. 'And there's a rumour going about that he'll never be well enough to work again.'

'I don't see what I can do to help,' her father said.

'You could speak to the committee about paying Ruth more,' suggested Caroline.

'It's hardly my place. I'm not even a committee member.'

'Perhaps that's why it should come from you. The committee members need someone to point out that what they're doing isn't fair. They're taking advantage of Ruth.'

'I suppose they are,' mused her father.

'If they have to appoint someone else – a man – they'll have to pay him the full wage. So if Ruth is doing a good job, why shouldn't they pay her?'

'Women are never paid as much as men,' her father pointed out.

'But why not?' persisted Caroline.

'Because they are women. If I were to pay my women workers as much as I paid the men, I'd never be able to afford to run the mill. It costs too much.'

'That doesn't make it fair,' Caroline replied.

Her father shook his head. 'It's business. It's how things are,' he told her. 'What you're suggesting is ridiculous. It would never work.'

Caroline felt frustrated by his response. She'd thought that he would be on her side. It was obviously an unfair system, but it wasn't something that had ever concerned her before. She wasn't sure if she'd even known that her father paid his women workers less.

'But could they not pay her a bit more?' she went on. 'She's not doing the same job as before. And supervising is harder than just helping.'

Her father seemed irritated by her persistence.

'All right,' he agreed. 'I'll speak to Mayor Hutchinson the next time I see him and tell him what you've said. But that doesn't mean he'll agree. In fact, I would be surprised if he did. The money for the soup kitchen is coming from donations,' he reminded her. 'It would look bad if the committee squandered it.'

Caroline thought that paying Ruth fairly for her work was hardly squandering money, but she said nothing more and smiled at her father and thanked him. She'd done what she could, but now that she was learning how the world of work and business ran, she was beginning to see that it was organised by men with their own best interests at heart. It was something she'd learnt little about in the past. She'd known her father ran a mill and that her grandfather did all sorts of clever things with money, but none of it had been her concern. It was only since she'd begun to mix with the girls who had to earn money at the soup kitchen that she'd realised how disadvantaged they were.

–

'What were you discussing so earnestly with your father?' her mother asked when she went to sit in the parlour to wait for dinner to be served.

'I was talking to him about Ruth Hodgson. Her father's had a stroke and she's having to do his job.'

'I might have known it would be about that soup kitchen. You're becoming obsessed with it,' remarked her mother as she reached to ring the bell for Jenkins. 'I don't know why he hasn't already come,' she muttered. 'It's three minutes past and the food should be on the table by now. Anyway,' she went on, turning her attention back to Caroline. 'It'll have to stop before we announce your engagement to Thomas Dutton.'

Caroline stared at her mother. 'Engagement?' she repeated. 'Aren't you getting a little ahead of yourself?'

'Not at all,' her mother replied. 'I've sent a note to Mr and Mrs Dutton to say that if Thomas comes to speak to your father, then he will meet with an affirmative reply.'

'And do I not get a say in the matter?' demanded Caroline, angry at her mother's interference in her life. She suspected that her mother was only keen to arrange a marriage for her because she was still cross about her going to work in the soup kitchen without her permission.

'Don't be argumentative, Caroline,' her mother rebuked her. 'I don't have the patience for it this evening. At last!' she exclaimed as Jenkins appeared at the door. 'I do hope your father is ready to join us. Between the two of you my life is almost unbearable,' she grumbled.

Chapter Thirty-Four

Ruth hurried home at the end of the day. Even though the soup making had all gone to plan and there had been no hitches, she was still worried that the mayor and his committee would decide to give the job of supervisor to someone else. Her only hope was that Caroline Haworth would remember her promise and speak to her father about it – and that Mr Haworth would succeed in persuading the mayor to keep her on and pay her properly.

She let herself in the front door with a feeling of trepidation, wondering how her father was. Agatha would have left some time ago and she wasn't sure if her sister Naomi would have managed to come. It was difficult for her when she had the girls to care for and Amos's tea to put on the table when he came home from the printers.

'Hello!' she called. 'Only me!'

'There you are!' her sister exclaimed as she opened the kitchen door. 'I thought they finished serving the soup at two o'clock.'

'They do,' Ruth told her, irritably. 'But then there's the clearing up to do and setting everything ready for tomorrow. I can't just walk out – not when I'm doing father's job. Goodness' knows they're already looking for an excuse to get rid of me!'

'I'm sorry,' Naomi said. 'I know you're doing your best, but Amos doesn't like it if his tea isn't ready when he comes in.'

'You'd better get going then,' Ruth said. 'Where are Hope and Nora?'

'With Amos's mother. She wants to help. But I can't ask her to have them every day. It'll tire her out.'

'How's he been?' Ruth asked, nodding her head towards the bedroom above them. 'Has he been out of bed?'

Naomi shook her head. 'He keeps saying he's better, but it's obvious he isn't. He wants to get up, but he just isn't strong enough.'

'Do you think he'll be all right for half an hour whilst I get some shopping from the market?' Ruth asked. 'I've not had the chance before and we've nothing in.'

'I'm sure he will. He's had a cup of tea and he's settled. He may even be sleeping. He didn't call down when you came in. You could be there and back before he wakes if you don't disturb him.'

'I'll have to go up,' said Ruth. 'I need some money and I'm not sure where he keeps it. I hope there is some. Has he said any more to you about borrowing from the bank?'

'Not a word. He obviously doesn't want to discuss it. Have you nothing at all in your purse?'

'No.' Ruth shook her head. 'Not a penny until they pay me at the end of the week.'

'Here.' Her sister took out her own purse and handed Ruth a shilling. 'Take this,' she told her. 'You can pay me back later.'

Ruth was grateful and she hoped that Amos wouldn't be angry about Naomi giving her the money. She knew he didn't earn enough to support two families. She hurried back out into the cold afternoon. It wasn't far to the market square on King William Street. Some of the stalls were beginning to pack up for the end of the day. Normally, they would have stayed later to cater for the workers coming out of the mills but there wasn't much point now. Most people could shop earlier when they collected their allowance from the relief committee.

Ruth bought bread and potatoes and oatcakes. Then used what was left for a small piece of cheese and some bacon. It would keep them fed for a few days and she was still hoping that at the end of the week, the soup kitchen committee might agree to pay her the wage they'd agreed with her father.

The temperature had fallen again and the remains of the snow and ice were sparkling in the light cast by the gas lamps as Ruth hurried home. She shut and locked the door and went upstairs to see her father. He was awake and Naomi had lit a candle by his bed.

'How did it go?' he asked her.

'Well,' she reassured him. 'The soup was good and everyone was fed. All the helpers seem to know what's required of them now and even the committee ladies are getting better at the preparations. How are you?' she asked him.

'I'm getting better too,' he told her. 'I'm thinking of getting up tomorrow. You can tell Mr Yates and Mayor Hutchinson that I'll probably be back next week.'

'I will,' replied Ruth, even though she had no intention of telling them what her father had said. She doubted he'd even be out of bed by next week, let alone whether he'd ever be fit to go back to the soup kitchen. He looked so ill and frail that she had to turn away before he noticed she was crying. 'I'll go down and get the tea on,' she said.

'Has Agatha left something good?' he asked.

'There wasn't anything for her to cook,' Ruth told him. 'I hadn't had a chance to shop, but I've just been to the market now and I thought I'd make some toasted bread with cheese on it. How does that sound?'

'Delicious.' He tried to smile but his face looked more like a grimace. She wondered whether to broach the subject of the housekeeping money with him, but decided to leave it for the time being. She didn't want him to be upset again.

The meal she made was nothing like the food that Agatha usually cooked for them, but it was fresh and warm and her father didn't want much anyway – and Ruth had had hot soup earlier so a little bit of bread and cheese was enough for her. She was so tired that she knew she couldn't have faced a big meal and then all the washing up.

Once they'd eaten, she helped her father to settle for the night. She was becoming accustomed to helping him with the chamber pot now and it didn't appal her as much as it had the first time. It was surprising what you could get used to, she thought as she went down to the privy to empty it. It wasn't that long since her main worry had been helping at the soup kitchen. She'd had no idea then how much was going to be asked of her. And what the future held, she was too afraid to contemplate. Even if her father's debt was somehow paid, there was the added worry about whether he would be fit to open the shop again once this crisis was over. If he couldn't go back to his sweet making, the threat of them losing their home and everything that she'd once thought was secure hung over her like a black cloud.

Chapter Thirty-Five

Sally woke up and mentally calculated how many more times she would wake in this familiar room. Even though she was still sleepy, she reckoned it was seven. They planned to catch the train to Liverpool on the twenty-third to be in good time to board the boat before she sailed. It was no time at all before everything would change. The thought filled her with a frisson of fear. Even though she was excited by the prospect of going to America it would be strange to leave the home she'd known all her life.

She dressed herself quickly, her teeth chattering with the cold. Would it be snowy like this in America, she wondered. They'd asked the agent, Mr Grady, all sorts of questions about the town they were going to – the mill, the houses, whether there were shops, a doctor, a church – but they'd never thought to ask him about the weather. Sally hoped it would be sunny and warm. She'd had enough of this winter.

When she went down to the kitchen, she saw her father was up and dressed, ready for his work at the quarry. Her mother had found some old rags to protect his hands and he was sitting by the cold hearth winding them around his palms. He smiled when he saw her.

'Seven days,' he announced. 'Then we'll be on our way. We can manage a week, can't we?' he asked.

Sally kissed his cheek. 'It'll pass in no time,' she reassured him, knowing how much he hated the stone-breaking work he'd been given.

She ate a cold breakfast knowing that they would make a hot cup of tea for everyone at the soup kitchen in another hour or so, and the fires there would soon warm her. Her work was so much easier than the task that had been set for her father and she wished he didn't have to go.

'I'm sure we could manage without the shilling they'll pay you,' she told him. 'Why don't you just stay at home?'

'They'll take away all our relief if I do that,' he reminded her.

'But it's only for a week,' she said. 'Are you sure we can't manage?'

He shook his head. 'I don't mind really,' he reassured her. 'Now that I know it's not for ever, I can put up with it, and the money means the youngsters don't need to go hungry.'

Sally hugged him before she went out of the door. He was a good father and she loved him. He always did his best for them and she believed he was right to take them to America even though her mother still had some doubts.

–

The routine at the soup kitchen was familiar now. She greeted Ruth Hodgson when she arrived and asked after her father, then tied on an apron and began to fill the water pots ready to pour into the vats. The foundry grew warm as she worked and the sight of Freddy Fry was always a welcome one. He grinned at her and she asked him what he was planning to do later.

'Sit and brood over a half pint,' he told her. 'It's all I can afford now that Mr Yates has me on reduced pay. Not that I should grumble. This work isn't hard and it has the added bonus of all ye bonny lasses.' He winked at her and then smiled at Ruth, and for a fleeting moment Sally wished she was staying in Blackburn. Discreet enquiries amongst her fellow mill girls had revealed that Freddy wasn't spoken for and wasn't even courting – although how he remained single was a subject of their amazement. They would have thought some lucky lass would have snared him long ago. And it wasn't as if he was backward at coming forwards. He was a natural charmer who seemed well aware that the girls found him attractive. Maybe he was setting his sights higher, mused Sally as she followed his gaze towards the door where Caroline Haworth had just arrived. If he thought he stood a chance there he was very much mistaken.

'Did you speak to Mr Haworth?' she heard Ruth ask Caroline as they settled on their stools at the preparation table and picked up their knives to peel the vegetables.

'I did,' Caroline replied. 'He promised to have a word with the mayor. He didn't sound hopeful though.'

Sally saw Ruth frown. It had been the main subject of conversation yesterday that Ruth Hodgson had asked for the same wage as her father. Some of the other girls had been scandalised by the effrontery of it, but Sally thought Ruth was right to ask and she admired her for it.

'He said he's calling in later,' Caroline added. 'Perhaps he'll be able to speak to the committee then.'

'Thank you for asking him,' Ruth said. 'I appreciate it.' She hesitated. 'The truth is that I need the money,' she told them. 'I suppose I shouldn't say anything. My father wouldn't like it. But he's got into debt and we may lose the house if we can't pay back the loan.'

'That's awful!' exclaimed Sally. 'I always thought you were well off. Who does he owe money to? Not one of those loan sharks, is it? I've heard they're no better than thieves, the way they take money from people.'

'No. He owes it to the bank,' Ruth told her. 'But if they don't get it back, they may take the house and the shop off us. That's what my brother-in-law Amos says anyway.'

'Why does he owe them money?' Caroline asked her.

'The shop hasn't been doing well,' Ruth explained. 'None of the workers has money for sweets.'

'That's true,' agreed Sally. She'd thought that she was deprived because she hadn't had the money to treat herself to a bag of toffee each week. It hadn't occurred to her that the Hodgson's might be struggling because of it.

'Please don't tell anyone,' Ruth begged them. 'I shouldn't have said anything, but I'm so worried, and I wanted to explain why I need the wages. It isn't greed,' she assured them.

'Of course it isn't greed!' Caroline exclaimed. 'You deserve them. And I won't say anything. I promise.'

'I promise too,' agreed Sally. 'I'm not a gossip,' she added.

–

Later, when the soup was almost cooked, Sally heard a commotion at the door. Mr Haworth and Mr Yates jumped up from the committee meeting they were holding on the far side of the room, where they were no doubt discussing Ruth's wages, to see what was going on. The threat of rioting was never far away, and Mr Yates called to Freddy Fry and the other lads who were still at the foundry to join them in case force was needed.

The banging on the door came again and Freddy was sent to open it whilst the other men stood behind him, ready to repel any ensuing rush of workers who thought they were being let into the kitchen early.

Sally didn't recognise the two men who were allowed in, but she could see by their anxious faces that they had brought bad news. She wondered if there was rioting in the town centre. Maybe they'd been sent to tell them not to open the kitchen after all.

She walked over to where they were in earnest conversation with the mayor and the other men. Their faces were serious and she heard them saying that help was needed.

'Do you think they're rioting?' she asked Ruth who had come to join her.

'I do hope not,' she replied. 'We have enough to worry about.'

Then Sally saw Mr Haworth look directly at her. His face was grim and he left the men gathered around the newcomers and came towards her.

'Did your father take work at the quarry?' he asked.

'Yes.' Sally wondered why he was asking.

'What about your George? Is he there too?'

'No, Dad wouldn't let him go even though he wanted to. Why?' she asked, hoping that her brother hadn't involved himself in a riot and got into trouble.

Mr Haworth frowned and looked uncomfortable. 'There's been an accident,' he told her. 'At the quarry. These men say there was a rockfall and some of the workers are trapped. They've come to ask the foundry lads to go and help dig.'

Sally saw that Freddy and the others were putting on their coats and Mr Yates was unlocking a door to a store-room where shovels were stored.

'Is my dad all right?' she asked Mr Haworth.

'I don't know. They couldn't say who the trapped workers were. I'm going up there with them. Do you want to come?' he asked. 'I'm sure you can be spared here.'

'Yes.' It was an easy decision. Once she had reassured herself that her father was safe, she could come back. But until then she would have no peace.

'Get your hat and coat,' said Mr Haworth.

-

They set off immediately. Sally walked between Mr Haworth and Freddy and both men tried to keep her spirits up as they climbed the steep hill towards Shorrock's Delph. As they approached, Sally saw a freshly fallen heap of stone that had left a ragged hole in the side of the moorland.

'Wait there,' Mr Haworth told her before he followed Freddy Fry and the other foundry workers across the uneven, boulder-strewn ground towards the rockfall where men were frantically picking up rocks and moving them aside. Sally looked for her father, but when there was no sign of him she grew uneasy. The workers weren't achieving much, and even when the foundry lads, who all looked bigger and stronger than the out-of-work cotton weavers, joined them, the progress was slow.

She watched, shifting her gaze from one worker to the next, desperately hoping that she would recognise her father amongst the rescuers. But he wasn't there and Sally began to fear he was one of the unfortunates who had been buried by the rockfall. If so, he was almost certain to have been hurt and she worried that it might mean he would be unable to travel to America.

The digging went on and she was joined by other women who had heard about the accident. Most called out in relief to see their sons and husbands and fathers. Some even ran across the rocks to embrace them they were so thankful. Sally wondered if her mother had heard what had happened. She considered going home to fetch her, but then decided that it would achieve nothing. If her father was found unhurt, she would have caused her mother worry and stress for nothing. So, she decided to wait until she had better news.

The fierce wind up on the hill added to the biting cold and soon Sally's feet were numb. She paced restlessly up and down, trying to keep warm and distract herself although she never moved far away from the quarry.

As the distant clock in the market square fired its one o' clock salute, a sigh of disappointment rippled across the delph. Sally approached the group of men huddled around what looked like a bundle of rags they had pulled out of the stones. It was a moment before she recognised the form as a body. It was lifeless. And although it wasn't her father, her heart raced with fear as she realised the chances of him being found alive were diminishing by the minute.

The body was covered in an old piece of sacking to await the cart that would take it away. The men began to dig again, but their enthusiasm was tempered, as if they had less hope now of finding anyone alive.

It was about three in the afternoon when someone gave a shout of *Quick! Over here!* All efforts were now focused on one area and a few minutes later another body was uncovered.

'He's alive!' cried Freddy Fry. 'Bring the board!'

An old door that had been brought for use as a stretcher was rushed to the scene and the men laid someone on it. Sally pushed through the crowd and recognised her father. He was white from head to foot with the dust from the rockfall, but as Freddy held a cup of water to his lips she saw he was living and drinking and she hoped that he wasn't too badly injured.

'Let me through,' she pleaded. 'It's my dad.'

The onlookers parted for her and she scrambled across to him and grasped his cold hand.

'Dad. It's me. It's Sally. You're going to be all right. They're fetching a cart and they'll take you to the infirmary.'

His eyes were open and he managed a slight smile and squeezed her hand, but the dust was in his mouth and he couldn't speak. He began to cough and Freddy gave him more water. He spluttered on it, then seemed to gasp and the hand Sally was holding went limp, and his eyes seemed glazed. Sally stared at him, willing him to acknowledge her.

'Give him another drink,' she urged Freddy. But Freddy shook his head.

'I'm sorry,' he said. 'He's gone.'

'Gone?' Sally looked from her father to the foundry worker and back again. 'You don't mean...?' But when she looked back at the body lying on the ground beside her she saw that it was true. Her father had died. 'No!' she cried as she held onto his hand and rubbed it, determined to make him live again. 'He can't!' she wept. 'He can't die. We're going to America next week.'

Sally felt Freddy gather her in his arms.

‘I’m sorry, Sally. I’m so sorry,’ he said as he rocked her against him. ‘I wish I could have done more, but he was too badly hurt.’

She sobbed and clung to the strong body that held her as a hush fell across the quarry. She would have to tell her mother, and her brothers and sisters. How was she going to do that? How would they bear it?

She held onto Freddy as he cradled her against him and hoped that in a moment she might wake from the nightmare. But she didn’t and soon Freddy moved her gently aside as someone covered her father’s body and two men lifted the board.

‘Where are they taking him?’ she asked.

‘It’ll be a job for the coroner,’ Freddy told her. ‘He’ll have to establish a cause of death.’

But Sally already knew the cause. It was this famine, this cotton famine, because if the cotton had kept on coming her father would have been safe in the mill, not working in this God-forsaken quarry, breaking up stone to make a footpath.

Chapter Thirty-Six

That afternoon, after the soup had been served, the mayor came to speak to Ruth.

'The committee has reconsidered your request for more wages,' he told her. 'Mr Haworth was very vocal on your behalf and pointed out that the job you are doing does carry more responsibility than the task you were originally employed to do. Now, whilst we can't pay you what we were paying your father, we have decided to increase your wage and you can have ten shillings each week.'

'That's less than half of what he was getting,' protested Ruth.

'It's a substantial increase on what was originally agreed for you.' Mr Hutchinson looked astounded. 'I would have expected you to be grateful!'

'I am,' Ruth replied, realising that this was the best offer she could hope for. 'I am grateful.'

The mayor didn't seem convinced and Ruth hoped she hadn't spoiled her chances of keeping the job – although she was still costing the committee much less than employing a man, she reasoned.

'We'll see how you cope,' continued the mayor. 'Hopefully it won't be too long until your father is fit to come back.'

Ruth nodded. She hoped her father might yet surprise them all and make a good recovery, but realistically, she knew it was unlikely. What was clear was that they could no longer afford to pay Agatha.

'I'm grateful to you for taking it up with your father,' Ruth told Caroline when the mayor had gone. 'I think what he said has made a difference. I'll thank him myself when I see him,' she added. 'Do you think he's still up at the quarry? Sally hasn't come back either.'

Ruth had been so busy all afternoon that it was only now that she began to grow concerned about her friend.

'I do hope her father hasn't been hurt,' she said.

'So do I,' echoed Caroline. 'But Freddy Fry and the other foundry workers haven't come back either, so I think it may have been a serious accident.'

The two of them exchanged a worried look. Neither of them had known Sally long, but the work at the soup kitchen had drawn them closer and Ruth hoped that the mill girl would soon return and reassure them that everything was fine.

It was Mr Haworth who was the first to arrive. He was covered in dust from the quarry and he looked weary. Ruth saw him speaking to Mr Yates, but they were too far away for her to hear what was being said, although it was clear from their faces that the news he was imparting was not good.

Caroline abandoned the dishes she was drying and went across the foundry to ask her father what had happened. Ruth dried her hands on a towel and followed her. There was no sign of Sally.

'No! That's terrible!' she heard Caroline exclaim as she approached the group of men that included Mr Yates and the mayor.

'What is?' asked Ruth, fearing the worst as Caroline turned to her with shock written starkly across her face.

'Sally's father has been killed in a rock fall,' she said as if she couldn't quite believe it was true.

'No!' Ruth found it hard to believe too. 'But they were going to America,' she said. 'What will happen now?'

'There'll be an inquest,' said Mr Haworth, 'and a funeral. I'll make sure it's paid for and that he gets a headstone. He'll not be put in a pauper's grave, not when he was one of my best workers. Damn this cotton famine!' he swore. 'Jimmy should have been at his work in the mill, not up there in that dangerous quarry.'

Ruth could see how upset he was. It was clear that he was blaming himself for having to lay off his workers, but what else could he have done? No one could run a cotton mill without cotton.

She saw Caroline put a hand on her father's arm. 'It isn't your fault,' she said to comfort him.

'It feels like it is,' he replied as he wiped his face with a handkerchief.

'Where's Sally now?' asked Ruth.

'Gone home to tell the bad news to her mother. I offered to go myself, but she went with Freddy Fry. I'll call round later and offer what help I can.'

'I'll come with you,' Caroline said.

Ruth wanted to offer to go as well, but she knew that her father would need her when she'd finished work here. So, she was relieved that the Haworths were going. But she knew it wouldn't be an easy visit.

They quickly finished off cleaning the tables and left everything ready for the next day. Then Ruth hurried home. As she walked, she pondered gloomily on how things could change in an instant. One moment someone could be alive and strong and well and the next moment they could be gone. Whoever would have thought this morning that Sally's father would be dead by the end of the day?

She let herself into the house and was relieved to see her sister and nieces sitting in the kitchen waiting for her.

'How is he?' Ruth burst out, somehow fearing that she would be the recipient of bad news as well.

'He seems a little better. Certainly no worse,' Naomi told her. 'Are you all right?' she asked. 'You look upset.'

'There was an accident,' Ruth said as she took off her hat and coat.

'At the soup kitchen?'

'No. Up at the stone quarry. Sally Grimes, one of the girls I work with, her father was killed there today.'

'I hadn't heard,' Naomi said. 'We've been here all afternoon. What a shame. I'm sorry.'

'It was a shock,' Ruth replied. 'I didn't know him, but Sally has become a friend. I don't know what she'll do now.' She went on to explain that Mr Haworth from the mill had offered to pay for the funeral and Naomi agreed it was good of him.

'Don't say anything to father,' her sister warned her. 'It won't help him if you go up there with a long face talking about death. Try to keep him cheerful. Dr Skaife says that looking on the bright side will help him along.'

Ruth nodded. She had intended to tell her father, but she could see the sense in not upsetting him too much, because he would be devastated when she had to explain that they must let Agatha go.

'Will you be able to call in and give him his dinner each day?' she asked her sister when she'd told her about the wage she'd been offered. 'I know it's going to be hard without Agatha to cook and nurse him, but there simply isn't enough money to pay her.'

It would be hard for herself too, she thought. The prospect of having to do the housework had been bad enough when she'd had all day to do it, but fitting it in around her work at the soup kitchen and looking after her father made it seem almost impossible. But she knew she would have to do her best. Other women worked longer hours and looked after their families.

'I'll do as much as I can,' promised Naomi as she prepared to go to her own home.

After she'd gone, Ruth took a moment to compose herself and forced herself to seem cheerful before she went up to her father with a cup of tea and a dish of stew.

Chapter Thirty-Seven

That evening, Caroline walked with her father from Richmond Terrace to Primrose Lane to visit the Grimes. Even though it was cold and a fine drizzle had begun to fall her father had said that, considering the circumstances, they should go on foot rather than take the carriage. Caroline agreed. The last thing she wanted was her friend to think that she had come as some sort of lady bountiful to dispense charity.

Although she knew where her father's mill was, she'd never walked in the streets that surrounded it before. The houses here were much smaller than the ones on Richmond Terrace. The front doors opened directly onto the street and were separated by just one window, giving the street the appearance of having as many dwellings as possible crammed into it.

She waited nervously after her father had knocked on the Grimes' door. One or two of the neighbours were peeping out from behind their curtains to see who had come and she felt conspicuous in her coat and bonnet when every other woman she'd passed had a shawl clutched around her head and shoulders.

After a moment the door was opened and a young man looked surprised to see them.

'Hello, George,' her father greeted him. 'Can we come in?'

'Yes. Of course.' He stepped back to allow them inside and Caroline was surprised to find herself standing in a parlour without there being any hallway to receive them. The room was unlit and only sparsely furnished. The fireplace was empty and it looked like the family had moved out already. But then George opened a door at the far side of the room and light spilled out from beyond it.

'It's Mr Haworth from the mill,' he announced.

Caroline followed her father into the small kitchen where a fire was lit in the range and the Grimes family were sitting around a scrubbed wooden table. She only recognised Sally.

'No, don't get up,' her father told the older woman who must be Mrs Grimes. 'I've just come to offer my condolences and ask if there's anything I can do to help.'

'Thank you,' whispered the woman. She couldn't be much older than her own mother, thought Caroline, but the contrast was stunning. Mrs Grimes looked gaunt and her hair was already streaked with white at the temples. She seemed an old woman, well past her prime, even though her children were young. They stared at Caroline, wide-eyed, but said nothing, clearly overwhelmed by their loss.

'Please, sit down,' invited Sally, offering Mr Haworth the chair by the hearth.

'I won't,' he said. 'We won't intrude, but I wanted to come to tell you that I'll pay for the funeral and for a headstone.'

'That's generous,' Sally said.

'I wish I could do more. I wish I could have kept Jimmy on at the mill.'

'We've brought a few things,' Caroline told her friend as she placed the basket she was carrying on the table. 'I knew you wouldn't have had time to shop,' she added, hoping that Sally would accept the food. She knew how fiercely independent she was.

'Thank you,' Sally said. 'That's very thoughtful. Did you manage to get everything done at the soup kitchen?'

'We did. We missed you though,' admitted Caroline.

'I'll be there tomorrow.'

'But are you sure? Won't you be needed here?'

'We need the money,' Sally replied as she moved aside the cloth that covered the basket to look inside. 'We need it even more now that there's only me earning a wage.'

'I'm sure the committee will understand if you need to take some time off,' Mr Haworth told her.

'No. I'll come,' repeated Sally.

'Well...' Caroline saw her father rub his hands together. It was a habit that always betrayed his nerves and she felt awkward too, standing in the Grimes's kitchen unable to offer anything more than sympathy, food and the prospect of a gravestone. 'If there's anything else I can do, you only have to ask.'

Sally nodded. She looked weary, thought Caroline. She longed to step forward and hug her to try to relieve her grief, but she knew it would never do. It would embarrass them both to step so far outside their social spheres and all she could offer was a sympathetic look as she and her father turned to leave.

'I never realised just how small those houses are,' said Caroline as they walked back to Richmond Terrace. 'And there are so many children. Where do you think they all sleep?'

'They'll share a couple of beds,' her father said. 'They're used to it. And those houses are much better than some of the hovels around the town. They have fireplaces and a cold-water tap. Families are grateful to live there.'

Caroline thought he sounded defensive, as if he thought she was criticising the accommodation he provided for his workers. But she'd been shocked. The house had been much smaller than she had expected.

'Why weren't they sitting in the front room?' she asked him. 'It seemed odd that they had another room but they weren't using it and they were all crowded into that small kitchen.'

'They would need to light another fire,' her father explained. 'And the relief committee are rationing the amount of coal that families are given so they probably only have enough for the fire they use to cook.'

'It didn't have any furniture either,' Caroline replied.

'They'll have sold it. They have tickets for America.'

'Yes. Sally told me they were going. What a shame they'll have to go without Mr Grimes.'

'It's a tragedy,' agreed her father. 'And I feel partly responsible. If only I'd kept the mill open it would never have happened.'

'It wasn't your fault,' she told him again, seeing how much he was blaming himself. 'You couldn't keep running the mill without cotton.'

'The trouble is there is cotton,' he replied. 'But not at the prices I can afford. It's what I tried to explain to your grandfather. In a way I suppose he's to blame as well!'

Caroline was shocked by the anger in her father's voice. 'How is grandfather to blame?' she asked, not understanding his reasoning.

'He's been speculating on cotton,' he told her.

Caroline wasn't sure what he meant.

'I don't understand,' she admitted.

'He's been buying up cotton hoping to sell it on at a higher price. It's common practice amongst businessmen,' her father explained. 'When something is in short supply, the price increases because the people who want it are prepared to pay more. But the price of the cotton is now so high that no mill owner can afford it, so it's sitting in the warehouses and the mills are closing. That's why I was so angry on Sunday,' he told her. 'Your grandfather thinks I should buy the cotton and then sell on the finished cloth at a price that will cover my outlay. He doesn't believe me when I tell him that the markets are saturated. And of course, your mother believes him rather than me.'

'I'm sorry,' Caroline said. She could see how upset her father was. So upset that he was unburdening himself to her when he would never normally have shared anything about his business. 'Is there nothing you can do?' she asked.

'Nothing,' he replied as he put out an arm to prevent her from crossing the street until a brewery wagon had gone past. He stared after it. It belonged to the Duttons' brewery. 'What did you think of Thomas Dutton?' he asked her suddenly. 'He seems a nice young man.'

'He's all right, I suppose,' Caroline replied, surprised by the sudden change of topic.

'Would you consider marrying him?' her father asked.

'I don't know.' Caroline was shocked that her father was raising the topic now, as they were walking along. She'd thought it was her grandfather who was keen on the match and she'd been counting on her father to help her out of the difficult situation. She hadn't expected him to mention marriage himself.

'Of course I wouldn't insist if you weren't keen,' he said.

Caroline sensed he was holding something back. 'Would you like me to marry him?' she asked.

'It would help,' he replied.

'Help? I don't understand.' They were approaching the house on Richmond Terrace and Caroline slowed her pace. She wanted to know more about her father's thoughts on the matter before they reached the door where the conversation would be bound to stop.

'I'm sorry. I've said too much.' He increased his pace as if the matter was finished, but Caroline caught hold of his sleeve to pull him back.

'No,' she protested. 'If there's something I ought to know, then tell me.' Their eyes met under the light of a gas lamp and she saw that he regretted what he'd said. 'I'm not a child,' she reminded him. 'Don't treat me like one.'

He gazed at her for a moment. 'You're right,' he said at last. 'It must be your decision. I don't want to put pressure on you, but...'

'But what?' She'd stopped walking now, determined to have this out with her father before he could go inside and hide himself in his study. 'And don't tell me to ask my mother,' she warned him. 'Tell me.'

He hesitated and then began to speak. 'I'm in some financial difficulty,' he confessed. 'I wanted to keep the mill open for as long as I could because I thought things would get better, but it's cost me a lot and I'm on the verge of bankruptcy. Your mother has no idea, and neither does your grandfather. Promise me you won't tell them?' he pleaded, grasping hold of her hand. 'I know I shouldn't be burdening you with this, but perhaps it's better if you understand the situation before you make any decision.'

'Decision?' she asked.

'About whether to accept Thomas Dutton.'

'What does that have to do with you being short of money?' Caroline asked. Her father was talking in riddles. She wondered if he was quite well. Maybe she ought to get him inside out of the cold. The freezing air seemed to be muddling his brain.

'Mr Dutton has offered me a loan,' explained her father. 'His brewery hasn't been so badly affected by the lack of cotton as the mills have. And he's happy to wait for the repayments, unlike the bank who will set a time limit on when they want their money. He never said that the agreement was dependant on you marrying Thomas, but it was implied. The Duttons have money, but they desire social standing. It would raise them up in society if their son married the granddaughter of Sir Walter de Lacy.'

Caroline stared at her father in disbelief. Was he really asking her to marry Thomas Dutton to save him from financial ruin?

'I can't,' she managed to gasp, pulling her hand away from his. 'I can't,' she repeated as she hurried towards the door and rang the bell for Jenkins to let her in. Tears were choking her and her heart was racing with alarm. She didn't want to be forced to marry Thomas Dutton. It wasn't fair of her father to ask her.

The door opened and she almost fell into the hallway. She didn't even wait to stamp the snow from her boots but fled up the stairs still wearing her outdoor clothes, leaving a trail of melting ice in her wake. She didn't pause until she reached her room where she slammed the door behind her, grateful that Lottie had already lit a fire and the candles to welcome her.

It took her a moment to regain her breath and then she sat on the edge of the bed and cried without even taking off her bonnet. It was how Lottie found her when she tapped on the door and then came in unbidden.

'Get out!' shouted Caroline. 'Leave me alone!'

She pulled off her bonnet and threw it across the room at the maid. Lottie's shocked face immediately made her regret her outburst.

'I'm sorry,' she said as she watched Lottie pick it up.

'Miss Caroline, whatever's the matter?' she asked. 'Are you ill? Shall I call your mother?'

'No! Not that!' Caroline told her. 'Oh, Lottie. I've just had the most awful news,' she confessed.

'I can see that you're upset, Miss. What can I do?'

Caroline wished she could ask the maid to hold her in her arms and give her some comfort, but it wouldn't do at all. She knew she must pull herself together and stop making an exhibition of herself. It was most unseemly.

'Would you bring me a cup of tea?' she whimpered, not knowing what else to ask for.

'Of course, Miss.'

When Lottie had gone out, Caroline took off her coat and boots herself and set them near the fire to dry. She was so shocked by what her father had said that she didn't know what to think. Would he really try to persuade her to marry Thomas? And what would happen to them if she refused? It was inconceivable that he had got into debt. Although she was aware of how much poverty the cotton famine was causing, she thought it was only the poor who were really suffering. She knew her father had no income without the mill. It had just never occurred to her that he had lost money to the extent that he needed to borrow more. Did her mother know? She suspected not, and she felt angry that her father had chosen to burden her with the knowledge.

She went to the window and drew back a curtain to stare out into the night. She'd begun the evening by feeling sorry for Sally Grimes and her family, but she was ending it by feeling sorry for herself, even though she had to remind herself that her situation was nowhere near as bad as theirs. But the prospect of being locked into a loveless marriage, similar to her parents', filled her with dread. She wanted to love her future husband.

She wondered if she could run away with Freddy Fry and let her father take care of his own problems. But what sort of future would that be? The prospect of living in a house like the one she'd seen earlier wasn't appealing. She'd previously had the idea that she could raise him up if only he'd give her a sign that he wanted her. She'd imagined her father giving him a good job, providing them with a house. She'd thought she might make Freddy into a gentleman, but it wouldn't be possible now if there was no money, only debt. And it had only been a dream, she told herself. Freddy Fry charmed all the girls. Why should she think she was special?

Chapter Thirty-Eight

After Sally had thanked Mr Haworth for coming, and for his generosity, she walked slowly back to the kitchen. It was strange for her father not to be there. Part of her expected him to come whistling in at any moment. She was finding it almost impossible to believe that he was really gone. Even though she had seen him die and witnessed his body being taken away on a cart to be examined by the coroner it all seemed unreal, like a bad dream, and she struggled to accept that it had really happened.

Freddy Fry had brought her home to break the news to her mother. He'd asked if she wanted him to do it, but Sally had said no. It wasn't the sort of news that should come from a stranger.

Her mother had smiled when she went in and then her smile had faded when she saw Freddy covered in filth from the quarry. She'd stared at Sally in alarm as she'd realised that something was wrong.

'What is it? What's happened?' she'd asked anxiously as she'd got up from where she'd been packing their belongings into a big wooden crate for the journey to Massachusetts.

'It's Dad. He had an accident,' Sally began. She'd been trying to find the right words to break the news as she'd walked down from Shorrock's Delph. But there were no words that she could find that would help. There was nothing she could say that would make it easier for her mother to hear the dreadful news.

'Is he hurt?' her mother had asked in alarm.

'There was a rockfall. He was buried beneath it. They pulled him out and I held his hand and spoke to him, but…' Sally had hesitated, but the shock and horror on her mother's face revealed that she'd already guessed the truth. 'He died,' Sally said in an anguished whisper. 'Just all of a sudden. He was there and then he was gone. It was horrible.'

Her mother had gathered her in her arms and they'd sobbed together, each trying to comfort the other. Freddy must have slipped away unnoticed because when at last, they'd sat down at the table and Sally had managed to tell her mother the few details she knew, he was no longer there.

Sally made a pot of tea. Her mother had seemed calmer then, as if she knew it was something that she couldn't change and that she must accept it.

'Where is he now?' she'd asked and Sally had explained that her father had been taken to the infirmary.

Her mother had insisted that she must go to see him and she'd pulled her shawl around her shoulders.

'Stay here until the others come home,' she'd told Sally.

'Shall I tell them?' she'd asked.

Her mother had nodded. 'If you can,' she'd said, acknowledging how hard it would be. So, whilst they waited for their mother to return, it had fallen to Sally to tell first the twins, then her little sisters and finally George that their father wasn't coming home. Each of them in turn had stared at her with a blank expression as if they didn't comprehend her words. It had almost broken

Sally each time she had to repeat the news. The pain had stabbed at her heart over and over again as she'd seen the grief on her siblings' faces. Everything had changed for them in almost an instant and now she had no idea what they would do.

'It was good of Mr Haworth to come,' said her mother. 'Do you think we should have offered him a cup of tea? I hope he didn't think we were ungrateful.'

'I'm sure he didn't,' Sally soothed her. She'd been surprised and thankful for the mill owner's offer to pay for the funeral. She would have hated to see her father put in a pauper's grave, and it was nice that he would have a headstone, but she still felt an unaccountable anger towards their former employer. It was true that her father would have been safer in the mill and deep down she felt that Mr Haworth was at least partly to blame for what had happened. His offer, and the basket of provisions that Caroline had left on the table were welcome, but they seemed inadequate when they did nothing to right the terrible wrong that had befallen her family.

She looked around at her brothers and sisters – all sitting in silence, bewildered and afraid. It was past the twins' bedtime, and even though they looked worn out, she hated to suggest that they should be sent up the stairs to be alone in the small truckle bed they shared. Her sisters looked exhausted too and Ellen was visibly shivering, even though the room was not that cold. It was the shock, realised Sally. Ellen had been their father's favourite, his devoted little shadow. She'd adored him and Sally knew this was something from which she would never fully recover.

George was trying to be strong, but the tears kept welling in his eyes and his chin trembled. Their father had been their rock and Sally knew they must all feel as she felt, lost and cut adrift with no clear path to guide them in what they must do next.

The practicalities would need to be dealt with, of course. The inquest attended and then the funeral arranged. She had no idea how long that would take. And then there was the question that none of them had dared to ask. What about America? Were they still to go? Or would they need to remain in Blackburn now? And if they remained, how would they survive?

Her mother had said little since she'd come back from the infirmary. They had allowed her to see her husband's body, she'd said, but the visit had been short. The coroner wanted to make his examination.

'We can't bury him until it's done,' she'd said. 'Though I'm not sure what they hope to find. I hope they don't cut him open. I can't bear to think of them cutting him open.'

'I don't think they will,' Sally had reassured her, although she had no idea if they would. It wasn't something she knew anything about, and she simply wished they could bring her father home so that they could wash him and lay him out in the front room in his best clothes – the ones in which he'd planned to travel.

'Are you really going to the soup kitchen tomorrow?' her mother asked her, after a while.

'I think I must,' she replied. 'I'm the only one earning any money. We'll need to have something coming in.' She didn't know what the situation would be with the relief money. Hopefully they would still receive something, but she wasn't sure. It certainly wouldn't be as much as they had before, and they would pressure George to find work.

She just hoped they wouldn't be so callous as to suggest he work at the quarry.

–

The younger children had been put to bed and Sally and George were sitting with their mother, not knowing what to say when there was a knock on the door.

'I'll go,' George said. Sally followed him, wondering who was calling so late. She expected it to be another well-wisher, come to express their sympathy. Someone from the relief committee perhaps? Or even Mr Hutchinson, the mayor. But when George opened the door, she recognised Mr Grady, the American. He took off his hat to reveal his grave face.

'I've come to offer my heartfelt condolences on your loss,' he said. 'I was shocked to hear the news. May I step inside momentarily? Is your mother at home?'

'Come in,' Sally said.

'I hope I'm not intruding,' the American said when he reached the kitchen and stood, turning his hat in his hands. 'I know it's a difficult time. But there's some urgency in the matter.'

'Is it about the tickets?' asked Sally's mother.

'It is, indeed, ma'am.' Mr Grady was obviously ill at ease and it was clear to Sally that he hadn't brought them good news. 'Thing is,' he went on, 'the loss of your husband has changed matters. It's men we are mainly offering work to. Men who would be able to provide for any family they brought with them. As things stand…' His voice trailed off and he looked around at them appealingly. 'How would you manage on women's wages? How would you build your house?' he asked.

'I could do it,' George told him. Sally thought he sounded brave and determined, but Mr Grady shook his head.

'How old are you?' he asked.

'Fifteen,' George replied. Sally knew her brother liked to think of himself as a man. But he wasn't and wouldn't be for a few years yet.

'I'm sorry,' said Mr Grady, looking awkward. 'I have to ask for the tickets to be returned. There are other families waiting. And besides, I doubt you'd be ready to sail by next week,' he added.

Sally knew that was true. It had been worrying her. They couldn't go until her father had been decently buried and they couldn't make any arrangements for the funeral until the coroner had delivered his verdict.

She watched as her mother stood up and took down her purse from the shelf where she kept it. She opened it and took out the tickets, smoothing them flat before giving them to Mr Grady without saying a word. He mumbled his thanks, offered his best wishes once again and moved sideways towards the doorway, keen to leave. When Sally took him to the front door, he stepped out briskly and wished her goodnight before putting on his hat and hurrying off down the street.

'Someone will get good news this evening,' remarked her mother after Sally had pulled the bolt on the door and gone back to the kitchen. 'But I can't say I'm sorry that we're not going. How could I have left your father here with no one to tend his grave? It wouldn't have been right,' she said as she began to cry again. 'I wish I'd tried harder to persuade him not to go to that quarry. We would have managed, and he would be here with us now.'

Sally saw the disappointment on George's face. Like her, he had been counting down the days until they sailed.

'Perhaps it's for the best,' she said, although the thought of what they were to lose, added to the loss of her father, weighed heavily. The prospect of the roomy house, secure jobs and good pay had been helping her to cope through the difficult days at the soup kitchen and she'd counted each one off as she'd walked home in the afternoons. But now everything had been taken from them in a few short hours and she had no idea how they would manage to survive.

Chapter Thirty-Nine

Ruth was surprised when she saw Sally at the soup kitchen the next morning. She hadn't thought that she would come, and she found herself unsure what to say as she watched her friend hang up her shawl and roll back her sleeves to begin work.

'I'm sorry,' she told Sally after a few moments of awkward silence. Sally nodded. 'I didn't think you would come,' she added. 'You didn't need to. We can manage.'

'But my family can't,' Sally replied bluntly. 'My wage is all we have now, unless we can still get some relief.'

Ruth nodded. 'I understand,' she said, thinking that the need to support their families was something they had in common.

She was saved from having to say more by Freddy Fry, who, after dumping a heavy bag of coal next to the furnace, came across to speak to them.

'How are you?' he asked Sally.

'Middling,' she replied as she began to peel a potato.

'Let me know if there's owt I can do,' he said. The sympathy was clear in his eyes and he looked at Sally with such concern that Ruth felt a stab of jealousy. It took her by surprise.

He was such a gentleman, which wasn't what she'd expected when she'd first met him. She realised now that he'd only shouted at her about Caroline's skirt being on fire because he'd been upset and concerned. He'd never raised his voice again and he was always ready to help her in any way he could, just as he had the night she'd fetched the doctor for her father. She was still grateful to him for that. She'd never expected a working man to be so caring.

Sally managed to smile at Freddy, but her face was full of sorrow. Her usual demeanour when he was around was absent. This morning, she responded to him as a true friend and the usual teasing and banter was forgotten as he repeated that whatever she needed, she only had to ask him.

'Remember that goes for you too,' he said to Ruth as he turned his blue gaze on her. 'I know how hard things are for you as well – with your father.'

'Thank you,' she said, feeling herself blush.

She watched as he went back to shovel the coal. He was so kind and considerate, and although she would never join in with the giggling and nudging of the mill girls every time he walked by, she had grown to like him very much.

She was glad that the morning was busy and that she had a lot to do. The other mill girls came across to hug Sally and offer their sympathy, and even Caroline Haworth seemed to find the right words to say to her new friend. Sally seemed grateful and Ruth hoped that she knew she cared as well, even if she wasn't as good at expressing it.

When the doors opened for dinner the men who trooped in seemed downcast, as if the bad news of the previous day was preying on their minds. They were all without work and as Ruth went around the tables, she heard them discussing the stone quarry.

'I'll not accept work up there. It's too dangerous,' she heard one man say.

'Aye. But if it's offered and tha refuses, they'll not give thee tickets for this soup,' replied another and a gloomy silence fell as if they all knew they were trapped in a situation that was not of their own making and from which there was no chance of escape.

At the end of the day, Ruth walked home counting her blessings. Yesterday's events had made her reassess her own situation. She'd been so worried about her father being ill that she'd felt envious of both Sally and Caroline for having fathers who were young and healthy, but the accident at the stone quarry had made her realise that life was precarious and anyone could be struck down in a moment.

Her father had seemed a little better when she'd taken him a cup of tea early that morning. He had more use of his leg and had managed to use the chamber pot without help.

When she went in, she was pleased to hear his voice coming from the kitchen.

'He insisted on coming down,' her sister explained. 'I didn't want him to, but he took no notice and came down one step at a time. I was terrified he would fall.'

'There's no need to talk about me like I'm not here,' their father said. His voice still sounded strained and slightly slurred, but it was easier to understand him now and Ruth gave thanks for the improvement. He was alive. He was getting better. And she felt a glimmer of hope that he might be able to work again and that maybe he could pay off his debts and they wouldn't have to worry about losing the house after all.

She went across to where he was sitting in his chair by the fire and kissed him. 'It's good to see you up and about,' she told him.

'I'll send Amos round to help him get back upstairs,' promised her sister as she prepared to leave with Hope and Nora. 'We don't want any accidents.'

'Thank you.' Ruth appreciated what her sister was doing now that Agatha was no longer here to cook for them. She felt a pang of guilt about Agatha. The maid had been devastated when Ruth had told her that they would have to let her go. She'd thought for a moment that Agatha was going to offer to come for no wages, but she would never have allowed it.

'My father will give you a very good reference,' she'd said. 'I'm sure someone will be glad to employ you.' She hoped it was true. She hadn't heard that Agatha had found a new job and Ruth worried that she was holding on, hoping to come back when things improved. It would be a long time before they could afford to pay a maid again.

The hotpot her sister had made smelt delicious. When Ruth began to spoon it onto the plates, she saw it contained far more meat than she'd been able to afford to buy and she wondered if her sister was hoping she wouldn't notice that she was subsidising their food supplies. But then, she had a responsibility towards their father too, and Dr Skaife had said that a good nutritious diet would help him in his convalescence.

She took a dish and a spoon to her father and he made a good attempt at feeding himself.

'I'm getting feeling back,' he told her. 'My arm seems more like my own again. I'll be back at work in no time.'

'There's plenty of time for that,' she replied. 'The soup kitchen is running well without you.'

'Are you telling me I'm not needed?' He looked a little crestfallen.

'Of course you're needed. But we're coping,' she said in an attempt to soothe him. 'Besides, you need to concentrate on getting strong so you can open the shop again,' she told him.

'I hope I'll be able to,' he said. 'I need to set things right. I've made such a mess of it all, putting us into debt like I have. I shouldn't have done it,' he told her. 'But like a fool I was tempted. With every pound I borrowed I told myself that I could pay it back once this crisis was over. I never thought it would go on for so long or that things would get so bad. I expected the government to step in and send gunships to ensure the cotton left the ports. I never expected them to abandon us like this.'

Ruth put aside her own meal to go to him as she saw tears roll down his cheeks. She hated to see him cry. He'd always been so strong for her and now his fears made her afraid, even though she knew she had to be strong for him. How quickly their roles had been reversed, she thought, as she tried to comfort him. The cared for had become the carer, and she suspected that their relationship would never return to what it had been before. It was up to her to be the strong one now.

'Things will get better,' she told him. 'But you mustn't take on all the worry yourself in future. You must let me help. You must show me how to keep the accounts rather than just having me serve customers in the shop. I can do it. I'm sure I can. I'm proving myself at the soup kitchen,' she reminded him.

He gazed up at her lovingly. 'I never wanted to trouble you,' he said.

'It would never have been a trouble,' she said, sitting down again. 'And I'm sure I could understand the account books. Someone will have to take over from you eventually,' she reminded him.

It was something they'd never spoken of before. Ruth didn't think that either of them had really considered it until now. Her father had always been there and as she'd grown from a child into a woman, she'd never thought to question it. But his illness had made her realise that he wouldn't be with her for ever, and the thought frightened her. She had no idea how she would cope without him. But working at the soup kitchen was opening her eyes. It was the first time she'd been given any real responsibility and she was enjoying it now that she'd realised she was capable of doing the job. And although she wished that the crisis would end and she could return to working in the shop, Ruth knew that she wouldn't be content to simply serve customers in the future. For her father's sake as well as her own, she needed to learn everything there was to know about the business, because the day would surely come when she had to take it over – because it was either that or lose her home and maybe have to rely on the charity of her sisters and brothers-in-law. Ruth hated that idea. The soup kitchen had given her a taste of independence and she was determined to hang on to it.

It wasn't long before there was a knock on the door and Amos came in. Ruth was glad to see him. She knew she would have struggled to get her father back up the steep stairs. But Amos put his arm under her father's shoulders and before long he was safely back in his bed.

'How are you coping?' Amos asked her when they were back in the kitchen. 'You don't have to go to that soup kitchen, you know,' he told her. 'We'll all pull together and manage somehow. We'll not see you go hungry.'

'I can manage it,' Ruth told him. She didn't say that she was beginning to enjoy it. She didn't want Amos to think that she was choosing the easy option and leaving the nursing to Naomi. 'It brings in some much-needed money,' she reminded him, even though they both knew it was barely enough to feed her and her father.

'I thought I might go to talk to them at the bank, with your father's permission,' said Amos. 'Given the situation, I'm hoping they'll agree not to call in his loan just yet.'

'I'll come with you,' Ruth told him. Her brother-in-law looked doubtful.

'There's no need,' he said. 'If your father signs a letter to say I'm his representative, I'm sure they'll talk to me.'

'I want to come,' she said. 'I want to know how bad things are and how much we owe. I want to be sure that we can open the shop again and that we won't lose the business.'

Amos seemed surprised. 'I can take care of it,' he insisted. 'There's no need for you to worry.'

'It's not just a matter of worrying, although I am worried,' she admitted. 'But I've just been talking to Pa about it and I've told him that I want him to show me the account books and explain them to me. I want to understand the business,' she went on. 'I want to be able to help him properly and take some of the burden from him.'

'But you'll be getting married before long,' argued Amos. 'Then you'll move out. So what would be the point?'

'I may not marry,' she replied.

'Of course you will.' He dismissed her argument.

'But what would happen to the sweet shop then?' she asked.

'I don't know,' Amos admitted. 'I've no interest in it, and I doubt Deborah and her husband would want it. I suppose it would be sold once your father retires, or when he…' He left the word unspoken.

'And what would happen to me then, if I wasn't married?' asked Ruth. It was all very well everyone presuming she would marry, but she had realised that she needed to make plans in case she didn't.

'If you didn't marry you could come to live with us,' offered Amos.

Ruth saw that the idea of her taking over the confectionery business was something Amos would never understand, and yet it made her even more determined to make plans to do it.

'I will come to the bank with you,' she told him. 'We can go after the soup kitchen is finished for the day.'

He nodded. 'I'll ask for an hour off work,' he said. 'I'm sure Mr Tiplady will understand if I promise to make up the lost time later. Maybe on Friday?' he asked.

'Yes,' replied Ruth. 'Come and call for me before you go,' she said, hoping that he wouldn't forget, or change his mind, and go alone after all.

Chapter Forty

When Caroline arrived home from the soup kitchen the following afternoon, she found that her mother had a visitor. Mrs Dutton was sitting in the parlour with a cup and saucer on the small table at her elbow. She looked uncomfortable, but smiled when she saw Caroline, as if she expected her to welcome the encounter.

Caroline felt irritated. All she wanted to do was go upstairs to wash herself and change out of the clothes she was wearing. They stank of vegetables and she knew that she looked a mess, with her hair in lank strands and her nails in need of scrubbing. She'd been astonished when her mother had called her in from the hallway rather than waiting until she had made herself presentable. She was in no fit state to take tea with a visitor.

'Mrs Dutton has come to talk to you,' announced her mother. She seemed relieved that Caroline had come home and Caroline suspected that she was finding it a challenge to entertain the brewery owner's wife who was not a part of her usual social circle.

'You must excuse my appearance,' said Caroline. 'I've been helping at the soup kitchen.'

'Yes. Thomas told me that you'd talked about it. I think it's admirable,' announced Mrs Dutton. It wasn't the response Caroline had been hoping for. The only way she could see out of this marriage proposal was if the Duttons decided that she wasn't a suitable match for their son after all.

'My daughter takes her philanthropic duties very seriously,' replied Caroline's mother. 'It pleases her father. He's always been keen to help the poor.'

Caroline sat down and accepted the cup of tea that Lottie poured for her. She was tired and thirsty and would have preferred to lie down for half an hour rather than become the object of a conversation between her mother and Mrs Dutton. She even wondered if her mother had invited Mrs Dutton to call at this particular time so that she would see her in her work clothes, looking like a downstairs maid rather than a lady. Even Lottie was better dressed than she was and when she exchanged a glance with her maid, she saw that Lottie was finding the situation quite amusing.

'Whatever would Thomas say if he could see Caroline now?' asked her mother with forced laughter. But it was a direct challenge to Mrs Dutton. Caroline despaired. It was impossible to know what her mother was up to. She'd seemed keen on the marriage when her grandfather had suggested it, but now Caroline wondered if her father had spoken out in favour of it and she'd changed her mind simply to spite him. It was just the sort of thing she would do.

'I'm sure he would think that Caroline looks like she's been working very hard,' replied Mrs Dutton. It wasn't the approval that either Caroline or her mother wanted.

'Is Father not home yet?' Caroline asked, putting down her empty cup and nodding to Lottie to refill it. She knew he would be furious if he came in and saw her sitting with Mrs Dutton, unwashed and in her work clothes.

‘He’s gone off somewhere,’ said her mother, sounding irritable. ‘I expected him back by now.’

So that was it, thought Caroline. Her father was supposed to be here to witness this. Her mother wanted to provoke yet another argument.

‘I think he said he had a meeting regarding re-opening the mill,’ Caroline told her, knowing that he had planned to speak to Mr Dutton about the prospect of a loan.

‘Really?’ said her mother. ‘How strange that he should have told you that.’

She turned to Mrs Dutton. ‘Of course I take no interest in the mill,’ she told her. ‘It keeps my husband amused, but I wasn’t brought up to associate myself with trade.’

The insult was clear, although Caroline wasn’t sure if it was intended. Her mother was not known for her tact. She saw Mrs Dutton recoil as if wounded. Her husband had risen from being an ordinary working man to being a brewery owner, and although they moved amongst the higher classes now, her mother’s words emphasised the social gap between the two women.

‘My mother said you wanted to talk to me,’ Caroline said, trying to defuse the situation. She was angry with her mother now and beginning to feel sorry for Mrs Dutton.

‘Yes. I did. Thomas very much enjoyed meeting you at lunch last Sunday. He wondered if he might meet with you again. My husband and I would like to invite you to take tea with us at Yew Tree House on Saturday afternoon.’ Mrs Dutton’s smile had genuine warmth, and it was clear that she believed Caroline was attracted to Thomas.

Caroline didn’t reply immediately. She wondered how she could politely refuse the invitation without giving offense.

'Shall we say three o' clock?' persisted Mrs Dutton.

'I would still be working at that time,' replied Caroline, thankful for a genuine reason to turn the woman down.

'I didn't realise you worked at the soup kitchen on Saturdays,' Mrs Dutton said, sounding disappointed that her plan had been thwarted.

'I work there every day. It's the least I can do to help during this crisis,' Caroline told her. 'Times are hard for so many people.'

'They are,' agreed Mrs Dutton. 'Perhaps five would suit you better?' she went on, clearly not intending to accept a refusal.

Caroline looked at her mother, hoping that she might provide a reason to put the visit off, but she seemed bored with her game now and with no other option than to offend Mrs Dutton, which she would have hated to do, Caroline reluctantly agreed to go, even though she realised that turning up for tea on Saturday would be as good as telling Thomas that she was agreeing to a marriage. It was not what she had intended.

At least her father would be pleased, thought Caroline when Mrs Dutton had gone and she was lying in the warm bath, which Lottie had prepared for her. Hopefully he would get his loan. But if she could just hold out until the cotton situation improved, maybe he would be able to pay back the Duttons without her having to go through with the marriage. It was a hope that she decided to cling to.

Her father smiled warmly when she went down, dressed in pink silk with her hair in ringlets thanks to Lottie's ministrations.

'You look nice,' he complimented her.

'Better than she looked earlier when Mrs Dutton came to call,' remarked her mother.

'Mrs Dutton?' He sounded alarmed at the news.

'Yes. She was here when Caroline came in from that soup kitchen, looking like a common washer woman.'

Her mother delighted in telling him every detail until she reached the part where Mrs Dutton had invited her to tea. She left it to Caroline to tell her father about that.

'So, you're invited to Yew Tree House?' he asked after dinner, when Caroline's mother had retreated to her room.

'Yes. Although I think mother was trying to scupper it,' she told him. 'I think she may have changed her mind about the Duttons.'

'Only to spite me,' her father confirmed. 'I ought to have known that, as soon as I told her I thought it was a good idea, she would decide it wasn't what she wanted after all.'

'Did you tell her why you thought it was a good idea?' Caroline challenged her father. He frowned. She'd known that he wouldn't have. He hated to discuss his money troubles with her mother, because her mother never seemed to believe him and took the view that when he said he couldn't afford things, such as a country house, he was only saying it to make her miserable.

'Did Mr Dutton agree to the loan?' persisted Caroline when he didn't answer. She was becoming increasingly angry that neither of her parents seemed inclined to take her wishes into consideration.

'Not yet. I think he's waiting until an engagement is announced. But we're moving towards that, aren't we? You won't let me down, will you, Caroline? With a loan I can buy some cotton to tide me over until I can make arrangements to ship in cotton from India. It will provide work and I'll be able to open the mill again.' He sounded hopeful. 'So many families are relying on me,' he said.

Like the Grimes', thought Caroline. If there had been work at the mill, then Jimmy Grimes would still be alive. She remembered Sally's sad face and the way her friend had worked all day without a word or a smile. She was a shell of her former self. Caroline would hate the same thing to happen to anyone else who had been employed at Haworth's. And it was in her power to prevent it. But it would mean a huge sacrifice.

'Of course, I won't insist if you're set against it,' her father conceded. 'But you could do a lot worse than Thomas Dutton. He's a decent lad and his family are rising in the world. They have money. You'd be comfortably off.'

Caroline was about to protest that she barely knew him, let alone loved him, but she kept her thoughts to herself. Her own parents were a poor example of a love match and they would both point out its dangers to her. And if there was one thing that they agreed on it was advising her that security and money were the things she ought to be seeking.

Perhaps they were right, mused Caroline. She thought of Freddy Fry again. Perhaps, if the mill re-opened, she could persuade her father to take Freddy on and allow him to rise through the ranks to mill manager or something similar, so that a marriage to him might just be possible.

'I would like to help you,' Caroline told her father. 'If there was another way.'

'There is no other way,' he replied. 'And if I do have to be in debt, it's better to be in debt to family than the bank. Mr Dutton is very understanding and has assured me he will put no pressure on me to repay the loan until I am able.'

Caroline sighed. She was caught in a trap and could see no way out of it.

Chapter Forty-One

The inquest into the death of Jimmy Grimes was held on the Friday following his death on the Monday. It was held in the courthouse on King Street. Sally and her family attended and sat on the benches, which had been reserved for them, at the front of the court.

Sally watched as the twelve men of the jury were sworn in one by one. She was familiar with most of them and waited anxiously until they had taken their seats and the inquiry began. Several men who had been working at the quarry that day were called to give evidence and they were asked about the rockfall.

'There were ten quarrymen engaged in filling the wagons with stone that morning,' explained the foreman of the quarry, John Spencer. 'About fifteen minutes past ten a loud rumbling noise was heard and the place suddenly darkened with a thick cloud. One of the men shouted an alarm, and the other workers threw down their tools and quickly fled, panic-stricken, in different directions. Almost immediately, five or six tonnes of limestone came sliding and crashing down. Seven men escaped, one of whom was partially injured by the falling debris, but two were buried in the mass of earth. A number of men at once set to work to recover those who were buried. Thomas Connolly was found after a search. He was quite dead. Some time later, with the help of men who had come up from Yates's Foundry, James Grimes was found. He presented a ghastly appearance, being torn and bruised all over. He was still alive when he was pulled out, but died within a few minutes.'

Every word tore at Sally's heart and beside her, her mother sobbed at the description of what had happened. Sally held her hand and wished that it was all over and that they didn't have to hear any more about it. Her father was dead, and no matter how the blame was apportioned it would not bring him back.

Next another of the quarrymen was called to give evidence. 'We had no suspicion of it coming,' he said. 'I believe it was melting snow that caused the accident. It would appear that the freezing and thawing caused the earth to become loosened.'

Next Mr Shorrock himself was called. 'I was informed shortly after half past ten that there had been a slip at the quarry,' he said. 'I went up to find two men had been buried and that both had been taken away dead. I have no doubt that it was the weather we have endured recently that caused this terrible accident.'

After not much deliberation, the jury agreed that no one was to blame, even though some of the workers, particularly those who had been mill hands, maintained that Mr Shorrock was responsible and ought to go to prison for the deaths. Sally had some sympathy with their anger. She was angry too, but she realised that hatred and blame would achieve nothing. All she wanted was to take her mother home where they could make arrangements for her father's burial.

The coroner gave a verdict of accidental death and Sally held her mother upright as she almost collapsed. She was weakened by hunger, thought Sally. She'd eaten hardly anything all week, insisting that the scraps of bread Ruth had given Sally to bring home should go to the children.

'Let's get her home,' she said to George as they came down the steps outside the courthouse.

'Sally!' She heard her name being called and turned to see Mr Haworth approaching her. 'Is your mother all right?' he asked, looking concerned.

Sally almost snapped back that of course she wasn't. What did he expect? But she managed to reply politely.

'She's upset, that's all. She'll be better when we get her home.'

Sally saw Mr Haworth take in the faces of her brothers and sisters who were staring at him.

'Have you eaten today?' he asked, and her little sisters and the twins all shook their heads.

'We're still waiting for the relief committee to decide our entitlement,' Sally told him.

'Come to the soup kitchen,' he said. For a moment Sally thought he was ordering her back to work. 'All of you,' he added. 'You can eat there.'

'We've no tickets,' Sally told him.

'Tickets be damned!' he replied. 'I'll sort it out if anyone makes an objection. Come just before twelve. I'll tell Freddy Fry to look out for you and let you in ahead of the queue.'

'Thank you,' said Sally, feeling immensely grateful to the mill owner.

'It's the least I can do. I'm so very sorry about your husband, Mrs Grimes,' he said to her mother who was slowly recovering her wits. 'He was a good worker, and I had a lot of respect for him. I wish there was more I could do for you.'

–

At fifteen minutes before noon, Sally and her family arrived at the door of the foundry on Cleaver Street. There was already a queue and Sally wasn't sure how they would get past it, even if Mr Haworth had said they should go in first, so they stood at the end of the line, waiting patiently and hoping that the mill owner would be as good as his word and get them something to eat. The aroma of the soup was wafting down the street and it smelt appetising.

When she heard Freddy call her name urgently, it was a moment before she saw him at a smaller doorway further down the street.

'Sally! Come in this way!' he called.

'Where are they going? That's not fair!' she heard people mutter as she and her family hurried to where Freddy was standing.

He ushered them in. 'Quickly!' he warned as the men and women who had followed them tried to get in behind them. He slammed the door shut in their faces and Sally heard them banging on it with their fists and shouting their displeasure. She felt guilty as she and her family were taken through two or three empty rooms and into the familiar space where she worked.

'Over here,' said Freddy. 'This table's been reserved for you. Sit down,' he urged. 'We'll bring it to you.'

Sally looked round and saw Caroline Haworth coming to them with a tray of bowls filled to the brim with soup. She was followed by Ruth Hodgson with a platter piled high with bread and a jug of tea.

'Are you sure this is all right?' Sally asked Ruth anxiously. 'I don't want there to be trouble if the tickets don't match what's been handed out.'

Ruth put a hand on her shoulder. 'You know there's always extra,' she said. 'You and your family deserve some kindness today, and besides, you've earned it with all the help you've given me. I'd never have coped here without you.'

Sally's eyes filled with tears as she looked up at her friend. 'Thank you,' she said. She knew that, at first, she'd dismissed Ruth as being useless and had resented having to show her what needed to be done. But Ruth was a quick learner and had soon begun to suggest ways that the work could be made easier by better organisation. Even so, Sally was grateful that Ruth had expressed her appreciation.

'I think some of the people waiting are annoyed at the queue-jumping,' Sally admitted as they heard shouting from outside. She followed Ruth's gaze towards the door where Freddy Fry was waiting to pull back the bolt.

'Freddy will sort out anyone who says a word against you,' Ruth replied.

Sally smiled at the thought of Freddy being her saviour as she turned her attention to the twins, handing out the bread and warning them to blow on the soup because it was hot. They were ravenously hungry, but she didn't want them to burn their tongues.

Chapter Forty-Two

That afternoon, when everything had been left in good order at Cleaver Street, Ruth hurried home to change her clothes. Her brother-in-law Amos had made an appointment to see the bank manager, Mr Catterall, at four o' clock and she wanted to make a good impression.

Her sister was sitting with her father, and her two nieces were playing quietly at the table with their dolls.

'You're not going like that, are you?' asked Naomi, looking at her stained clothes.

'Of course not. I'm getting washed and changed,' Ruth said, filling a basin with hot water to take to her bedroom.

Upstairs she hung her soup kitchen clothes to air and quickly washed herself down to get rid of the pervading smell of the cabbages. Then she put on her Sunday best clothes, arranged her wayward hair into a neat bun and went back down to the kitchen where Amos had arrived to wait for her.

Her father smiled up at her. It was still a crooked smile, but he was looking more like himself with every day that passed.

'What are you up to?' he asked when he saw Ruth putting her hat on. 'Where are you going?'

'I'm going with Amos to see the bank manager,' she reminded him. He was still forgetful.

'We're going to see what can be done, so that we can keep living here.'

Ruth saw her father's face fall into a look of despair. 'I'm sorry,' he said. 'I've made such a mess of everything. I'd be better off dead rather than being a burden to you all like this.'

'Don't be silly. That's nonsense,' Ruth told him. 'We just want to help, that's all.'

He nodded morosely. 'I'm thankful for it,' he said.

Ruth walked with Amos to King William Street, where her father had an account with the Manchester and County Bank. It was a building she'd passed many times, but she'd never been inside. The heavy oak doors had always seemed imposing, and she'd always imagined that what went on behind them was slightly secretive and not a matter she should ask about. So, it was with some trepidation that she stepped inside when Amos held the door open for her.

She was met with the feel of a thick doormat beneath her feet, inviting her to wipe her boots, and a refined silence, broken only by the scratching of pens and the ticking of a large grandfather clock that stood in the hallway. A clerk got up from his stool and came across to greet them. Amos explained they had an appointment, and after a moment they were shown through another door and into an office with a thick rug on the floor and a large fire burning in the grate. Sitting behind the oak desk was Mr Catterall, the bank manager. He was neatly dressed in a dark jacket and grey waistcoat and had wire-rimmed glasses perched on the end of his nose, which he took off and dropped onto the open ledger set in front of him as he invited them to be seated.

'Mr Smith, Miss Hodgson,' he greeted them. 'How may I help you?'

Ruth watched as Amos withdrew the letter from an inside pocket and handed it to him.

'My father-in-law has appointed me to overlook his affairs,' he explained, telling Mr Catterall about Ruth's father's illness and apologising for the poor handwriting on the letter. 'He has signed it,' he explained, 'although it may not closely match his usual signature as he still has some weakness in his hand.'

Mr Catterall replaced his spectacles and studied the letter for a moment then nodded. 'That all seems to be in order,' he said. 'I have Mr Hodgson's account here.' He pointed to the ledger in front of him. 'He is a long-standing and valued customer of the bank. But I'm not sure if you are aware, he has recently taken out a substantial loan.'

'He has told me that he owes money to the bank,' Amos agreed. 'That's why we're here. We've come to ask if the loan can be extended until Mr Hodgson is recovered from his illness and is in a better position to repay it.'

Ruth twisted her fingers together in her lap as the bank manager studied the account again. She wished that she understood it all more clearly. She wished she knew what all the figures neatly written in the endless columns really meant.

'I see that the premises on Queen Victoria Street are offered as collateral for the loan,' said Mr Catterall. 'I take it that this is the confectionery shop, which is currently closed?'

'It is,' confirmed Amos. 'But it is also the home of Mr Hodgson and Miss Hodgson. If you were to call in the loan, then they would be without a place to live.'

Mr Catterall raised an eyebrow as he met Amos's appealing expression. 'This is something Mr Hodgson was aware of when he asked for the money,' he reminded him.

'I understand that,' replied Amos. 'But these are desperate times.'

'And we are a bank, not a relief committee,' Mr Catterall reminded him.

Ruth felt despair creep through her. Mr Catterall looked unconcerned about her plight and she thought he was on the verge of asking for the money there and then.

'How much does he owe exactly?' she asked.

Mr Catterall seemed surprised that she had spoken, let alone asked a question.

'Five hundred pounds,' he replied after a moment. 'It's a lot of money,' he added.

'Yes,' Ruth agreed. It was far more than she had imagined. More than her father had admitted to them, and it made her wonder how long he'd been subsidising their shop with borrowed money.

'I think we were hasty to lend so much,' admitted Mr Catterall. 'But your father has been a client of this bank since our opening and has always been in credit before. I thought it was worth the risk, especially with the value of the premises to fall back on, but times have become much more difficult with the lack of cotton imports, and now, added to that, your father's illness…' He paused and turned back to Amos. 'What are the chances of him being well enough to open his shop again? Health wise?' he asked. 'You need to be honest with me, Mr Smith.'

'I don't know,' admitted Amos, looking gloomy.

'If there is no prospect of the shop re-opening then there is no prospect of this loan ever being repaid,' Mr Catterall went on. 'It would be better for the bank to call in the money now before more interest accumulates and the sale of the assets will cover the debt, rather than let it mount up even further. Could your father-in-law and Miss Hodgson live with you on the sale of Mr Hodgson's property?' he asked.

'But the shop will reopen!' Ruth protested. Both men stared at her in surprise. 'Even if my father is still unwell, I will reopen the business as soon as it becomes viable,' she told them. 'I will make sure the money is repaid. Every penny!'

It was a huge promise, and not one that she was sure she could keep. At a few shillings a week it would take her a lifetime to pay back what her father had borrowed. But she was determined that she would do it if she could. She would rather try to keep the shop open than be forced to fall back on the charity of her sister and brother-in-law.

Mr Catterall seemed wrong-footed by her declaration.

'Do you think that's possible?' he asked, appealing to Amos.

'I don't know,' he admitted. 'I'm not familiar with the running of the confectionery business.'

'I've worked there since I left school,' Ruth told them. She was surprised at how confident she made herself sound. Working at the soup kitchen had changed her, she realised. It had given her the ability to speak out without revealing that she was quaking with fear inside. It was a skill she'd had to learn quickly to do her father's job and it was a skill that she hoped would benefit her now. 'I'm familiar with the business,' she told the bank manager. 'If you will look kindly on me and my father and not call in the loan just yet then I'm sure that the money will be paid once this crisis is over and the mills get back to work.'

Mr Catterall looked unsure, but Ruth could see that he was considering it, and that gave her hope.

'You said yourself that my father has been a valued customer of the bank,' she reminded him. 'I hope that in the future you will say the same of me.'

'Do I take it that you intend to take over your father's business interests?' asked Mr Catterall. He sounded curious and seemed to take better notice of her, speaking directly to her now, rather than to Amos.

'I do. I know my father has appointed my brother-in-law as his representative, but I think that was because he was afraid you might not take me seriously.'

'You are very young,' Mr Catterall replied. 'But you aren't the first businesswoman the bank has dealt with, even though it's more usual for a widow to take over her husband's affairs.'

He looked down at the ledger in front of him again and was silent for a time that seemed to Ruth an eternity.

'It's a difficult decision,' he admitted at last. 'But the value of the property is there. You do understand that I would be forced to call in the loan if you missed any payments?' he asked her.

'I do.' Ruth nodded, wondering if she could really afford to repay the bank from her soup kitchen wages. She wasn't even sure how much would be needed.

'You seem a keen young woman, and I would like to help you and Mr Hodgson,' said Mr Catterall. 'Perhaps I could agree to accept just the interest payments until the shop is open again so long as that is no longer than, say, six months?'

'That sounds a very good compromise,' Ruth replied with a smile. She was sure she could manage that. If not, she would try again to persuade the mayor that she ought to be paid her father's full wage under the circumstances.

Mr Catterall nodded and closed the ledger. 'The bank will write to your father with the new terms and conditions,' he said. 'If they are agreeable and he signs them, then the loan will be extended.'

'Thank you,' breathed Ruth. It was a relief to know that she could sleep in her own bed for a while longer.

'You were quite impressive in there,' remarked Amos when they were back on the street. 'I saw a side of you I never knew existed.'

Ruth nodded. She felt shy again. The euphoria that she'd felt as the bank manager shook her hand had quickly subsided, leaving her feeling exhausted.

'We got the result we needed. Pa will be relieved,' she said.

'And do you really intend to take over the shop?' he asked.

'Yes,' Ruth replied. 'When it reopens.' She was certain now that it was the right thing to do – the thing that she wanted to do.

Chapter Forty-Three

The thaw continued into the following week and early in the afternoon on Wednesday, when Sally and her family gathered at the parish church to watch her father being laid to rest, the earth was wet and soft beneath their cold feet. A westerly wind stirred the trees that grew around the edges of the graveyard and even though the temperatures had risen, both Sally and her mother shivered uncontrollably as the vicar recited the solemn words of the burial service.

It was the day they should have been leaving Blackburn to travel to America. Sally looked up from the dark coffin, paid for by Mr Haworth, and stared at the leaden grey sky. She'd always pictured America as a place bathed in sunshine with blue skies and bird song. Whether it was true, she would never know now. Some other family had caught the boat train to Liverpool and before nightfall they would be aboard the *Alexander Marshall* ready to sail the next day. She thought that the disappointment lay even heavier on her brother, George. Despite his grief he was restless and frustrated by inactivity. He had been offered work at the stone quarry, but their mother had pleaded with him not to go, and the relief committee had been compassionate and not cut their money. Yet, George was keen to work. Like their father he hated to be idle or take handouts.

Sally watched as her mother grasped a handful of earth and dropped it onto the coffin lid with a thud, before gasping back tears as she brushed the clinging mud from her bare hands. Sally's sisters and the twins stood at the edge of the grave and looked on in disbelief as if it was incomprehensible to them that their father was lying in the deep hole. Sally found it hard to believe too. The day was like a dream and despite all the embraces and warm words from friends and well-wishers, none of it seemed real.

When the service was over, Sally led her family away from the graveside. The gravediggers were waiting with their spades to fill in the earth and she couldn't bear to watch. They were to go to the soup kitchen again. Mr Haworth had arranged for cups of tea and ham sandwiches to be provided for all the mourners, and hunger, combined with worklessness, had ensured a large turnout amongst their friends and neighbours.

Sally had been moved to see her new friends, Ruth and Caroline sitting alongside the mill girls in church. Ruth in her Sunday best and Caroline dressed in black from head to toe – the only one present who could afford to wear funeral clothes during such desperate times. She thought that she must be sure to thank them for coming when she got the chance.

The tables in the soup kitchen had been set with clean white cloths and had chairs arranged around them. In each place there was a plate and a cup and saucer. They didn't all match and Sally thought that they must have been brought from people's homes – their best china, much nicer than the sturdy mugs and bowls that were in usual service.

Mr Haworth had taken responsibility for all the arrangements, and it was he who guided Sally's mother to the top table, saw her seated and offered her tea and sandwiches. Sally organised her brothers and sisters and then sat down herself. The tea was hot and strong and there was sugar provided to sweeten it. The drink warmed her through after the chill of the graveyard and she accepted one of the sandwiches, although she didn't feel particularly hungry.

When she bit into it, the taste of the fresh white bread, the butter and the thinly sliced ham made her recall better days when such food had been plentiful. They had eaten sandwiches and cake for their tea on most Sundays, all the family sitting around the little table in the front parlour, enjoying their day's holiday. Sally couldn't help but think how much her father would have enjoyed sitting with them now. The thought provoked fresh tears, and she put the half-eaten sandwich down on her plate. At least the younger ones were enjoying the meal, she thought as she watched them tucking in eagerly. George was chewing on a sandwich too, but he looked as if his mind was miles away from the food. And her mother toyed with hers, cutting it up and moving it around on the plate, but seemed unable to put it in her mouth. Sally knew she was trying her best to be brave for the rest of them, but she'd heard her sobbing in the night when she thought they were all asleep. It was hard for her, especially in these troubled times when her loss was made worse by poverty and an uncertain future.

The soup kitchen continued to fill with mourners. There were more people than there were places at the tables and Sally saw Ruth directing some of the foundry men to find more chairs, benches, even boxes for the guests to sit down. Whether there would be enough food or even enough cups for everyone Sally doubted. Part of her felt that she should get up and go to help, but her desire to stay and support her mother was stronger. Besides, Ruth seemed to be coping well and Freddy Fry, always reliable in a crisis, was assisting her with a willing smile.

Sally suspected that Freddy liked Ruth, although she seemed completely unaware of it. But Sally had noticed that he always seemed to be on hand to do anything for her. And even though she was so sad, Sally felt a pang of jealousy. She wondered if she would have encouraged him herself if she hadn't thought they were going to America. As it was, she'd tried to put Freddy out of her mind because it would have been pointless to walk out with him when she was leaving so soon. But now things were different. She would be staying in Blackburn after all and, feeling bereft at the loss of her father, a strong kind man to take on part of her burden was appealing.

Sally put her thoughts aside. They weren't appropriate for today and Freddy was friendly towards all the girls. It was why they loved him. She even suspected that Caroline Haworth found him attractive. An unexpected laugh almost burst from her at the thought. That would be a match to be remarked upon.

She took another drink of her tea and was relieved to see her mother do the same. She must put aside her own feelings for the time being and concentrate on helping her mother, who needed her now more than she ever had.

'We must thank Mr Haworth for all this,' her mother said. 'I never expected such generosity.' Her eyes filled with fresh tears.

'It's his guilty conscience,' muttered George.

'Shush.' Sally frowned at him. He was right, of course, but this was not the time or place to say it. 'He didn't have to do it,' she told him. 'We ought to be grateful. And he hated having to close the mill. You know he kept it open much longer than Perseverance. It isn't his fault there's no cotton coming.'

Before long the plates were empty and the teapots were drained. The mourners began to get up from their chairs and come to speak to Sally and her mother before they went home.

'I'm so sorry for your loss,' they said.

'If there's anything I can do just let me know.'

'Jimmy was such a good man. He'll be missed.'

'I'll pray for you,' said one or two, including the vicar who'd accepted the invitation to come to the funeral tea.

Sally's mother thanked them all, but the good wishes made her weep with gratitude and Sally wished that it was time for them to go home where they could mourn their loss privately. But it would be bad manners to leave before their guests and she knew they must endure it.

When the room was almost empty, Sally sought out Ruth.

'Thank you for everything you've done,' she said. 'I know it must have been hard work for you after making the soup this morning. Is there anything I can do to help clear up?'

'No. It's almost done,' Ruth replied. 'The people who lent cups and saucers have taken them home to wash and Freddy is emptying the teapots for me.'

'It was good of you to help,' Sally told her.

'It was the least I could do after what you and your family have suffered,' she replied. 'Take your mother home,' she advised. 'She looks exhausted.'

Sally agreed, but she wanted to thank Caroline Haworth as well before she left. Dressed in her fashionable mourning outfit, Caroline had not flinched from making herself useful and Sally had seen her carrying around the huge, heavy teapots and topping up the cups of anyone who asked for more. It had been an incongruous sight, the lady serving the common folk as their maid. In different circumstances it might have been amusing, but Sally knew that Caroline wasn't doing it to bring herself any glory, but simply because she wanted to do something for her friend.

'Sally,' she said simply when Sally approached her and she put her arms around her and hugged her. She smelt of cologne and lavender and, for a moment, Sally gave herself up to the embrace. 'If there's anything I can do, you only need to ask,' she said and Sally knew that she meant it and that they were not just empty words. 'In fact, my father has something to tell you,' she added as Mr Haworth walked over to join them. Sally began to repeat her thanks to him, but he cut her off before she could finish the long list of everything he'd done for her family.

'It's the least I could do,' he replied. 'And I have some other news, although I wasn't going to bother you with it today.'

'Any good news would be welcome,' Sally told him. 'Is it about the mill?'

'Yes,' said Mr Haworth. 'I going to begin production again. I've managed to source some bales of cotton. I can't take all the hands back,' he explained. 'There isn't enough to run all the looms, but I'd like you to come back to work.'

It was just what Sally needed to lift her spirits. The thought of running her looms again delighted her, although her joy was quickly diminished by the thought that if her father were still alive, he would have been able to go back to his weaving as well.

'What about George? Can you take him back?' she asked.

Mr Haworth's face betrayed his answer before he spoke. 'I'm sorry,' he said. 'It seems fair to only take one from each family.'

Sally nodded. She could see that he was trying his best to do what was right.

'In that case, I'd rather you took on George,' she said. 'He hates being unemployed, and I'm terrified the relief committee will change their minds and insist he takes work in the quarry after all. He'd be safer at the mill. I know he's not as experienced as I am, but he's competent.'

'It's skilled weavers I need,' Mr Haworth told her. 'This cotton is precious. I can't afford to let an inch of it go to waste.'

'I could come in the afternoons when I'm finished here and help him,' she offered, thinking how good it would be to go back to her job even if it was unpaid.

She watched Mr Haworth's face as he considered her offer. He was obviously conflicted, but in the end he agreed.

'All right,' he said. 'Tell him to be at the mill first thing on Monday morning and I'll set him on.'

Sally thanked Mr Haworth again before saying goodbye to him and Caroline and walking home through the darkening streets with her family. She told George what the mill owner had said to her and was pleased to see his face soften from the hardness of his sorrow.

'He may not be able to pay you a full wage,' Sally warned him. 'But with my wages from the kitchen and what else we can get from the relief committee then we should be able to manage. It'll take some of the worry off Mam.'

George nodded. He was a good lad, thought Sally. She was proud of the way he'd helped her to hold the family together since their father's accident. She knew it hadn't been easy and that he was still disappointed about not going to America. But the mill re-opening was a glimmer of hope for them all and maybe it wouldn't be long before this crisis began to decline. It could never bring back their father, but it would at least make their lives a little more comfortable.

Chapter Forty-Four

When Caroline returned from the soup kitchen on the following Saturday, she saw that Lottie had laid out her pink gown for the visit to Yew Tree House. There was a tub filled with hot water for her to bathe in and a cup of tea on the bedside table. Lottie was a treasure, thought Caroline as she stripped off her clothes and stepped into the scented water.

By the time Simmons came to the front door with the coach, Caroline had been carefully prepared by Lottie, who was much more eager than Caroline at the prospect of her meeting Thomas Dutton again.

'Do you love him?' she'd asked as she'd arranged the front of Caroline's hair into plaits to soften the effect of the tight bun at the back.

'I've only met him twice,' Caroline had replied.

'But it's so exciting,' Lottie had insisted, and Caroline hadn't contradicted her. Even if the prospect of the visit was making her gloomy, she saw no reason to spoil the maid's anticipation of the event. She guessed that Lottie was hoping there would be a return visit and then she could see Thomas Dutton for herself and judge whether he was handsome enough to be a bridegroom.

The coachman had made a clear path from the front door earlier and Caroline went out in shoes rather than the boots she was becoming accustomed to wearing. Her feet were cold and she felt awkward as she got into the carriage, wishing for the ease of the clothes she'd worn earlier. They were altogether more practical and comfortable. Her job at the soup kitchen had spoiled her taste for high fashion, she lamented.

The struggle to get seated in the crinoline hoops made her recall her mishap at Cleaver Street and she indulged herself for a moment by allowing her imagination to dwell on Freddy Fry's blue eyes and strong hands. Then, she was jolted from her daydream back to reality as the carriage moved off. She glanced back at the door of the house, but it was closed. Her father was at the mill and her mother had thought it unfashionable to stand and wave her off.

The journey to Yew Tree House was not a long one. The house, newly built by the Duttons, was set back from the new road to Preston, in a wooded valley that screened it from passers-by. Simmons turned into the driveway through two sandstone pillars set on either side of the gate, so new that they were still unsullied by smoke and grime. They passed a small lodge and when the house came into view Caroline was surprised by its modernity. It had steeply pointed roofs and several chimney stacks. The porch was enclosed in glass with a mock Tudor façade and two lamps, one on either side of the steps that led up to the front door. The melting snow revealed a glimmer of green where lawns were laid up to the walls and ivy was already beginning to cling to the brickwork.

By the time Simmons had opened the carriage door to help her down, a maid in a white apron over a dark blue dress had opened the main door to the house. Caroline climbed the stone steps with a smile and went into the hallway, furnished with thick carpet, deep armchairs and an array of mahogany tables. A grand staircase swept upwards to the next floor and everything looked brand new. It was a far cry from the shabby and faded furnishings of her grandfather's mansion.

'This way, ma'am,' said the maid after she'd taken Caroline's hat and coat and handed them to another maid who was waiting by the door to a downstairs cloakroom. She took Caroline into a drawing room, equally well furnished, with a marble fireplace and a huge mirror above it, which reflected the ornate plaster ceiling. Here, Mrs Dutton was waiting to greet her. Although still small and fragile in appearance she seemed to have grown in stature since Caroline had last seen her. The fine surroundings of her own house enhanced rather than diminished her and she appeared confident here and at ease.

'Come to the fire,' she invited Caroline. 'It's still very cold and you must be chilled from your journey.'

'Thank you,' said Caroline. She was relieved to see the ornate screen set on the hearth. She would have hated to set her skirts on fire again.

'Here's Thomas,' said Mrs Dutton as her son came into the room. 'I'll leave you with him for a moment whilst I go to check if the tea is ready in the dining room.'

It was an obvious ploy to give them a moment alone together and Caroline prayed that Thomas wasn't intending to make a proposal. He smiled and seemed shy.

'Thank you for coming,' he said. 'It's nice to see you again.'

Caroline managed to return the smile, even if she couldn't bring herself to say that she was pleased to see him. Although he was well-dressed with a jewelled pin glistening in his cravat and neatly brushed hair, the best word Caroline could find to describe him was nondescript. There was nothing remarkable about him at all.

'I hear you're still working at the soup kitchen,' he said.

'I am. And I intend to carry on until it's no longer necessary,' she warned him.

He nodded, unperturbed. 'I've heard it may close after the worst of the cold weather has passed. There's talk of cotton imports arriving from India in the summer and the mills re-opening. My father said Mr Haworth intends to begin manufacturing again as soon as next week.'

'He is hoping to start up some of the looms again,' Caroline replied, still unsure how much Thomas knew of the arrangement between their fathers. 'But it's still a long way from full working. I fear that will take much longer.'

'Do you take an interest in your father's business?' he asked, sounding surprised.

'I do. Why shouldn't I?' she challenged him.

'There's no reason you shouldn't,' agreed Thomas. 'I hope you'll take an equal interest in brewing in the future.'

Caroline didn't reply. The words confirmed her fears that as far as Thomas was concerned she was to be his wife.

'I know nothing about brewing,' she told him. 'I don't even like the taste of beer and the smell from the brewery can be very unpleasant,' she said, thinking of the yeasty aroma that pervaded the town on many mornings of the week.

'We don't smell it here,' he replied. 'Although my mother never complained when we lived in town. She said she liked it.'

Caroline must have expressed her distaste in her facial expression because Thomas laughed. His eyes twinkled at her discomfiture and he relaxed now that he believed he had the upper hand.

'I won't make you live near the brewery,' he promised her. 'If you agree to marry me,' he added as if suddenly uncertain of himself again.

'I'm very pleased to hear it,' Caroline replied. How could she ever extricate herself from this situation? Events were speeding on towards a marriage she had never agreed to and which she didn't want.

She was saved by Mrs Dutton coming back in to tell them that tea was ready. Thomas offered Caroline his arm. He was quickly learning the ways of the gentry, she thought. She placed her hand lightly on his jacket, appreciating the quality of the fabric, and walked with him to the dining room where Mr Dutton was waiting to greet her. He looked extraordinarily pleased with himself, as well he might, thought Caroline. His loan to her father had bought him a potential daughter-in-law who was descended from ancient, landed gentry. It was certainly a feather in his cap.

Thomas, rather than the manservant, pulled out a chair for her to sit down. Caroline seated herself and accepted one of the dainty finger sandwiches as the tea was poured for her.

'I'm so pleased you could come,' Mrs Dutton said as she fussed over the handing out of the food. 'Perhaps when we've eaten, I can show you the house. It is rather lovely,' she added with a smile for her husband. He beamed back at her.

'My wife is thrilled with her new home,' he told Caroline. 'I think she invites people to tea merely to give her an excuse to show it off.'

'From what I've seen it's well worth showing,' Caroline replied.

'It's a pity it's so cold or you could have seen the gardens as well,' Mrs Dutton said.

'I'm sure Miss Haworth would like to return when the weather improves to see them,' Mr Dutton told her. 'Perhaps when the snowdrops are on show. We planted as many as we could get hold of,' he told Caroline. 'We're hoping that in time they will give a wonderful display.'

'I'm sure they will,' replied Caroline. 'The grounds at Salesbury Hall are overrun with them in the springtime.'

'Well, of course, the gardens here will take time to become established,' said Mr Dutton. 'But we're hoping they will give us great pleasure.'

Caroline smiled and nodded. It was clear that the Duttons were immensely proud of their house and its grounds. It was also clear to her that they liked one another. The smiles and glances between them seemed genuine and not put on for show as was the case with her own parents when they invited people to dine – although that rarely happened. They had few mutual friends, and her mother preferred to do her own entertaining in the afternoons when her father was out at the mill.

She began to relax a little in the Duttons' company as the conversation flowed easily. They asked her about the soup kitchen and seemed genuinely interested in her work there and not in the least judgemental. She found that she could talk to them about it without worrying about what she said. The constant state of tension that accompanied her meals at home was absent here and when she told them the story of setting her skirt on fire she found she could laugh about it now, even though their faces were shocked as she recounted how the fire had burnt away her skirts and left her legs on show.

'How distressing for you,' said Mrs Dutton. 'I think you were very brave to go back.'

'I felt I had to help,' Caroline replied.

'You make me feel ashamed that I haven't done more,' said Mrs Dutton. 'We've given donations, of course, but it doesn't seem the same as actually doing something practical. I think you're an exemplary young woman. I hope that we can be friends,' she said, reaching across the white damask tablecloth to lay her hand on Caroline's.

'I'm sure we can,' she replied as she found herself welcoming the overture. She was growing to like Mrs Dutton.

When the meal was finished, Caroline was given a tour of the house from the basement kitchens to the attic rooms where the maid servants slept. Everything was fresh and modern, and no expense had been spared in the furnishings. Even the servants' quarters looked luxurious compared to the little rooms that were provided at Richmond Terrace for Jenkins and Lottie.

'I know Thomas was very quiet earlier,' Mrs Dutton said as they came back down the grand staircase to the drawing room. 'He's a shy boy. But he does like you. I hope you will give him a favourable answer when he garners the courage to speak to you on the matter of marriage?'

It was a question. Caroline could see the doubt in Mrs Dutton's eyes, as if she couldn't quite believe that she would be so lucky as to welcome her as a daughter-in-law. Caroline found she didn't want to disappoint her, but still she hesitated.

'I know it seems a convenient arrangement,' Mrs Dutton admitted. 'But I would dearly love to have you as a part of my family.'

Caroline nodded. She would like to be part of this warm and welcoming family too. It was just a pity that she needed to marry Thomas to achieve it.

When Mrs Dutton took her back into the drawing room, he was waiting for her. He stood up as they entered, looking anxious.

'I'll give you a moment alone,' said Mrs Dutton before she discreetly withdrew and closed the door behind her.

Caroline looked at Thomas. He seemed lost for words, and she hoped that he might not find the courage to ask her to marry him and she would be spared. But he stepped closer to her and grasped her hand in his. His felt hot, but thankfully not sweaty. Then he cleared his throat a couple of times and began what was obviously a well-rehearsed speech.

'Caroline, I know we're not very well acquainted, but what I've seen of you has impressed me greatly, to the point that I can admit I am in love with you. As you know, I have good prospects. As an only son I stand to eventually inherit the brewery and until then my father makes me a very generous allowance. I would be able to provide for you amply.' He paused and seemed uncertain of himself as she betrayed no look of encouragement but stared at him in despair. 'Caroline,' he went on in an uncertain voice. 'Would you do me the honour of becoming my wife?' he asked.

She kept him waiting for an answer until the silence between them was unbearable. Then she just nodded her head in acquiescence. She found herself unable to say the word *yes* and wondered if she might be able to claim later that it had all been a misunderstanding.

But what else could she do? The agreement that had been made between their fathers meant that at least some of the weavers were going back to work. George Grimes would be employed and bringing in a wage that would help her friend Sally and her family. And once people had wages in their pockets, Ruth Hodgson and her father might be able to open their shop again. Caroline felt as if there were so many people depending on her. All she had to do was put aside her inappropriate attraction to Freddy Fry and resign herself to being the wife of Thomas Dutton.

Chapter Forty-Five

Ruth slept better following the visit to see Mr Catterall at the bank. She no longer feared the knock of the bailiffs at their door telling them that the house must be sold to pay off their debts.

Her father had seemed relieved by the news of the extension to the loan as well. He'd cried when Amos had explained to him the agreement with Mr Catterall and had repeated over and over again how sorry he was that he'd got them into this mess. Ruth did her best to comfort him, as he had once comforted her, but she knew she must face the truth – things had changed.

'It's become too much for him,' Amos had said after her father had been put to bed. 'He's kept too much to himself these past months. No wonder it's made him ill.'

He didn't add that her father was getting older, but Ruth could see it. Even if he recovered from the stroke, he would never be the same as he had been before. She knew that if they were to keep their home and the shop then it was up to her to take on the burden of running it. Amos had said that he would help where he could, but Ruth knew she couldn't sit back and let him try to do everything. He had his own work and family to take care of. It was up to her to make the business a success once more and pay off the debt.

Strangely, the decision had made her feel better rather than filling her with dismay and she found that she was looking forward to the day the soup kitchen closed so that she could open up the shop again. As she prepared to go to work the next Monday morning, she decided that when she came home, she would go to the storeroom and inspect the jars of sweets. If they were still fit for sale, she would find time to wash down the shelves in the shop and mop the floor. Even if they couldn't reopen straight away, she would feel better knowing that everything was ready.

She walked across town to Cleaver Street feeling more optimistic than she had for a long time. Freddy Fry greeted her with a smile as he shovelled coal. His friendship warmed her. He was always cheerful, a hard-worker and had a kind word for everyone. He took the teasing of the mill girls in his stride and even seemed to enjoy it, although Ruth noticed that he didn't tease them back so much these days, not when she was around anyway.

She tied on her apron and began to direct the workers to their tasks as they arrived. Now that she was used to the job it was nowhere near as hard as she'd first thought it would be, and she hoped she would find the same when she took over the sweet making. The vats would need to be very well scrubbed, she mused as the girls began to fill them with water. It wouldn't do to produce sweets that had any hint of turnip and onion about them.

She went to help put out the spoons and basins on the serving table, and as she worked, she saw the mayor come in to speak to Mr Yates. They both glanced across to where she was, and after a moment the mayor came over to speak to her.

'There may not be as many men today,' he said. 'A few have gone back to work this morning.'

'What? To the mills?' Ruth asked in surprise.

'Aye,' Mr Hutchinson went on. 'Haworth's Mill is beginning some manufacturing again. Did you not know? I thought Miss Haworth would have told you.'

'There's been no time to chat,' she replied.

'Aye. Well, it seems Mr Haworth has got hold of some cotton and he's set a few millhands back on. We may not need this kitchen much longer,' he warned her. 'It seems the worst of the crisis may be over.'

Ruth hoped that it was true. It would mean she could begin work on getting the shop open again. She would tell her father as soon as she got home. It was bound to cheer him.

'I hear your father's opened his mill again,' she said to Caroline when she returned to the preparation tables.

'He has,' she agreed although it seemed the news didn't please her much. Ruth wondered if it was because she would miss helping at the soup kitchen when it closed. It seemed strange that Caroline would actually prefer peeling vegetables to a life of leisure. 'Mr Dutton has offered him a loan to buy in cotton,' she told her, 'but it seems to be dependent on me marrying his son.'

'Do you not want to marry him?' asked Ruth, surprised that Caroline Haworth would agree to anything against her will.

'He wouldn't be my first choice,' she replied, her gaze drifting towards Freddy. Ruth saw that her friend was smitten with the foundry worker. But surely she had never seriously considered him as a husband? He was a lowly working man and she was gentry. It would be an impossible match.

'Mr Haworth has given our George a job,' Sally told them with a smile of relief. 'However he's come by the cotton, I'm grateful for it. And I'm going into the mill to help out this afternoon. I'll be glad to be weaving again, although I'll miss coming here,' she admitted. 'It hasn't been all bad.' Her eyes tracked Freddy Fry as he walked past, and Ruth saw that Caroline was watching him too and she had tears in her eyes.

She left them to their tasks and went to check on the soup. She dipped in a spoon and blew gently on the hot liquid until it had cooled enough for her to taste it. It was as good as usual, flavoured with meat and plenty of salt and pepper. Unlike those who complained they were sick of the sight of it, she thought she would miss her dinnertime food when the kitchen closed. She supposed she could try to make it herself at home, in a big pan. If she had time, she mused. They wouldn't be able to afford to employ Agatha again and she suddenly realised that all the housework and cooking as well as the shop would be her responsibility from now on.

She must have frowned at the thought.

'Is it not so good today?' asked Freddy. She looked up to see him studying her. 'The soup,' he said. 'You didn't look pleased with it.'

'No. The soup's all right,' she assured him. 'I was just thinking of something else.'

'It's not your father, is it? He hasn't taken a turn for the worse?'

'No. He's getting better,' she told Freddy. He continued to look at her quizzically. 'I was just thinking about when the kitchen closes,' she admitted. 'I'll have everything to do at home as well as opening up the shop. My sister's coming round every day at the moment, but I can't expect her to keep house for me for ever.'

'Will your father be able to manage the shop?' Freddy asked her.

'I don't know,' she said. 'I hope he can do some things, but I'll have to do more than just serve the customers in the future. I've asked him to show me how to make the sweets. He's always done it himself before, but I think it's time I learnt the trade.'

'It'll be heavy work, lifting those vats,' Freddy observed.

Ruth looked at the size of the big metal pans, filled with the simmering soup. She suddenly realised that she would struggle to lift them, even though they wouldn't be so full or heavy when they were filled with sweet mixture.

'Your father'll not be able to do much heavy-lifting either,' went on Freddy.

Ruth suddenly felt dejected. Her father could barely stand without holding on to the furniture. He certainly wouldn't be able to manage the pans. And even if he did show her how to mix the sugar and spices and fruits, what good would that be if she was too small and weak to pour the mixture into the moulds? She almost blamed Freddy for spoiling the plans she had made in her head. Why did he have to burst her bubble like this? It didn't seem fair. But on the other hand, Ruth knew that what he was saying was right. Why had she not realised it before? Her plans to run the business seemed to have hit an insurmountable problem before she'd even begun.

'I could help,' Freddy offered.

Ruth wasn't sure she'd heard him right.

'Sorry. What did you say?' she asked.

'I could help you,' he repeated. 'There'll be nothing for me to do here when the soup kitchen closes. I doubt Mr

Yates will reopen the foundry until all the mills are back at work.'

'I can't offer you a job,' said Ruth, feeling awkward. It was just like when all the mill girls had come to the shop before Christmas looking for employment.

'I'm not asking for a job – not a paid one,' Freddy told her. 'I was just saying that I could help.'

'Why would you do that?' Ruth asked, genuinely puzzled.

'I want to,' he replied. He seemed awkward and Ruth wondered why. 'I'd like to help you – and spend more time with you,' he added. 'I like you.'

She stared at him and saw a faint blush of colour creep across his cheeks.

'I'm sorry,' he said. 'I've spoken out of turn.'

'No!' She reached a hand out and put it on his arm to prevent him walking away. She'd had no idea that he liked her and the thought of it filled her with a rush of unexpected pleasure. It also solved the problem of lifting the vats. 'I'd like to spend more time with you too,' she told him and was rewarded with a huge grin that spread across the whole of his face.

Chapter Forty-Six

When Sally got home, she found her mother sweeping the floor. It was a good sign. Ever since her father's death, her mother had done nothing but sit in his chair by the fire and brood. But now, she seemed to have made the effort to shake off her inertia and busy herself with the tasks around the house that still needed to be attended to, even in this time of grief.

'I've brought some soup home,' said Sally, putting the jug down on the hearth. 'It's still hot if you want some. Ruth sent a loaf of bread as well. She said you were entitled, even if you didn't want to come to Cleaver Street to eat.'

'I'm not sure we are entitled now that both you and George are in work,' her mother replied, sounding doubtful.

'Sit down and eat,' Sally told her. 'There's plenty, so we can save some for the little ones when they get back from school and I'll take some for George now. There was a lot left over,' she explained. 'We made the usual amount but there were less people came because of the mill being back open.'

'They'll stop giving out the tickets soon,' predicted her mother.

'Maybe,' Sally agreed. 'But until then we can enjoy it.'

‘Are you not having some?’ asked her mother when she saw that Sally had set only one bowl on the table.

‘I’ve already eaten and I need to get to the mill,’ she reminded her mother as she pulled her shawl back on and hurried out again.

When she opened the mill door and breathed in the familiar, distinctive aroma of cotton, she paused for a moment to listen to the rhythmic clatter of the looms as they rose and fell for the shuttles to fly backwards and forwards with the thread.

‘How is it going?’ she shouted to her brother above the din when she found him.

‘Good,’ he grinned as he powered down the looms and accepted the soup she’d brought for him. ‘It’s a relief to be back. Everyone says the same. They were all shaking Mr Haworth by the hand and thanking him for what he’s done for us. He’s a good man.’

‘He is,’ agreed Sally. ‘Let’s hope he can get more cotton soon, enough to set all the workers back on. Then this crisis will be over and done with.’

‘It’ll not bring father back though,’ said George. ‘No matter how much the cotton flows in the future, it’ll never change that.’

‘I know.’ Sally hugged her brother. ‘But he wouldn’t want us to be sad,’ she reminded him. ‘He’d want us to get on and do our best and look after Mam and the little ones.’

George nodded, but Sally knew the loss was hard for him. He’d adored his father, as they all had. It had been a cruel blow to lose him in such a pointless accident, but it was something they couldn’t change. They had to be brave and carry on.

'If only the tickets for America had come a day or so sooner,' he mused as he ate.

'Don't think like that,' Sally advised him. 'It'll do no good.'

'I did wonder about going on my own,' her brother confessed. 'But I don't think I will now. I'll stay here and work hard to look after you all.'

Sally hugged him again. He was so young, and so determined. It wasn't fair that any of them should have been dealt this blow, but life rarely was fair, she thought. There was no sense to it. You just had to make the best of what you were dealt.

'Perhaps you'll get another chance in the future,' she said. 'Don't think you have to stay here for my sake or Mam's. We'd manage. You must do what you think is best for yourself.'

She would be so sad to be parted from him, she thought, but if America was where he believed his future lay, then maybe he ought to go. Maybe he would be able to get a good job and build a big wooden house and then they could all go to join him there. Her father would have liked that.

Chapter Forty-Seven

Caroline had told Simmons that there was no need to keep collecting her from Cleaver Street. She'd become embarrassed at finding the carriage at the door waiting for her when she and the other girls came out in the afternoon. She preferred to spill out onto the chilly streets as one of them, and she often pretended, for a moment, that she was just an ordinary lass, doing a job of work.

On Tuesday afternoon, the mill girls had called goodbye to her as usual as they'd linked arms and set off across Blackburn to seek some new adventures to fill the rest of their day. Caroline had watched them go, wishing that just once they would take her arm and show her the delights of whatever it was they found to amuse themselves. But she knew they never would. They still regarded her with some suspicion. It was only Sally Grimes who seemed to accept her as an equal and today she'd been in a hurry because she was going to help her brother at the mill.

'Shall we walk together?' Caroline had asked, hoping she wouldn't be rebuffed. Sally had nodded and they'd set off together in the direction of the marketplace. As they'd walked, Sally had nudged her arm.

'Look at that!' she'd exclaimed.

Caroline hadn't been sure what she'd meant at first and had stared about trying to see what had amazed Sally.

'Over there!' Sally had continued and Caroline realised she meant the couple who were walking some way ahead of them on the other side of the street.

It had been a moment before she'd recognised the couple as Ruth Hodgson with her hand tucked into the crook of Freddy Fry's elbow. As she'd stared at them, a feeling of deep disappointment and sorrow had crept through her, making her feel colder than even the hardest of the recent frosts.

'I wonder how long that's been going on,' Sally had mused. 'Mind you, I'm not entirely surprised,' she'd continued. 'I've noticed the way he looks at her, but I wasn't sure if he would ever dare to ask her. She's out of his class, really. But there she is with her arm in his so she must have agreed. I wonder if her father knows.'

'Out of his class?' Caroline had asked, not understanding what Sally meant.

'Yes. He's just a labourer,' she'd explained. 'Ruth's father is a shop keeper – a businessman.'

'I see,' Caroline had replied, although she didn't really. She'd always known that Freddy Fry was in a class below her, but she'd never considered that he might be seen as inferior to Ruth. 'Do you think her father might object?' she'd asked, wondering what her own father would have said if it had been her holding onto Freddy's arm.

Sally had shaken her head. 'I couldn't say,' she'd admitted. 'But he's a good worker. Ruth could do a lot worse. Even so, I'm still surprised.'

When they'd reached the marketplace, Caroline had parted from her friend and walked thoughtfully towards Richmond Terrace. Even though she felt the hurt of disappointment sharply, she kept reminding herself that Freddy Fry would never have been so presumptuous as to ask her to walk out with him. From what Sally had said it seemed he had almost over-reached himself by asking Ruth.

She wondered if Sally was disappointed too. She'd always thought that she was her rival for Freddy's affections. It had never occurred to her that it might be Ruth. Still, it meant that she really must put him out of her mind now. He was spoken for, and so was she, she remembered, because her engagement to Thomas Dutton was on the verge of becoming official. The loan to her father had been paid, the cotton purchased and the mill re-opened. How could she change her mind now? How could she throw her father back into debt and put George Grimes and all the other millhands out of work again? How would she reconcile herself to being the cause of so much misery and confusion? She knew she couldn't. And Thomas was nice enough. She had no reason to dislike him.

She rang the doorbell and Jenkins let her in. She went up to her room and undressed and got into the bath that was waiting for her. She washed herself thoroughly with the scented soap, dressed herself in the gown Lottie had put out on the bed and went downstairs.

Her father was at the mill and her mother was in the parlour.

'There you are,' she said, glancing up. 'I'm planning a tea party to announce your engagement. I suppose I'll have to invite Mrs Dutton. I hope it won't be too overwhelming for her. She seems so quiet and mousy,' remarked her mother, wrinkling her nose in distaste.

'I think she'd like to come,' said Caroline. 'She's going to be family, so I think it's only right she should be asked.'

'Family,' repeated her mother. 'That does seem a strange idea. All right. I'll add her to my list. You'll have to look after her though. She'll be your responsibility. I can never think of anything to say to the woman. Now, who else will come, do you think?'

Caroline watched her mother making notes in her little book. When did she become such a snob? Surely she must have been different when she was young and in love with her father?

'You seem very morose,' remarked her mother the next time she glanced up.

'There's a lot of sadness about,' remarked Caroline, without explaining her own despondency at seeing Freddy Fry with Ruth. She knew that her mother wouldn't understand.

'Perhaps it's time you stopped going to that soup kitchen,' her mother told her. 'It's becoming embarrassing. My friends pretend it's very commendable, but I can see that they don't really approve. Besides, I suppose we'll have to start planning the wedding before long. Your grandfather's very keen for it to go ahead without delay.'

The words sent a shiver through Caroline. She'd resigned herself to agreeing to the engagement, but her plan had been to put off any wedding for as long as possible.

'I was hoping for a long engagement,' she protested.

'I was hoping he would get cold feet and not ask you,' confessed her mother. 'I think you could do much better, but your grandfather's keen and now that your father wants it too, I'm outnumbered. Not that they ever listen to anything I say,' she grumbled.

–

When Caroline's father came home, he looked as if a weight had been lifted from his shoulders. He brushed his lips across her mother's face and then turned to her and kissed her cheek warmly.

'Is everything all right?' she asked him, although she could see that it was.

He nodded. 'It's good to hear those looms running again. I'm grateful,' he whispered. 'And I think it will turn out for the best for you.'

'Perhaps,' said Caroline, unenthusiastically.

'You won't change your mind, will you?' She could see that he was alarmed at the prospect.

'No,' she reassured him. 'Too many people are depending on me.'

'Don't look at it like that,' he pleaded. 'This marriage will be so beneficial to you. You'll never have to worry about living with a father who might lose everything. You'll have a home that's secure for the rest of your life now.'

'Might you have lost everything? Really?' she asked. He looked grave and then nodded. 'It came close,' he admitted. 'Although I hoped that your grandfather would take you and your mother in if I had to give up the house.'

The prospect of having to live at Salesbury Hall and spend her days being reminded of how feckless her father was made Caroline shiver. She told herself that at least when she married Thomas she would have her own home. And he was agreeable. He would let her do as she chose. He might even allow her to continue her work with the poor. Perhaps it wouldn't be that bad, after all.

Chapter Forty-Eight

Ruth allowed Freddy to walk her home after the soup kitchen had been cleaned and locked up. She enjoyed holding his arm as they headed towards Queen Victoria Street. It made her feel special, and she still couldn't quite believe that he had singled her out as the one he wanted to spend time with.

'Will you come in?' she asked when they reached the door, beside the shop window with the blinds pulled down.

Freddy hesitated.

'I know my father will be pleased with your offer to help us,' she told him, hoping it would prove to be true and that her father would agree to it.

'All right.' He pulled off his cap and raked his fingers through his dark hair in an attempt to make himself presentable, but he had a smear of coal dust across his cheek. Ruth longed to wipe it away for him, but felt too shy to initiate such an intimate touch.

When she pushed open the door she was surprised to see her father in the shop, lifting jars of sweets onto the shelves.

'Be careful!' she warned him as he reached up with one. He was still unsteady on his feet and his left arm didn't have the strength it needed for the heavy glass jar.

'Allow me, sir,' said Freddy, taking it from him and putting it on the shelf. Ruth sighed inwardly. All the jars would have to come down again because she hadn't had time to wash the shelves yet.

'Do I know you?' her father asked, studying Freddy.

'This is Freddy Fry,' Ruth told him. 'You must remember him. He works for Mr Yates. He helps with the fires at the soup kitchen.'

'I thought I'd seen you before,' her father said. 'What's he doing here?' he asked Ruth, looking concerned. 'There isn't trouble, is there?'

'No,' she reassured him. 'Everything is just fine. Freddy walked me home because I wanted to show him where we make the sweets. He's going to come and help us.'

'Help us?' asked her father doubtfully. 'What sort of help? What do you know about sweet making?' he asked Freddy.

'Not much,' he admitted. 'Working metal is my trade, but there's no work at the foundry so there'll be nothing for me to do when they close the soup kitchen. I thought I could help here with the heavy-lifting and suchlike.'

'Why did you bring him?' Ruth's father asked her. 'You know how I'm fixed. I can't take on an employee.'

'He doesn't want wages, Pa,' she explained. 'He's just offering to help us.'

Her father looked at Freddy suspiciously. 'Why would he do that?' he asked.

Ruth began to explain but Freddy put a hand on her arm.

'I'll tell him,' he said. 'Mr Hodgson, I like your daughter very much and I really would like to come and help her with the sweets. And I hope…' He paused and glanced at Ruth. 'I hope that, with your permission, I can ask her to walk out with me.'

She watched as the glimmer of understanding registered on her father's face.

'Ruth!' he exclaimed. 'You've got yourself a young man! I never thought I'd see the day!'

It was such a relief to Ruth that her father seemed pleased, if surprised.

'So, you don't mind?' she asked.

'No. Of course not,' he said before turning his attention back to Freddy and looking at him as if he was seeing him for the first time. 'I'm very pleased,' he said, putting out his hand tentatively to shake Freddy's.

'Likewise, sir,' said Freddy. Ruth watched as he took her father's hand gently. He was careful, aware that her father was still very frail and it made Ruth like him even more.

Chapter Forty-Nine

The thaw continued and the daylight hours grew longer as February came in with its promise of spring. The trees in the churchyard began to form early buds and snowdrops raised their brave heads amongst the gravestones, including the newly carved one which marked the resting place of Jimmy Grimes.

A few more mills began part-time work again as the Indian cotton began to trickle into the ports, and although there was still no prospect of an end to the American war, there was a feeling of optimism in the town that the bad times were coming to an end and things could only improve as the weather warmed.

At the end of February, the relief committee took the decision that the soup kitchen was no longer needed and would close at Easter.

–

Sally was sorry when the last day came. It was a Saturday. The day before Easter Day. Even though Mr Haworth had offered her work on two looms, and she would be glad to return to a paid job at the mill, she knew that she would miss the soup kitchen and the friends she had made there.

She went in to find Ruth already directing operations, although the truth was that everyone knew their jobs so well now that there wasn't much need for her guidance. She seemed a changed person, thought Sally, as she watched her friend, so different from the shy lass who'd first come to help her father in the kitchen. Her confidence had grown and she was blossoming since she and Freddy Fry had begun to walk out together.

'I can't believe we won't be doing this tomorrow,' Ruth said. 'I was dreading it at first. I thought I'd never manage to make even one dish of soup.'

'It's been interesting,' Sally said. 'To tell the truth, I wasn't sure how it was going to work out myself. I only came because Mr Haworth pleaded with me.'

'And now you'll be going back to the mill. Are you looking forward to it?' asked Ruth.

'I am,' replied Sally. 'It won't be the same though. It'll be odd not having my father there. And I'll only be running a couple of looms. It won't be as busy as it was when I had four on the go. But I'll still be helping my brother George to weave. If he can become as skilful as my father was then hopefully he'll always be able to find work in the future.'

'Here? Or in America?' asked Ruth.

'That's a good question,' Sally told her. 'The trouble is no one can be certain what the future will hold for the mills here. Even if the American war finishes, we can't be certain that the cotton will come in the quantities it used to. Suppose the Americans decide to keep it for themselves to spin and weave it in their own mills? If that happens then America may be the place for him to go.'

'Will you go?' asked Ruth.

'I don't know. It sounds exciting and I think I'd like to, but I'm not sure my mother would agree. She was very reluctant to go when my father got the tickets, and

I'm not certain I could persuade her now – even though there would be work for her. I suppose we'll just have to wait and see what happens.'

'Well, I won't be going anywhere,' Ruth told her. 'I just hope that there are enough people back in work to make the sweet shop profitable again.'

'You're keen to get it re-opened then?'

'I am.' Ruth smiled. 'I'm sure I can do it with Freddy's help.'

'Is he going to work for you permanently then? What about his job here at the foundry?' asked Sally.

'Well, Mr Yates has no plan to begin production again just yet, so I suppose I'll have to wait and see. Freddy may want to come back to his real work in the end. If he does, I'll have to employ some other help.'

'It sounds as if you're planning to build quite an empire,' Sally remarked. Ruth didn't disagree.

'I'll be happy to have just the one shop for now,' she said. 'But like you said, none of us knows what the future might hold.'

They both smiled as they saw Caroline coming towards them.

'What are you two talking about so seriously?' she asked.

'We're talking about our futures, now that the kitchen is closing,' said Sally. 'But of course you know exactly what your future is going to be!'

'Yes.' Sally felt sad that Caroline didn't sound more enthusiastic. Both she and Ruth knew that their friend wasn't excited about her forthcoming marriage to Thomas Dutton.

'You'll be able to be a lady of leisure,' she reminded her. 'No more peeling potatoes.'

'I'm going to miss coming here, though,' Caroline told them. 'I've come to enjoy it even if I had no idea what to do at first. I still can't believe I was so stupid as to wear that huge crinoline and set myself on fire!'

As she spoke Caroline glanced across to where Freddy was setting the fires under the vats. She looked pensive and Sally knew that her friend was struggling to shake off the attraction she felt for Freddy. Sally wondered if Ruth had guessed Caroline's feelings. She'd given no sign, but to Sally it had been obvious. Ever since the day of the accident, Caroline had looked at Freddy Fry with a wistfulness that clearly revealed her wish that he would grasp hold of her once again. But it would never have been possible. They lived in such different spheres that their orbits could never have collided – it would never have been allowed.

–

Caroline tore her gaze away from Freddy Fry and back to her friends. It was strange to think of these two women in those terms, but during the winter months, as they'd worked in the soup kitchen, they had become friends. Circumstances had thrown them together and given them an opportunity that they might never have otherwise had. If the cotton crisis hadn't come, then Sally would have remained just one amongst dozens of her father's workforce – a girl she might have vaguely recognised but one she would never have spoken to. And Ruth would have remained nothing more than a shop assistant – someone she might have exchanged pleasantries with when she went to buy sweets, but someone who would have remained outside her social circle. Her days would have been spent helping her mother organise tea parties, trying to keep the peace between her parents and enduring the awkward visits to her grandparents, where she was regarded as not quite good enough for an excellent marriage, but a girl who must nevertheless be found a husband, because that was all she was good for.

The soup kitchen had been a revelation for her. It had shown her a glimpse of other people's lives and she had discovered that they were not that different from her after all. They all had their hopes and dreams, their wishes and desires. They loved their families, or sometimes didn't, the same as herself. They felt grief and happiness in the same way she did, and the only thing that really set them apart was just an accident of birth.

She'd been brought up to consider herself lucky, but now Caroline wasn't sure how lucky she really was. Her homelife had never been easy, and at first, she'd been jealous of Sally Grimes when she talked about her parents and her brothers and sisters. Caroline had longed to be part of a big, happy family like hers even if times were tough at the moment. And when Sally's father had been killed, she had been shocked and appalled at the tragedy – and she'd felt that her own family was partly responsible. Ruth too had seemed so happy until her father became ill – and Caroline knew that his stroke had been brought on by his worries. Ruth had admitted one day that he had borrowed money to try to keep his shop open and Caroline thought about the loan her own father had received from the Duttons. It had sealed her fate, in the same way that Ruth's father's illness and Sally's father's death had sealed theirs. Fate had dealt them all a harsh blow in one way or another and it was up to them to face their setbacks and make what they could of their lives in the future. For her, that meant the prospect of marrying

Thomas Dutton, and although she knew that neither Sally nor Ruth would regard that as a hardship, it was not what she would have chosen if she hadn't been compelled to.

–

Ruth smiled at her friends. These past few months had been her first taste of real friendship, she realised. Before this she had only known people – people from church, customers at the shop. Apart from her sisters she'd never felt so close to other women before. And if anyone had told her that her two closest friends would be Sally Grimes, a mill girl, and Caroline Haworth, the mill owner's daughter, she would never have believed them. If her previous life had continued as she'd always believed it would, then the only contact she would have had with either of them would have been across the counter of her father's shop. And then there was Freddy. She felt a warm glow as she thought of him. She would never have met him if it hadn't been for the soup kitchen. She might have had to face the prospect of being an old maid as her sisters had predicted. But now her future was set on a different path. One she had never dreamt was possible. Of course, the cotton crisis had brought almost insurmountable problems for her, but it had brought good things as well and she hoped that her friends Sally and Caroline would be able to find some of the good that she felt. Caroline, of course, had never been in any danger of going without a thing. She was privileged. But she'd never put on airs and graces, and she'd worked hard. Ruth hoped she would be happy in her marriage and not forget her and Sally.

Ruth thought that Sally had probably had the worst ordeal with the loss of her father. Every day when she went home and saw her own father getting better, she felt a pang of guilt that Sally would never see her father again.

'Don't look so sad,' Sally said to her. 'I know it's our last day, but we'll keep in touch, won't we?'

'Of course we will!' Caroline exclaimed.

Ruth nodded. She hoped that it was true because these two women had come to mean the world to her and, she hoped, to each other.

Author Note

My inspiration for this book, and the two that will follow in the same series, was the terrible hardship that hit the Lancashire mill towns from the close of 1861 until the spring of 1865, when the supply of raw cotton completely dried up because of the American civil war.

In the 1860s the Lancashire spinning and weaving mills were totally dependent on imported cotton from plantations of the southern states of the American Union. Some politicians had warned that relying on one supplier for the raw goods to support a staple industry was foolish, and some steps had been taken to source raw cotton from other countries, including India. But no one had foreseen the sudden catastrophe that the outbreak of war in America would bring.

When the northern states, led by Abraham Lincoln, blockaded the ports of the southern states to prevent them profiting from sales of their cotton, Lancashire was reduced to abject poverty as the mills were forced to close and workers were laid off with no wages.

In 1861, the population of Blackburn was 61,126. Out of this number about 25,000 were directly employed in various branches of the cotton trade. But as the total population included dependants such as small children it's estimated that 79% of the inhabitants were directly dependant on the cotton industry. In addition to this, there were around 3000 people employed in engineering and machine making in the town and with the closure of the mills their work dried up too. Shopkeepers were also directly affected as is clear from an account given by my own great, great grandfather, William Eastwood.

In later life, William was interviewed by a local newspaper, *The Blackburn Times*, and this is what he said.

> *I first went to work at Brookhouse mill. I was put in the spinning room at eight years of age. There was no half time then. I remained at Brookhouse for about 15 years, then went to Plantation mill, run by Will and Tom Turner, but after a while this place was stopped and I started a grocer's shop on Primrose Bank. Later I took a shop on Peter Street. We had that shop during the Cotton Famine. We had to let people have a lot of groceries on credit, because they had no money to pay for them, and we lost a great deal as a result. In fact, it almost ruined us. We were owed nearly £100 out of which we got very little back. And, of course, £100 was a great deal to us at that time.*

On the 1861 census, taken in April of that year, William's occupation is given as Grocer and Cotton Spinner. His sons are all working in the cotton industry as cotton piecers, cotton creelers and his brother James who is living with them is a minder. The Cotton Famine must have hit them hard, putting most of the family out of work as well as causing them to lose a huge amount of money in the shop.

There was no welfare state back then and any help offered to those who had no money came from voluntary donations. In Blackburn, a relief committee was formed, although at first many of the workers were too proud of their independence to accept help. But as time passed it was clear that the only alternative was starvation. A soup kitchen was set up on Cleaver Street and I've drawn on contemporary accounts of this as background for my story. The ingredients I've mentioned, the amount made and the cost are all factual.

Much of the detail has come from a book named *The History of the Distress in Blackburn* written by William Gourlay in 1865 when the worst of the crisis was over. It's a fascinating account and I hope it has added a note of authenticity to the series, even though all my characters are entirely fictional.

Later, various classes were set up around the town to give the workers some employment for a small wage, and I've used this as inspiration for the second book in the series *The Sewing Class Girl*.

Some help also came from the northern union of America. Abraham Lincoln sent food, mostly flour, to alleviate the starvation of the cotton workers. The most famous of these shipments is the *George Griswold* and some of the barrels that contained flour still survive. I know there is one in the museum at Rochdale. And if you ever visit Manchester, you will see a statue of Abraham Lincoln in Lincon Square, which commemorates this aid. Of course there was a political strand to this help. The southern states had expected England to support them and send war ships to break the blockade. Lincoln was keen that this shouldn't happen and he wanted to express his gratitude to the cotton workers for supporting him and his fight for the abolition of slavery. As well as slavery being one of the crucial issues of the American war, it was an integral part of the cotton industry. The previous growth and prosperity of the cotton towns had been built on raw material picked by slaves. It's often said that the Lancashire workers put up with starvation because they supported abolition. I think the truth is more nuanced. Whilst they knew slavery was wrong, many simply wanted to get back to work and feed their families.

The American civil war dragged on until 1865, after which the cotton began to flow again, and the town saw a rise in prosperity.

By 1871, William is still a grocer. He has two children living at home, George, my great grandfather, and his half-sister, Ellen, who are both weavers. The cotton was coming again, with the main difference being that it was no longer being picked by slaves.

If you'd like to learn more about the background to my books, visit my website at www.libbyashworth.com or follow me on Facebook.